# Hayley Ryan was definitely going to have a baby

That made it a thousand times more foolish for her to be out here, in Jacob Cooper's opinion. "You're pregnant," he said simply. "Why didn't you tell me that? It puts a different spin on everything. You can't stay here!"

Hayley wheeled away from him and extended shaking hands toward the fire. "It's for me to say what I do, Jacob," she said with renewed ferocity. "Go away and leave me alone."

"Damn, Hayley. I worried when I thought it was just you. But you and a baby... It's craziness for a pregnant woman to be this far from a good road. You need—"

"Thank you very much for your flattering opinion of my capabilities. But I don't answer to you. It's my baby. My responsibility. My decision."

"Oh? So the kid doesn't have a father?"

Hayley's face crumpled. "He d̲___ band or father. Besides, ̲___ walked out on me."

"I didn't mean to open___ was me, I'd want to know I h___ works. A man deserves the chance to ṉ___ is child."

A haunting smile came and went. "Not all men have your sense of responsibility, Jake."

Dear Reader,

Before I moved to Tucson, I subscribed to the city's newspaper because I wanted to find out more about the community. I read an article that intrigued me so much, I cut it out and saved it. The article concerned a woman who'd discovered blue opals on a remote site near the Mexican border. This idea kept nagging at me, insisting there was a story to be told.

This is not Cheri Saunders's story, although her real-life adventure is, of course, fascinating, and you might learn part of it if you visit Cheri at the Jay-R Opal Mine Art Gallery in Huachuca City, Arizona. My tale about Hayley Ryan and Jake Cooper is totally a work of fiction. I don't even know where the Jay-R Opal Mine is located; I suspect it's a well-kept secret.

Any mistakes in descriptions of digging the ore and polishing or setting stones are mine alone. I did visit the wilderness ranch area around the old ghost town of Ruby. It was desolate and, in the true sense of the word, awesome. I think I know how Hayley—a pregnant woman determined to make her way alone—would feel while she camped there.

This is really a story about love. And about how Hayley, left pregnant and destitute by a scoundrel husband, learns to trust Jake with her life and that of her child. I hope you enjoy my efforts on Hayley's behalf.

I love hearing from readers. You can write me at the address below or e-mail me.

*Roz Denny Fox*

P.O. Box 17480-101
Tucson, Arizona 85731
e-mail: rdfox@worldnet.att.net

# MOM'S THE WORD
## Roz Denny Fox

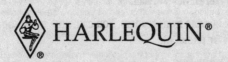

# HARLEQUIN®

TORONTO · NEW YORK · LONDON
AMSTERDAM · PARIS · SYDNEY · HAMBURG
STOCKHOLM · ATHENS · TOKYO · MILAN · MADRID
PRAGUE · WARSAW · BUDAPEST · AUCKLAND

ISBN 0-373-70926-9

MOM'S THE WORD

Copyright © 2000 by Rosaline Fox.

For Denny. I couldn't have written any of the previous books without your love and support. But with this one I *really* owe you—for driving to ghost towns where there weren't any roads. For finding a spring that, according to the map, was supposed to exist but turned out not to be so easily located. And especially for not complaining when the water was too deep to cross and we needed to reach the highway we could see in the distance. You probably felt like leaving me there, but you still had a smile after bouncing twenty long, dusty miles over terrain that was really only accessible on horseback. Thanks, with all my heart.

# CHAPTER ONE

"YOU'RE PREGNANT, Hayley." Kindly old Dr. Gerrard looked over the top of his half glasses at the young woman seated on the examining table. "Given your circumstances, my dear, I hate to be the bearer of bad tidings."

Hayley Ryan stopped pleating folds in the loose-fitting paper gown and gasped as she spread both hands protectively across her stomach. "But I...I've been losing weight. Not gaining. Are you sure your diagnosis is correct?"

The doctor patted Hayley's suntanned hand. "My practice here in Tombstone may be winding down, child, but I haven't been wrong in predicting blessed events in thirty years. Why, twenty-six years ago your mama sat in this very room, asking the same question." He chuckled. "Nine months later out you popped."

"I didn't mean to imply that...that you don't know what you're doing." Hayley swallowed hard to keep from crying. "It's just that this isn't the best time in my life to be learning I'll soon have another mouth to feed. I'm not sure how I'll take care of myself let alone a baby."

Dr. Gerrard sobered at once. "I know. Gossip's running rampant about how your husband left town with that sassy-faced Cindy Trent from the nail-painting place." The doctor removed his glasses and gazed with unfocused sympathy into Hayley's turbulent eyes. "What kind of man, I'd like to know, leaves his wife while she's still grieving from burying her grandpa? I said it before, girl, and I'll say it again—Joe Ryan's worse than a snake-oil salesman."

Hayley glanced away. She could do without having that fact driven home. A little more than a year ago, Grandpa O'Dell and many of his friends had cautioned her against marrying Joe. If she had a dime for every person in Tombstone who'd warned her Joe Ryan was the kind of guy who blew into town on his own wind and would likely blow out the same way, she wouldn't be sitting here now, alone and worrying about how to feed herself and the baby Joe had planted before he pulled his vanishing act. "It's easier for me to see now that Joe only married me so he could get his hands on the Silver Cloud mine," Hayley murmured.

"Big Ben O'Dell would turn over in his grave if he knew that four-flushing louse stole his mine and left you in this fix."

"What's done is done. There's no use crying over it, Dr. Gerrard." Even as the words left Hayley's lips, tears slid down her cheeks.

"This isn't something I'd normally suggest—" Dr. Gerrard hesitated "—but you might think about terminating the pregnancy. I don't perform the procedure, but I'll recommend a reputable clinic in Phoenix. I calculate the child is due around Christmas." He turned and picked up a calendar. "Let's see, it's June. You're eight to ten weeks along. You'll have to decide soon. The surgery does carry some risk, but you're still within the limits set by the state."

Hayley looked horrified and linked her fingers across her stomach. "I appreciate your concern, really I do. But the good Lord entrusted me with a new life. I expect He'll eventually put my feet on a path that'll allow me to take care of myself and this baby.''

''I wish I had your faith, Hayley. If the Man upstairs takes care of His own, He shouldn't have let Joe and that floozy forge your name on the Silver Cloud's deed. Wasn't more'n six months ago that Ben told me he felt so poorly he'd decided to sign it to you. Joe was sittin' right here. If you ask me, that's when the lowlife hatched his plan.''

''Probably so. Then I suppose you could say I brought this mess on myself,'' she said glumly. ''Gramps didn't like Joe to drive him to his breathing treatments. That day, Dee Dee Johnson phoned and asked me to go to the gem show in Tucson with her. I'd never been to a gem show, even though I've lived in Arizona all my life. I practically begged Joe to take Gramps for me.''

''Don't be taking the blame, girl. Joe's the bad apple. He and that deputy-sheriff pal of his would steal a cross from the church if they thought they could melt it down and sell it for a dollar.''

''You don't mean Shad Tilford?'' Hayley frowned.

''The very same.''

''He…he's in charge of my complaint. Sheriff Bonner assigned Shad to my case when I asked the law to go after Joe for half the money from the mine sale. Shad hasn't been very helpful. He insinuated it was Joe's right, as my husband, to sell the Silver Cloud. He finally said he'd issue a warrant to bring Joe in for questioning.''

''Humph! I'll wager Tilford got a cut of the money Joe received from the deal. I've suspected for some time that our deputy's a little shady. How he ever wound up wearing a badge is beyond me.''

"Francesca said he was an L.A. city cop before he came to Tombstone."

"Just 'cause a chicken's got wings don't mean it can fly. I know Francesca has her fingers in a lot of pies in town, but how does she know Tilford didn't dummy up those fancy recommendations he flashed at the city council meeting?"

Francesca Portolo was one of the former lady friends of Big Ben O'Dell, and as such, she'd had a hand in raising Hayley. Hayley's dad had died in a mining accident when she was only a few weeks old. When she was three, her mother succumbed to breast cancer. Hayley's maternal grandfather, Ben O'Dell, a local prospector who'd—more than once—lost his shirt mining for silver, gold and copper, became guardian and caretaker of his grandchild. He, in turn, relied on the women who fostered dreams of becoming the second Mrs. Ben O'Dell to raise Hayley.

She had a soft spot in her heart for all of them, but Francesca, owner of the local fabric store, had taught Hayley how to sew and cook. In addition, she'd shown a lonely little girl tricks she needed to know about becoming a woman. So Hayley tended to believe Francesca.

"Like I said, Dr. Gerrard, I'm in a fix and it's not likely to change. Gramps had more downs than ups, but he was never a quitter. Nor am I. To tell you the truth, I'm relieved to hear it's a baby making me sick and not cancer, like killed Mama. If my health's otherwise okay, I'll get by without Joe."

"You're fit as a fiddle, Hayley, though a mite on the skinny side. Ask Esther at the front desk for the booklet I give all my prospective mothers. Tells you pretty much everything you need to know about prenatal care. Follow the book's advice and eat right. You'll have a healthy baby.''

''Thanks, Dr. Gerrard. I guess my biggest worry, then, is how to earn the money to keep the rent paid, eat right and pay for my delivery.''

''Your grandpa and I went back a long way. I'll arrange terms to make it easy on you, Hayley. Tell Esther that, too.''

Hayley smiled, the first real smile since her grandfather's chronic asthma facilitated a persistent bacterial pneumonia from which he never recovered. Thank God, she thought, the world still held a few good men like Dr. Gerrard.

As Hayley left the clinic with the booklet and a supply of prenatal vitamins clutched in her hand, she set her sights on doing whatever was necessary to make a life for herself and the new life growing inside her.

Which seemed easier said than done when she returned home and found the mail had brought overdue notices on her utilities. Not only that, rent on the house was due in three days. She phoned Sheriff Bonner and voiced her concerns about Shad. Bonner said she had to be patient. They'd issued a warrant for Joe. It seemed he'd disappeared.

On hanging up, Hayley reviewed her options. She had the thousand dollars' guilt money Joe had left on the kitchen table. In the note he'd clipped to it, he'd said the money should tide her over until she found work. Of course, Joe ignored the fact that in a community-property state, he owed her half of the two hundred and fifty thousand he'd received from a mining consortium. Even so, it wasn't his taking the money that hurt so much. It was his betrayal. Never very outgoing, Hayley hadn't made a lot of friends her own age before Joe had come to town selling mining explosives. She'd been flattered by his interest. He was good-looking and charismatic. And he'd centered his attention on her.

Gramps had said disparaging things about Joe. So had several of the old-timers in town. Now Hayley wished she'd listened. But no one, especially not Gramps, understood how lonely she'd been for most of her life. Ben O'Dell had been a tough old codger who liked his solitude. He often took off for weeks on end, prospecting. When he was home, he was preoccupied with the Silver Cloud mine.

Mining was virtually all Hayley knew, too. And mining was tough. There hadn't been money for college at the time she graduated from high school. While her contemporaries moved on, Hayley had been stuck in Tombstone. Was it any wonder that at twenty-five, she'd latched on to Joe like a drowning woman with a life preserver? It was painful now to admit she'd been hoodwinked—that she'd been stupidly trusting despite all the warnings.

Not a chance she'd make *that* mistake again. No, siree! Hayley Ryan was through with men. Anyway, she had bigger worries now. A thousand dollars wouldn't pay two months' rent, let alone keep up with utilities and buy food.

She needed a long-term plan. She needed a job. But...doing what? Hayley drew stars on the back of her electric bill. Shoot, she didn't have a lot of skills, and Tombstone wasn't exactly a job mecca. Sometimes months went by without an opening being listed in the paper. If she knew anyone in Tucson or Phoenix, she could go there, where unskilled jobs were more plentiful. Thing was, she didn't even have transportation. Joe had traded in his car and Ben's sedan on a flashy convertible—or so she'd heard. The pencil lead broke as she bore down on the last star.

"Lord," she muttered, propping her chin in one palm, "if you're going to show me a path, now would be as good a time as any to do it." Idly she sorted a stack of bills while gazing blankly around at the meager accumulation of a lifetime. Dinnertime came, but she had no appetite. Although now she had to think about someone besides herself. The first item in Dr. Gerrard's prenatal care booklet said to eat nutritious meals.

Hayley finally settled on a salad with some grated cheese for protein. She was in the middle of halfheartedly tearing apart limp lettuce when someone knocked timidly on her door.

For a moment her stomach pitched. *Had Joe repented?* As quickly, Hayley knew she'd never take him back even if he crawled in on hands and knees.

It wasn't him she saw, anyway, as she peeped through the window beside the door. It was Virgil Coleman, one of her grandfather's retired mining buddies.

"Virgil, hi," she greeted the crusty gentleman who stood on the porch, crumpling a battered hat between his gnarled hands.

"Hate to bother you, little lady, you being in mourning and all." The old fellow carefully picked his way through condolences, as men his age were prone to do. Clearing his throat, he added, "My oldest boy, Hank, is coming tomorrow to move me up to his place in Flagstaff. We're putting my property up for sale. I wondered if you'd mind moving Ben's old pickup and camp trailer out of my shed? The Realtor said I gotta clean the place up."

"Pickup and camp trailer? I thought all of Gramps's

equipment went to the consortium that bought the mine.''

"Ben never used this stuff at the Silver Cloud. It's his prospecting outfit. In fact, the whole kit and caboodle was once your dad's. So I guess you know it's old. Truck still runs okay, though.''

"I'd forgotten those things.'' Hayley could barely contain her excitement. "The unit is self-contained, right?''

When Virgil scratched the fringe of hair that ringed his bald pate, Hayley elaborated. "I mean, the trailer has a kitchen, bedroom and bathroom, doesn't it?''

"About the size of a postage stamp, but yep. Once Big Ben stepped inside, he filled the place. I reckon it served his purpose, though. A man huntin' ore travels light. He made do with it when he worked his claim down Ruby way.''

"Wait—are you saying Gramps had a mine other than the Silver Cloud?''

"Not a mine, but a claim site.''

Hayley was floored by the news. And thrilled. And suddenly hopeful. "A duly registered claim?'' she asked, her heart beginning to flutter excitedly.

Virgil stammered a bit. "'Spect so. Don't rightly know. If Ben worked it, I knowed he'd have filed right and proper.''

"A name, Virgil.'' She grabbed the old man's scrawny wrist. "If you know what he called his claim, I can find the location in the recorder's office.''

Shaking his head, the old man backed out the door. "Wish I could help you more, missy. Ben was real secretive about that claim. So can I tell Hank you'll pick up the truck and trailer tomorrow or the next day?''

"Yes. You bet. Virgil, you just made my day.'' Hayley flung her arms around his wasted shoulders and gave him a resounding kiss on his leathery cheek. Typical of an old miner, Virgil blushed and hurriedly stammered out a goodbye.

Hayley spent only a moment hugging herself in glee and dancing around the room. Then she went to the one place she thought her grandfather might have kept a record of the claim. The same antique strongbox where he'd stored the deed that Joe had stolen. But even if Joe had found placer or lode claims for the Ruby site, she'd still have the pickup and trailer.

As she took down the box with hands that shook, Hayley recalled reading a magazine in Dr. Gerrard's office about campers who parked their RVs for free out on the desert near Quartzsite. If nothing else, it'd be a place she could live rent free until the baby arrived. A place where she could stretch the money Joe had left her.

It'd be too much to hope for—to think she might actually have claim rights to a parcel of land.

After a deep breath, Hayley began unloading the strongbox. She found her birth certificate and her parents' certificate of marriage, along with old family photos. She paused to look at one of her mom before reverently laying it aside. Taped to the back of her grandmother's photo was her worn gold wedding band. Old-timers in town said that Hayley, except for her lighter hair color, resembled her grandmother, a full-blooded Apache.

Hayley lightly traced the woman's high cheekbones and straight black hair. She saw a resemblance both to herself and her mother. It was easy to see why Grandpa had never given his heart to another woman, even though he'd taken numerous females to his bed. There was a strength and beauty about her grandmother that made her very different from softer ladies Ben squired around town.

Hayley neared the bottom of the box and her hopes of finding a claim dimmed. Suddenly, stuck to the lining, there it was. A claim form, yellowed with age, stapled to a hand-drawn map. Hayley could tell by the dates stamped on the form that Ben had refiled on the same site for ten years. To retain rights to any claim, a miner had to do a minimum of a hundred dollars' worth of work on it every calendar year. The recording calendar ran from July 1 to June 30.

*Yikes!* She had a week left to ready an outfit and refile on the property.

*A week!* Yet it felt like a beautiful, wonderful, stupendous reprieve. Hayley hugged the papers to her breast and skipped across the threadbare living-room carpet. She had no idea what Gramps thought he'd find near the old ghost town of Ruby. But certainly something worth going there for year after year.

Gold? Arizona had a rich history of gold deposits. Ben had fascinating stories to tell about placer-gold and flourgold strikes. He'd taken Hayley prospecting in her younger days. Those trips had been idyllic. Out of her memories, Hayley suddenly formed a vision of cottonwoods shading a lazy stream. It was a vision she couldn't shake throughout a sleepless night or as she walked over to Virgil's the next day to claim her truck and camp trailer. Once again life held purpose. Purpose and dreams.

By the end of the following week, she'd paid her bills and said her goodbyes to the people who mattered. Only a very few people knew she'd bought stores for a lengthy outing. Cradling her still-flat stomach, she smiled.

"Hang in there, wee one. Your mama's going to find gold. You'll never have to worry about where your next meal's coming from—and you'll never have to rely on a man to take care of you."

Monday morning she left Tombstone behind and aimed the old pickup toward the county seat to renew Ben's claim.

When she got to the courthouse in Nogales, she filed for a divorce from Joe Ryan and posted her filing fee on the claim. Her dreams didn't stretch so far that she dared believe she'd ever become a millionaire, though she did allow herself to hope that Ben's secret claim would produce enough ore to provide her child with the kind of life she'd always wanted herself. Including a house. A permanent home in some friendly city that no one could ever take away.

After leaving the courthouse, she began the trek to Ruby. Twice she had doubts—although she never considered turning back. Once when she lost sight of the jutting red rock known as Montana Peak, which she'd been using as her compass since leaving the highway, and a second time when she passed the ghost town of Ruby. One-hundred-degree heat sizzled off the dented hood of the pickup. The remnants of dilapidated buildings depressed her. They stood as grim reminders that this scorched earth had beaten stronger men and women than Hayley Andrews Ryan ever thought of being.

She touched her stomach, where the flutter she felt was fear, not the movement of her child. What insanity had possessed her to come to this desolate land alone? *Pregnant* and alone.

Then, when the vegetation became greener and Hayley spotted a frolicking white-faced cow and calf, she reminded herself how alone she'd been in Tombstone.

"There's just you and me, kid," she murmured, patting her stomach again.

The trailer bumped when she hit a rocky dip. Hayley bounced on the seat and settled back with a giggle. "I hope you like roller coasters, kiddo. The track from here on is a real washboard."

According to the map, she was near the claim. While she'd hoped for an oasis of deer grass and cottonwoods, what lay ahead was an occasional mesquite, ironwood and rock. Sheer cliffs of reddish rock. Turning left around a promontory, Hayley saw a cascade of water falling between the two sentinel rocks drawn on the map. The falling water formed a natural spring. But it didn't feed the Santa Cruz River as she'd hoped.

A crushing disappointment descended as Hayley stopped her rig in the clearing also indicated on the crude map. So her grandfather hadn't been panning for gold. What riches had enticed him to come to this desolate place year after year—and to keep it such a secret?

She pulled the trailer beneath the shade of a huge mesquite. Maybe this *wasn't* the place, she thought as she climbed down from the cab.

But a hand-carved wooden sign carefully wedged in a stack of rocks said Blue Cameo Mine. Tears sprang to her eyes and it suddenly seemed absolutely right that she be here. A cameo carved in blue was the only memento she had of her mother. Another legacy stolen by Joe Ryan. Losing the cameo had hurt worse than his selling the Silver Cloud.

Ben O'Dell had carved his name in the sign. That was how prospectors staked a claim. Hayley could expect to find a similar mound at each of the claim's four corners. Twenty acres in all was the limit one person could work.

Night was sneaking up on her. The sun had slipped

behind the Sierrita Mountains. Tomorrow would be
plenty of time to take stock of the land Hayley planned
to call home for at least the next six months. What she
needed to do in the remaining daylight was unhitch the
pickup and level the trailer. With luck, she'd have time
to gather a bit of wood and build a campfire. The trailer's
utilities ran on butane, but she wanted to save that for
when inclement weather drove her inside. She hadn't
passed a convenience store or gas station, in the past
thirty miles. Twenty of those miles had been unpaved
road. Yes, she'd do well to save her store-bought resources and live off the land for as long as possible.

One indulgence she'd bought—a portable radio. And
she'd laid in a good supply of batteries. It had seemed
a frivolous purchase at the time, but as she snapped it
on and twirled the dial until she found the faint strains
of Tejano music coming from across the border, Hayley
thanked whatever had prompted her to make the impul-
sive buy. With music, she didn't feel half so alone.

As she built a fire, hammered pegs to hold the trailer's
awning and dragged out the two lawn chairs that had
belonged to Gramps, Hayley paused a moment to appreciate a truly glorious sunset. Life wasn't so bad, she
decided on a rush of emotion. In fact, things had turned
out pretty darned good. The thought ended abruptly.
Over a lull in the twangy music, Hayley heard the steady
clip-clop, clip-clop of a horse's hooves.

Holding her breath, she lowered the music. Yes, a
horse and rider were definitely coming closer. The
squeak of leather told her the horse was saddled. Gramps
had taught her well to listen for and delineate sounds in
the wild. And he obviously didn't consider this site totally safe; in the pickup's window rack, Ben had left a

twelve-gauge, double-barreled shotgun and a well-oiled rifle.

Hayley dashed to the truck and grabbed the shotgun. She'd never shoot a person, but scaring someone, now, that was a different story. No stranger to guns, Hayley counted on being able to run a good bluff. She carefully put the crackling fire between her and the approaching rider.

Unfortunately he came at her out of the west, forcing her to look directly into the brilliant red glow of the sinking sun. Horse and rider rounded an outcrop of granite, appearing as a huge dark shadow. The horse snorted and blew as if he'd been ridden hard. The man sat tall and menacing in the saddle. These few facts registered with Hayley as she raised the gun to her shoulder and said in the toughest voice she could muster, "Stop right there." Squinting, she saw that the stranger wore a battered Stetson. His shoulders were wide, his legs long, and he looked like he hadn't shaved in a while. Even in modern times, Tombstone attracted its share of saddle tramps; Hayley had heard that the farther south one went, the more likelihood there was of encountering men who made their living rustling cattle or running contraband across the border. Just another show of her bad luck that she'd meet one of the unsavory types her first night out.

"Who the hell are you?" a rough voice asked. "This is private property. I'll give you two seconds to pack up and scram off Triple C land."

Hayley had to hand it to the stranger. He ran a fair bluff, too. "Scram yourself, cowboy. I have a piece of paper that says this twenty acres belongs to me as long as I work my claim. And I've got a loaded gun backing up my right to be here. I suggest you hightail it back wherever you came from.''

''You've staked a claim? For mining?''

''Not your business, cowboy.'' Hayley drew back one shotgun hammer. Instead of withdrawing as she expected, her visitor touched his boot heels to the big gelding and crow-hopped toward her.

Hayley didn't want to shoot, but the closer he got, the bigger he seemed. His sweating horse might as well have been breathing fire. Hayley panicked. She envisioned her life and that of her unborn child ending here in no-man's-land, where the buzzards would pick her bones clean and no living soul would care. Aiming above his head, hoping to make him think she meant business, she fired.

The force of the explosion slammed the stock of the gun against her shoulder and spun her sideways. But not before she saw a limb on the mesquite splinter. A thick limb, about to drop on the stranger's head. If she didn't do something, it could strike him dead. Hayley dropped the shotgun and lunged at the bay gelding.

''Are you plumb crazy, woman?'' The rider jerked back on his reins, which was the wrong thing to do. The limb hit him hard and scared his mount, who reared high on his hind legs and bolted, sending his rider flying.

The man landed hard enough to shake the ground.

''Oh, no. Oh, no!'' This was not at all what Hayley had intended. Muttering a prayer, she hurried to the stranger's side, fell to her knees and peered anxiously at his face. A great bloody gash spread above his left ear. Hesitantly she slipped her fingers beneath the red bandanna he had tied around his neck, checking for a pulse.

''Thank God.'' Hayley heaved a sigh and pillowed

his head on her knees. His pulse beat slow and steady. At least she hadn't killed him.

JACOB COOPER opened his eyes. He felt the world spin, so he shut them again. There was a hollow ringing in his ears. It took Jake several moments to realize he was no longer seated in his saddle but lay horizontally on the ground—with his head resting on something soft. Good, since his head hurt like hell.

What the devil had happened? It'd been years since he'd tumbled from a horse. Not since his rodeo days.

All at once Jake remembered the woman with the big eyes and the even bigger gun. Had she shot him? He struggled to sit up and, though woozy, nearly smacked his nose into a face peering at him from close range. Had he met his maker? Was this the angel of death? Somehow he'd never expected the angel of death to be so pretty.

So pretty, or so solidly real. It dawned on Jake that his head lay on the lap of a flesh-and-blood woman. He was so deliriously happy to discover he was alive he started to laugh.

His angel of death's beautiful eyes narrowed warily. Jake noticed they weren't blue as he'd thought at first but almost lavender—unless it was a trick of the light created by a fading sun.

"What's so funny?" the woman demanded, beginning to edge out from beneath his shoulders.

"You are," Jake said, planting a hand near her hip so he could lever himself into a sitting position. "If I'd been the kind of guy you thought I was—the kind who needed killing— you'd be in a heap of trouble about now, lady."

She scrambled backward, still on her knees. "I wasn't

trying to kill you. I'll have you know I generally hit what I aim for.''

Jake touched his bloody head. ''I'll vouch for that.'' He climbed shakily to his feet and whistled for his horse, who now stood quietly lapping water from the spring.

''I aimed over your head. The sun was in my eyes. I didn't know the shot would sever a dead limb on that big old mesquite.''

Jacob now understood why he couldn't hear so well. It'd been the nearness of the shotgun blast. He glanced at the ground, saw the size of the limb and thought it was a miracle he and Mojave hadn't both been killed. The base of the limb was as big around as his thigh, and the front portion looked like a spike. ''Loggers call limbs like this widow makers,'' he muttered. ''Only I don't have a wife.''

The woman obviously wasn't anywhere near ready to trust him. While he patted down his horse, checking him for injuries, she stretched out a hand to retrieve her gun.

It was then that Jake noticed how dark it had become. The only light now came from the woman's campfire. Yet he could clearly see what she had in mind. In two long strides he beat her to the weapon. ''Oh, no, you don't. I'm not letting you finish the job.'' As easily as taking a lollipop from a toddler, Jake divested her of her weapon.

''How about we start with introductions,'' he said when she shied away. ''I'm Jacob—Jake—Cooper from the Triple C ranch. I admit this spring is on Bureau of Land Management property, but it's got water crucial to our cattle. In fact, there are some ten ranchers in the area who need that water. July to October our range land is almost dry. The vaqueros we hire to help with roundup start that pump over there at intervals to feed water through the ditches. Well, it's not really a pump, but a set of four flow valves that work off the water pressure when someone turns the wheels and opens the valves." He pointed.

"I don't think so, Mr. Cooper." She crossed her arms. "I've recorded a legal claim to prospect here. My claim starts at that pile of rocks—at the sign declaring it the Blue Cameo Mine. This plot of ground is mine from now until next July."

"Sorry. I didn't catch your name."

"Hayley. Hayley Ryan. Feel free to check with the county recorder and the state BLM office. You'll find my paperwork in order and my fees paid."

Jake bent at the waist and scooped up his hat from where it had fallen. He jammed it on his head and then grimaced because it scraped the bloody reminder of his encounter with this woman. "I hate to burst your bubble, Hayley Ryan. You're claim-jumping. A man by the name of Ben O'Dell filed on this site—and the Triple C has an agreement with Ben. He promised to notify us when he's finished prospecting, and we're going to the recording office with him when he releases the mineral rights. Then we'll buy this twenty acres, plus the hundred that adjoins it."

"Did my grandfath…uh…Ben…did he put that in writing?"

Jake removed his hat again and slapped it against his thigh. "I shot the breeze with Ben a lot. We swapped stories and drank coffee or an occasional beer. I suppose you could call what we had a gentlemen's agreement. Are you and he related? He never mentioned having a family."

"Everyone has a family. Ben passed on recently. That

nullifies his claim. If you two had an agreement, he didn't tell anyone. My claim is good, Mr. Cooper.''

Jake's eyes narrowed suspiciously. ''Well, I hope you'll pardon me if I ride into Tombstone to see if you're telling the truth.''

''Be my guest.'' Hayley waved him off. ''Don't let me keep you. It's been a long day. I'd like to eat my evening meal in peace, if you don't mind, Mr. Cooper.''

''It's Jake, or Jacob, please.''

''Jacob, then,'' she said sweetly, extending a hand. ''And, if you don't mind, I'll take my shotgun before you go.''

Jake let his disgruntled gaze circle the isolated campsite before he silently handed back her gun. ''Ben never said what he was digging for. It must be something valuable for a pretty lady like you to bury herself in such a desolate place. Are you aware of how far it is to the nearest ranch house?''

When she said nothing, only clamped her pointed little jaw tighter, Jake went ahead and filled her in before he swung into the saddle. ''Your closest neighbor would be the Triple C. Eight miles from here as the crow flies. Closer to twelve if you follow the trail. Our ranch sits practically on the Mexican border.''

Again Hayley said nothing. She simply cocked her head.

''Dang! It goes against my grain to leave a lady alone among coyotes and wolves. To say nothing of any two-legged varmints who drift past here, or any illegals jumping the border. Say the word and I'll help you hitch up that trailer so you can park closer to civilization.''

''I just unhitched, Mr. Cooper, er, Jake.'' Hayley enunciated clearly, as if to a child.

"I'm offering you the Triple C's hospitality, woman."

"My name is Hayley," she said pointedly as he'd done with his earlier. "Nice try, but nothing you say is going to frighten me off my claim. You may as well give up. If you have eight miles to travel before sitting down to supper, hadn't you better take off?" Hayley delivered the advice through a dazzling smile.

Jake pinched the bridge of his nose. Stubborn didn't begin to describe Hayley Ryan. He could just imagine what his dad and his brother, Dillon, who lived with his wife in a separate house on Triple C land, were going to say when he delivered the news about this squatter. He'd catch hell from his mom and his sister-in-law, Eden, too, for leaving a defenseless woman to fend for herself. Jake was torn between going home to impart the news or sticking close to look after the damn little fool.

A sharp pain sliced through his skull. He changed his mind about calling the woman defenseless. She was one tough cookie.

Touching two fingers curtly to the brim of his hat, he wheeled Mojave and rode off the way he'd come. If she didn't run out of lead for that scattergun, she ought to be safe enough by herself—for one night.

# CHAPTER TWO

WADE COOPER met his son in the barn where Jake had stopped to rub down and feed Mojave. A Border collie Jake had raised from a pup yapped excitedly.

"Sit, Charcoal," ordered Wade, a lean handsome man in his midsixties. Without being asked, he pitched in to help Jake take care of his horse. "Expected you back by suppertime. Why don't you let me finish here? Go wash up. Your mother saved you a plate in the oven. You know Nell won't admit to worrying, but she still frets and peeks down the road when she thinks I'm not looking."

"Yeah, well, I'd have been here sooner, but I ran into a snag." Jake removed his Stetson and gingerly touched his swollen temple. It still hurt like hell.

"Literally a snag?" Wade stepped closer and frowned at the blood matted in his son's close-cropped sideburns.

"In more ways than one, I'm afraid." Jake left nothing out as he replayed his encounter with Hayley Ryan at Ben O'Dell's claim.

"Well, hell!" Wade exclaimed. His chin sagged to his chest by the time Jake finished his story. "I feel bad about Ben. Would've attended his funeral if I'd known about it. Your brother subscribes to all those damned papers—Tombstone, Nogales, Tubac. Wonder how he missed O'Dell's obituary?"

"You'll have to ask him. Perhaps Eden lined the bird

cage with it.'' Jake grinned. His brother was sappy in love with his wife. He'd do anything for her. But Dillon really had a hard time liking Eden's beloved parrot. Coronado talked a blue streak to everyone who walked into the couple's house—but reserved special treatment for Dillon, screeching at him and biting him every chance he got.

"Quit needling Dillon over that bird. Tell me more about the Ryan woman.''

Jake scowled. "What's to tell? She's no bigger than a flea. One of our stiff Baja winds will blow her and that tomfool toy trailer of hers right off the map.''

"That's not what I meant. Ben led me to believe he'd kept this claim a secret.''

"Hayley Ryan alleges she's Ben's granddaughter. But he never mentioned any kin to me. I wonder if she's trying to pull a fast one. She told me Ben never said a word about our water deal. And asked me if I had something in writing. I thought I'd drive to Tombstone tomorrow and snoop a little.''

"Let Mom and me go,'' Wade said. "We'll drive on to Tucson. Nell's been badgering me to go before roundup starts. She heard about a new pottery-supply store.''

"Fine by me. I'd just as soon not drive the pickup over that graveled track between here and Arivaca.'' Jake hunkered down to pat Charcoal, then let the dog lick his face.

"Probably wouldn't hurt if you were to ride back out and check on the woman tomorrow. Someone should warn her about the rattlers nesting back in those rocks. Ben tangled with a couple of big ones.''

"It's a waste of breath trying to scare her off. I

brought up wolves, coyotes and mentioned illegals coming through. Didn't faze her.''

''Hmm. Then turn on the Cooper charm and see if you can work the same deal with her as we set up with Ben.''

Jake snorted and wrinkled his nose.

''Wha-at? You think I haven't heard Eden and Nell talk about how all the ranchers' daughters around here make cow eyes at you? I hear Dillon teasing you about all those single artists in Tubac who'd like to become Mrs. Jacob Cooper.''

''You're forgetting Hayley Ryan took a potshot at me, Dad.'' Jake didn't tell his father, however, that she'd also cushioned his injured head in her lap. Falling off his horse had been humiliating. But her hands had felt cool against his skin, and she'd smelled good. Very, very good. Jake recalled enjoying the faint scent of apple blossoms when he'd come to. Thinking about it again made him go a little breathless. He took a step back, threw the brush into a box of supplies and led Mojave into a stall.

''What do you suppose Ben hoped to find?'' Jake asked Wade, to take his mind off the way Hayley Ryan felt and looked and smelled.

''Can't recall the old guy saying. I don't know if he just needed to escape town life for a month or so every summer, or if he actually found ore.''

''You'd think it'd have to be more than just an escape to drag a guy out to live in primitive conditions every year for some ten years.''

''I figured he was halfheartedly hunting silver. A couple of times he talked like the ore was slowly playing out of his mine near Tombstone. But then, I'm a cattleman through and through. I don't pretend to know what makes a prospector tick.''

''*There* you two are.'' Nell Cooper poked her head inside the barn. Still slender at fifty-five, she had smooth skin and warm gray eyes, which contributed to the fact that she didn't look much older than her sons, Dillon, thirty-five and Jacob, thirty-two. ''Goodness, Jacob, what happened to your head?'' Very much in command of the Triple C in her role as family caretaker, Nell silenced Charcoal and bustled the men toward the house.

She clucked sympathetically as Jake and Wade alternately explained Jake's clash with Hayley Ryan. ''Well,'' Nell declared as she gently sponged her son's wound, ''that woman sounds crazy. I say leave her alone, Jacob. We used to haul water from the ranch out to some troughs your father and his dad constructed from fifty-gallon barrels. I guess we can do that again.''

Wade and Jake exchanged a very male rolling of the eyes. ''After we successfully dickered to use Ben's spring, it cut our work by half,'' Wade reminded his wife. ''Not only that, we're running twice the summer herd now. Jake, Dillon and I can certainly handle one contrary female.''

As Nell got out first-aid supplies, she wore a look that said they should heed her advice and that the matter wasn't closed by a long shot.

Jake knew that look. ''Mom, don't you be doing anything dumb. You and Dad are going to Tombstone tomorrow to check out the Ryan woman's story. I'm counting strays that may have drifted up around Pena Blanca Lake. I'll keep tabs on her when I head out in the morning.''

''You'd better spy on her from a distance,'' his mother said as she rubbed antibacterial cream across

Jake's nasty-looking wound. "Her aim might be truer next time."

Jake sighed. "I told you she was shooting over my head. She stared square into the sun and didn't see the limb. I peg her as a stubborn female, not a criminal."

"Jacob Cooper." Nell wagged a finger. "Now, mind you, I'm not condoning what she did. But I hope you're not one to be calling her stubborn simply because she's a woman. If it were a man protecting his claim, you'd give him his due."

"Now, Mama, I give women their due. What I was trying to say is that Hayley Ryan isn't all that dangerous."

"Doesn't hurt to take it easy until we know more, son," Wade said, clapping Jake on the shoulder. "I mean, we don't know anything about her, and we don't know how old Ben died, now do we?"

"Oh, for crying out loud." Jake threw up his hands and stalked into the kitchen, away from his parents. As they entered the room behind him, he faced them again and ran a hand across his jaw with its three-day growth of beard. He directed his question at Nell. "Look at me. If I rode in and surprised you, and you were camped alone, wouldn't you pull a gun if you had one?"

Nell studied her second-born son. The love she felt for him shone from her eyes.

"Okay, so it's not a fair question," Jake allowed. "All I'm saying is I'm willing to cut her some slack."

Nell removed a warming plate from the oven and set it on the table, then motioned Jake to have a seat. "You can be respectful without being too trusting, Jacob. Oh, I know, females young and old fall naturally under your spell. At times it's music to a mother's ears, even if some of them insult me with their flattery when they're angling to become my daughter-in-law. But remember, this Hayley Ryan is a total stranger. Just because she appears helpless and vulnerable doesn't mean she is. Don't forget the women's prisons are full of baby-faced stinkers.''

A peal of laughter burst from Jake. His eyes, a shade lighter gray than his mother's, reflected his mirth. ''That must be lecture number ten million nine hundred and ninety-nine thousand. Dillon said you quit lecturing him altogether when he married Eden. Is that what I have to do to get you to ease up, Mom? Find me a wife?''

She looked sheepish for a moment, then playfully slapped one of his broad shoulders. ''Go ahead, laugh. You'll understand when you have kids of your own. A mother wants her children's lives to be perfect. They never get so old that you stop worrying.''

''You worry too much,'' Jake told her.

Wade looped his arms around his wife. He pinioned her arms and nuzzled her neck. ''Our boys are men, Nell. Time they worried about themselves. In fact, Jake and I were talking yesterday. After the next roundup we thought we'd start clearing that mesa he's had his eye on. You know, the one overlooking Hell's Gate.''

The news brought a happy cry from Nell. ''Jake. Does this mean you've made up your mind to put a ring on some lucky girl's finger? No, don't tell me. Let me guess. Cayla Burke.'' She glanced from her husband to her son and back again. ''Granted, Cayla can be a little chatty, but she knows ranching. No?'' She pursed her lips. ''Who, then? Oh, Jake, not Sierra Mackey. I know Eden said you danced with her three times at the grange dance last month. But she's…she's…''

''Well, don't stop there,'' Jake teased. ''Sierra's what?''

Nell gulped. ''If she's your choice, Jake, I don't want

to be critical of her. I'll support your decision and make her welcome here, of course.''

''I'm not marrying Sierra. Just because I'm ready to have a place of my own doesn't mean I've found a partner. Not that I'm not looking. I am. But I'm holding out for what you and Dad have. And I'll finish the sentence for you. Sierra is exactly like her mother. Myra drinks too much and she can't keep her hands off other women's husbands. I've got eyes, Mom.''

''And brains,'' Wade said, drawing his wife around for a more complete kiss. ''Enough said, Nell,'' he muttered. ''Let's retire and let Jacob eat.''

Jake watched them leave arm in arm. An emptiness washed over him. He despaired of ever finding a mate who compared to his mother or to Dillon's wife, Eden. Both were one-man women. Yet they were strong and independent. His mom was a talented potter. Eden, a silversmith. Her jewelry sold in fine stores all over the world. Underneath, at a very basic level, each loved the land. Jake wouldn't settle for less.

The ranch was important to him. Many of the women he'd dated over the past five years couldn't wait to shake the dust of the country off their feet. Jake had known from the time he was five that he never wanted to do anything but raise beeves like his dad. Maybe it wasn't meant for him to get married, he mused as he polished off the last of the casserole and carried his plate to the dishwasher.

Maybe, unlike his father and brother, he couldn't have both.

HAYLEY SAT BESIDE her campfire and toyed with the hasty meal of biscuits and stew she'd fixed after the cowboy had gone. She couldn't remember a night so dark. There must have been some, she thought. Those times she'd gone prospecting with her grandfather. But back then, his larger-than-life presence had dispelled all the fears a young girl might associate with the darkness.

Hayley wished Jake Cooper hadn't ridden into her camp. In doing so, he'd reminded her how isolated she was. As melancholy overtook her, Hayley recognized that she'd fallen into the grip of a terrible homesickness.

Not only that, her uninvited visitor's unsubtle warning had turned the surrounding blackness into a potential place of terror. No stranger to the yip of coyotes, Hayley now gave a start and shivered whenever she heard distant calls.

She'd intended to stoke the fire after doing her dishes and then read one of the Luke Short westerns she'd brought to spice up lonely evenings. When an owl hooted nearby and she practically jumped out of her skin, Hayley changed her mind about staying up. She scraped her uneaten food into an airtight container to be disposed of later, and banked the fire, instead of feeding it.

She made one last check of the food sacks she'd hung in a tree. Jacob Cooper hadn't mentioned bears in his list of things she needed to fear, but Hayley would rather be safe than sorry.

Collecting her shotgun and rifle, she retreated into the tiny trailer, where she tossed and turned for hours. One thought she couldn't shut out: What if Jacob Cooper didn't belong to any Triple C ranch? What if, even now, he was rounding up pals to jump her claim? Things like that happened with regularity in the books she read. Perhaps she should have stocked some contemporary novels. People didn't jump claims in the twenty-first century, did they?

It was the newness of the situation, she tried to tell herself, not Jake's warnings, that had her listening for every whisper of wind through the brush and turning it into a wolf attack or just a plain thief attack.

She'd tried to act brave when Cooper leveled his dire admonitions. Inside she'd been quaking. The man at the recorder's office yesterday had already informed her that two ranchers in this vicinity had reported jaguars killing their range stock. The friend of Ben's from whom she'd borrowed the shotgun had painted a more gruesome picture. He'd flatly stated that homeless individuals who wandered the hills would certainly kill her and make off with her pickup and trailer.

Inside, the trailer was hot as sin. At first she wasn't willing to open either of the small windows, not even if it meant she baked in this tin can. The screens would be no deterrent, she decided, from any man or beast who chose to break in.

She lay on her back in the close confines of the small alcove and laced her hands across her belly. Talking to her baby helped calm her. "This is our only chance to make a go of things, Junior," she murmured. "Francesca warned me I'd kill us both hauling rocks or blasting ore out of the ground. Hard work never hurt a pregnant woman," she said, more loudly than she intended. "Gramps said my grandmother took care of my mom, planted and maintained a garden, kept house and helped him haul copper out of his first mine."

Sweat beaded Hayley's brow and trickled between her breasts. Breasts that had grown increasingly tender in the past two weeks. She drew up her nightgown and fanned her legs. "It's not the hard work I mind." Her biggest worry was determining the best time to leave here so

Dr. Gerrard could deliver her baby. And would she have found anything worthwhile on this claim?

Hayley couldn't answer those questions. She did know that if she didn't manage to get some rest, she could forgo working tomorrow. Heavens, she ought to be able to stand a little heat tonight. Things would look better in the morning. They always did.

Ten minutes past midnight Hayley gave up suffering and opted for the possibility of a cooling breeze over the threat of death. Soon after she opened the windows, she felt such relief at the breath of fresh air that she began to cry. Unable to stem the flow of tears, she ended up crying herself to sleep.

LIGHT FILTERING in the window woke Hayley before 5:00 a.m. At first it seemed she'd barely gotten to sleep, and she tried to burrow under the pillow. Almost as fast it struck her that she'd successfully spent the first full night in her new home. Not one bad thing had happened. She derived an immense satisfaction from that. Greeting the day seemed far more desirable than lolling about in a hot trailer.

She showered in the cramped hollow carved in rock behind the waterfall. Refreshed, she hummed "Carrying Your Love with Me," a once-popular George Strait tune, as she started a fire and put on water for tea. She ate a bowl of berries and cottage cheese while she waited for the water to boil. In this heat the ice in her cooler would soon be history. "I can't be driving into town too often." She spoke matter-of-factly to her unborn child. "Fresh fruit and veggies are not going to be very plentiful after what I veggies in my cooler spoils. Maybe some farmer around Arivaca will sell me a milk cow and a few laying hens next time I go to town for supplies. I don't have a lot of the thousand dollars left after laying in prospecting tools and stuff. But if the price is right, junior, it'll be worth the money.''

She patted her stomach. "Dr. Gerrard said in a few months I can have an ultrasound done at the hospital to show how far along you are. It might also tell us if you're Junior or Juniorette." Hayley chuckled, but soon her laughter faded. "I'm not sure I want to know. Life needs some nice surprises." For the first time since learning of her condition, Hayley wondered if Joe would care that he'd left her pregnant. Probably not, but he deserved to know he'd fathered a child. If the law found him, she'd tell him.

Pouring herself a second cup of tea, Hayley firmly rejected further thoughts of Joe and set out to wander the low-lying hills beyond the waterfall. What she hoped to find was a stream that might indicate Gramps had been panning for gold. Swishing water around in a sieve would be much easier on her than blasting rock and hauling heavy ore down from a mountain.

Instead of flattening out into a valley that would support a stream, the terrain beyond the spring grew hillier. There were signs in numerous places that her grandfather had used his rock hammer to split rocks. Since some pieces were missing, Hayley surmised he'd taken sections to assay.

At the top of the second rise, she turned in a tight circle and surveyed the area all the way to her campsite. What had her grandfather expected to find?

Sighing, she hopped from rock to rock and picked her way back to the trailer. This would be a beautiful place to build a home. The trees were green, the water sweet and the sky so blue it hurt her eyes. But Hayley was no stranger to the laws governing mining claims. A miner could throw up a tent or move in a motorhome, but any attempt to erect a permanent structure on land open to claims was illegal. And each year the rules got stickier.

At her camp again, Hayley hauled out a couple of her grandfather's mineralogy books, plus the copies she'd made of his yearly filing papers. Each year he'd listed a different mineral. None were valuable. Mica, pyrite and chalcopyrite, all names for fool's gold. He'd once reported streaks of copper. Not a big deal. The area around this site was rife with small deposits of copper.

"Gramps was nobody's fool," Hayley muttered, pouring herself more tea. He knew that if a person wanted to preserve a claim until he made a big find, it was best to feed the county recorder unimportant facts. His last report included quartz and chalcedony. Totally negative geological findings.

Hayley settled into a chair with her tea, the books and a small journal she'd found in the strongbox. Her grandfather had never been much for writing. In fact, Hayley doubted he'd gone past sixth grade in school. Yet he'd painstakingly cataloged everything he'd found when he worked this claim. She noticed his last entry differed from the report he'd given the county recorder.

Was that significant? Hayley sipped her herb tea and stared into space. He'd written coordinates, and in a shaky hand penned in *hydrous silicon oxide*. Hayley wasn't familiar with the term. Did his unsteady writing mean he was excited, or was it simply a sign that he was growing older?

His death was sudden and unexpected. Hayley, as well as others, assumed he'd recover from his nagging bout of pneumonia. Would he have told her about this spot if he'd had more warning? Hayley liked to think he would've taken her into his confidence. However, the old man really detested Joe, so maybe he wouldn't have breathed a word, after all.

The thought saddened her, but Hayley could only be glad Ben had kept his counsel. Otherwise Joe and Cindy would have converted the truck and trailer to cash and sold this claim to the highest bidder. Probably to Jacob Cooper, if he'd been telling the truth.

To keep from sliding into gloom, Hayley set Ben's mineral books on a low camp stool and opened the first to page one. She might not know what hydrous silicon oxide was, but she had a lot of spare time to find out. If need be, she could drive into Tucson to the library. Although Tombstone was closer, everyone there knew her. The first time any local prospectors suspected she was on to anything, this place would be overrun with scavengers.

The thought had no more than entered her mind when a horse and rider and a black-and-white dog exploded from the trees between Hayley and her trailer. She tried but failed to scramble from the chair. She spilled tea everywhere. Her heart tripped over itself. Darn, she'd meant to keep one of the firearms with her at all times. She'd already forgotten and had left both guns in a closet in the trailer.

Before she could panic or even take a levelheaded look at her situation, a familiar voice rang out. ''Don't go for your shotgun until you see what I've brought you.'' A gunnysack dropped into Hayley's lap, and the fright it gave her slammed her heart up into her throat. The bay gelding she'd only seen in twilight kicked sandy soil all over her fire ring as he danced in front of her. The dog, at least, seemed civilized. He ran up and licked her hand.

''Well, open it. It won't bite,'' said the man who'd

introduced himself yesterday as Jacob Cooper. Hayley finally caught her breath, although she continued to eye him warily as he dismounted.

Her hands tugged at the string holding the sack closed even as she noted the changes between this man and the stranger from last night. Still dressed in the working clothes of a cowboy, yesterday's saddle bum now wore a clean shirt and jeans. His hat, instead of the battered Stetson was the summer straw variety, and it was as clean as his newly shaven face. The engaging smile he wore exposed a dimple in one cheek and a cleft in his chin.

Jake dropped on his haunches next to her chair. With a quick flip of his wrist, he spilled the sack's contents into Hayley's hands. Four vine-ripened tomatoes, an ear of fresh corn and two thick slices of ham. "It's home-cured," he said of the ham. "My brother, Dillon, has a smokehouse. Smoking ham, bacon and turkey is kind of a hobby for him."

Hayley met the twinkle in the man's gray eyes with a look she knew must reflect her incredulity.

"I know there's a thank-you on the tip of your tongue," Jake said, rising and barely holding back a grin. "It's not so hard once you get the hang of it."

"I do thank you," she finally managed. "It's just…it's more like…you took me by surprise. You don't even know me!" she blurted. "Why bring me food?"

Jake removed his hat and slapped it a few times against his right knee. "No one ever asks why. Neighbors out here share, that's all. Now you're supposed to reciprocate."

This time Hayley clasped the sack to her breasts protectively. She flattened herself tight to the back of the lawn chair.

"Coffee," Jake said softly. "In exchange, you offer me a cup of java. It's a dusty ride over here. I could use something to wet my whistle before I go hunting for strays."

"Oh, coffee. I'll make some. Goodness, where are my manners?" Hayley babbled. Nimbler than before, she untangled herself from the chair and swept up the pot. "I, uh, have coffee grounds in the trailer. I'll go put the things you brought in my cooler and grab a clean mug for you, as well."

"Sure would appreciate it," he drawled. Watching her hurry away, Jake thought she had to be one of the most naturally pretty females in all three of the surrounding counties. Thick corkscrew curls hung past her shoulders, indicating she probably wore braids. Her eyes were huge and expressive. They were more blue than lavender today. She had a generous mouth and even white teeth. Her skin was possibly her best feature. Bronzed a light gold, to Jake it appeared flawless. At least the part he could see. Dang, he'd barely met the woman. He shouldn't be wanting to see more of her skin.

*Ha, tell that to a certain part of him!*

To keep her from seeing how unsteady his hands were, Jake looped Mojave's reins around a scrub bush and tucked his fingertips into the front pockets of his jeans. No, he decided quickly. That was a bad move.

He snapped his fingers at his dog. When Charcoal dropped panting at his feet, Jake returned his hat to his head and knelt to pet him.

That was the position Hayley found him in when she returned, not only with the coffee grounds and promised mug, but with the shotgun she'd brandished last night.

"Whoa!" Jake tipped his hat to a rakish angle, then held up both hands.

"This isn't for you," she said with a laugh. "But when you rode in, I realized it was pretty stupid of me to be out here alone and unprotected." She leaned the big gun against a boulder and bent to measure coffee grounds.

The seat of her denims pulled snugly over a gently rounded backside. Jake's mouth went dust-dry. For a moment he forgot any objections he had to her walking around with a loaded gun. He swallowed a few times before he could speak again. "So, you haven't had enough of your own company yet?"

Hayley poured his mug full, even though the coffee wasn't much more than colored water at this point.

Jake blew on the liquid to cool it as he waited for her answer.

"I'm planning to stay until December," Hayley said forthrightly.

"December?" Jake scowled. "We're sitting on high desert here."

"Yes." Her tone held an unspoken *So?*

"I don't think you want to camp out when the snow flies."

"Flurries, right? Nothing major. Tombstone and Sierra Vista get a bit of snow. Generally it melts by noon."

"We get more than flurries. If snow happens to fall on the heels of a monsoon, it gives new meaning to the great South*wet.*"

"Why are you trying to run me off this claim, Mr. Cooper?"

"I thought we settled last night that you'd call me Jake."

"Either way, I'm not leaving." She gestured with her own mug, clamped firmly in her left hand.

That was when Jake noticed the white band of skin on her finger—the perfect width for a wedding ring, obviously recently removed. It drew him up short to think of her having been married to some faceless man. He let his face match his mood and he frowned again.

*Stubborn as she was, no wonder some poor bastard took a powder.*

He'd scarcely had the uncharitable thought when he remembered his mother's words, and they kicked in. His mom could be plenty stubborn herself. As could Eden. Both women lived in this valley spring, summer, fall and winter. They made daily trips from the ranch into Tubac, where they shared a shop in the arty community on what had once been the site of Arizona's first mission. The roads in and out weren't great, but their husbands didn't expect them to stop working because of a little bad weather. Jake knew he had no business questioning any of Hayley's decisions.

"Bringing me a few supplies does not give you the right to stick your nose in my business," she said.

Jake was jolted back to the present in the middle of her tart little speech. "You're absolutely correct." He rose to his feet in one rolling motion. "Thanks for the coffee, although it's a mite weak." Moving aside the books spread across a small square table, he set down the nearly full mug. His eyes scanned the pages she'd propped open with a fair-size rock. The chapter was titled: "How to Know Your Minerals and Rocks." Any doubts as to her true intentions were dispelled by her choice of reading material.

"What exactly do you think you're going to find,

hacking around through the rocks and brush, Ms. Ryan?''

"It's Mrs. Ryan."

"Mrs.?'' Jake hadn't expected that comeback and it threw him. He recognized that his reaction was equal parts shock and disappointment.

"Yes. Mrs. Joe Ryan." Hayley bit her lip hard and felt guilty for lying. But technically her divorce wouldn't be final for six months. By then, she'd better have uncovered whatever secrets this land held. Meanwhile, claiming to be married might discourage Jacob Cooper from making any more uninvited visits.

But as she saw him climb back on the big gelding, a pang of regret gripped her chest. These past few minutes had been quite pleasant.

Really, though, she'd be foolish to trust him. Since Joe's subterfuge, Hayley had been reluctant to trust any man. She certainly ought to know better than to let one as overtly charming as Jake Cooper get under her skin. She'd landed in this fix because she'd tumbled head over bootstraps for one beguiling frog she'd mistaken for a prince. She didn't plan to let that happen again.

Shading her eyes, Hayley gazed solemnly at Jake Cooper.

"I've got work to do," he muttered. "Can't stay here socializing all day."

"I didn't invite you here in the first place," she snapped. When guilt stabbed again, Hayley dropped her arm and leaned down to pat his dog. "Take care, old fella," she crooned. "Tell your master I'll enjoy my dinner of ham, tomatoes and fresh corn."

Jake glanced down at the straight-arrow part in her hair, and despite himself he smiled. She tried so hard to act tough. Something told Jake she was a lot softer inside. But two could play her go-between game.

"Charcoal, you tell the lady to bury her scraps deep. We'd hate to have her blood spilled by some marauding cougar or one of those Mexican jaguars sighted around here last fall. Honest," he said. "Oh, and tell her to keep an eye out for rattlers. They come out to warm themselves on the rocks by the spring."

That last bit of information stiffened Hayley's spine. "Ick. I hate snakes. I suppose you're telling the truth?" Her hesitancy indicated she hoped he was lying.

"Scout's honor. Ben collected a whole box of fair-size rattles over the years. Promise me you'll take care."

Hayley didn't know why she should promise him anything. But the concern in his deep voice melted her resistance. "Same goes for you," she offered in a whisper. "I mean, you take care around those steers. I noticed you have a scar running along the top of your cheek. Last man I saw with something similar said he'd tangled with a longhorn."

Jake brushed his thumb over the old wound. He tended to forget about it until he went to shave. "This was a present from the last rodeo bull I climbed aboard. My dad said at least the animal knocked some sense into me. And my brother claimed I finally realized a pretty face meant more to me than a trunkful of gold buckles."

Hayley enjoyed the verbal peek at his family. She envied his close relationship with his dad and his brother. But she couldn't allow herself to feel such things, to be anything but resolutely self-sufficient. Swiveling, she grabbed both mugs and hurried to the spring where she knelt to swish the cups.

Jake willed her to look his way again. When it became

clear she didn't intend to and that their visit was at an end, he whistled Charcoal to heel and galloped off through the trees. Hard as it was, he resisted taking a last survey of Hayley Ryan.

# CHAPTER THREE

HAYLEY WANTED TO CALL Jacob Cooper back. He, his horse and dog had brought some warmth to her day. She felt a sharp loss when they disappeared from sight. Though she'd never had a lot of close friends, in Tombstone she'd at least interacted with people. Every day she went to the post office, the market and the mine. She'd always thrived on the company of others, preferring it to the solitary life she knew too well. Maybe trying to work this site by herself wasn't such a good idea after all.

What choice did she have? Hayley trudged back to the trailer with the newly washed mugs, thinking it wasn't like Joe had left her any alternative. Here it was mid-July. Christmas wasn't all that far off. By then, she'd have the company she craved. A child. Her child. The thought of holding her baby made Hayley smile.

As she returned to the fireside and picked up her book, she gave herself a good talking-to. She hadn't come to her grandfather's claim to socialize. She'd come to wrest out a living for herself and for her unborn child. She didn't need the distraction of a good-looking, soft-voiced cowpuncher. In her limited experience, men who made nice were after more than a cup of coffee. Jacob Cooper wanted something. It was a cinch he wasn't bowled over by her great beauty or stunning personality.

The notion that he might find her attractive made her

laugh. She looked positively scruffy and she'd acted downright surly. If someone had taken a shot at *her,* she wouldn't be inclined to go back, let alone bring gifts. Not only that, Joe had made it abundantly clear in his note that she had nothing to offer a man—except her grandfather's mine.

So, yes. Jake Cooper had an agenda. He wanted free access to the spring. He'd said his family had plans to buy this chunk of land and all the acreage that adjoined it, if and when her grandfather relinquished his claim.

Well…maybe Cooper had a water agreement with Gramps, and maybe he didn't.

Hayley shook off the uncharitable thoughts that kept crowding in. Jake Cooper had made an effort to be friendly. She needed the fresh produce he'd brought. She needed milk and eggs, too. Why hadn't she asked him if he knew of anyone who might sell her a milk cow or a couple of laying hens? Instead of getting so touchy, she should have made inquiries of her own.

JAKE RETREATED to the top of a rise that overlooked Hayley Ryan's camp. Dismounting, he tied Mojave to a scrub oak and flung himself flat behind a slab of granite. Charcoal whined as Jake peeled off his gloves and trained a pair of binoculars on the Ryan woman.

"It's okay, boy," Jake murmured. "We'll hunt strays in a little while. For now, find a shady spot and rest your bones."

The dog flipped his ears to and fro, then stretched out under a tree. Eventually he settled his nose on his front paws, never taking his eyes off Jake.

Jake wasn't sure what he'd expected Hayley to do once he'd gone. He felt a vague disappointment when she returned to her chair and stuck her nose in one of the books she had piled beside her.

"Crazy woman," he growled. "Acts like she's at a resort, instead of smack-dab in the middle of the wilderness." He watched her read for the better part of an hour. Suddenly she glanced up and straight at his hiding place. Jake found himself yanking off his white hat, lest she spot him and get it into her head to take another shot. This time with her rifle.

Common sense told him he was too well hidden to be seen by the naked eye. *Her* naked eye. And brother, what eyes they were. So dark a blue they were almost purple. Still staring through his powerful binoculars, Jake all but drooled on the bandanna around his neck. He didn't relax until she returned her interest to the book.

That didn't last. She soon tossed it aside, stood and shaded her eyes, staring hard in his direction. She turned slowly as if searching the hills for something in particular. *Or someone.*

Jake realized the sun had shifted and was probably reflecting off the lenses of his binoculars. "Crap." He dropped the glasses and scooted back on his belly until he was safely into the trees. "Why don't I just send up a flare and announce I'm snooping?" he muttered disgustedly.

Lifting his head, Charcoal barked.

"Shh." Jake raised a hand. "Sound carries down these ravines, boy. And we don't want the lady to know the Triple C plans to keep her under surveillance for a while."

The dog cocked his head, gazing at Jake intelligently before slithering to his side.

Grinning, Jake rubbed a hand between the dog's ears. "I know. You think I've taken leave of my senses.

Which is precisely what Dillon will say if I don't hightail it out of here.''

Dillon was expecting him to report the total number of strays between the ranch and Hell's Gate, where they were to meet. He'd been at the number-five line shack all week, moving half the herd into summer pastures. Jake was due to connect with him at three o'clock to exchange head counts and… Jake winced. The produce he'd left with Hayley had been meant to replenish his brother's dwindling supplies. Dillon would have a fit when he learned Jacob had given away the food Eden had fixed for him.

Of course, Dillon would be grumpy, anyway, having spent four nights without his wife. They'd be apart a week all told. Hell, that wasn't Jake's fault. He'd offered to move the herd. It was a chore he used to do with his dad while Dillon oversaw the ranch. Last winter, though, Wade Cooper had tangled with a rogue cow and his bum hip hadn't fully healed. His doctor recommended Wade let the boys handle fall roundup alone. Dillon didn't have a good eye for spotting strays in the canyons. Not like Jake did. As a result, Dillon got stuck driving the steers to pasture.

Taking a last look through his binoculars, just to verify that Hayley Ryan had gone about her business, Jake climbed into the saddle again and set off to complete the job he'd started.

HAYLEY COULDN'T SHAKE the notion she was being watched. She'd closed her book once and let her gaze roam the nearby hills. Nothing moved and nothing appeared to be amiss. Refilling her teacup, she'd returned to her reading. The feeling persisted. Finally she felt so uneasy that she rose and walked to the edge of the clearing. Shading her eyes against the morning sun, she concentrated on a rocky promontory where she thought she'd seen a flash—like the sun reflecting off a mirror.

Hayley stared at the spot so long she became dizzy. Or had she gotten dizzy from self-imposed fright? Her heart was certainly beating fast.

When she could see no sign of any human presence, Hayley gave herself a stern mental shake. She decided that sitting around doing nothing but reading was making her paranoid. Why would anyone skulk around spying on her? No one other than that cowboy even knew she was here. He'd said his piece last night and had made amends today. She'd been perfectly honest about her reasons for being here.

As for the possibility of someone else keeping an eye on her, well, this wasn't exactly a people watcher's paradise. And it was too early for hunters to be combing the hills.

"There, see?" she exclaimed, marching back to her trailer, "You have an overactive imagination, Ms. Ryan. Get over it."

The best way she knew to allay her fears was through physical labor. Rather than digging willy-nilly when she had no information about what to look for or where to search, Hayley elected to conduct a survey of the site. Gramps must have left, if not an open shaft, then at least test holes that might give her an idea of what he was after.

She loaded a day pack with a rock hammer and a cigar box divided into small compartments to serve as a collection box for specimens. She slapped together a peanut-butter-and-jelly sandwich and added sunglasses and a baseball cap to her stash, before she filled a canteen at the spring. Despite the growing heat, the water was cool and sweet.

"This water could be lifeblood to a rancher," she said to no one. No one except two squirrels who frolicked on a nearby branch. Their presence, and the melodious trill of songbirds flitting about, dispelled the last of Hayley's anxiety.

Who needed human companionship when there was all this wonderful wildlife to serve as company and an early-warning system? Hayley took a measure of assurance from the fact that birds squawked and squirrels fled at the mere sound of her footsteps.

She trudged through the trees, walking a blanket of pine needles. For a time she was more interested in the flora and fauna all around her than in settling down to look for test holes in the pockmarked granite hills. She climbed steadily for the better part of two hours before she came to a man-made depression in the facer rock. Bits of broken rock lay strewn about. Hayley paused to inspect the dynamited debris. Quartz and pyrite were all she found. Obviously her grandfather hadn't wasted much time on this spot.

Hayley continued upward. Eventually the trail petered out and the going got tougher. She could tell that Ben hadn't taken his search this high. But now that Hayley had climbed all the way up here, she wanted to examine her claim from the ridge a little above her. Even if getting there appeared more suited to mountain goats than humans.

She was winded by the time she reached the sheared-off granite table. The view was everything she'd anticipated. Spectacular hills and valleys stretched out on all four sides. The binoculars she'd found in Gramps's trailer were old and one lens was scratched; however, they served her purpose and helped her pinpoint his dig sites.

Four were visible to the right and below her. All seemed to follow one deep arroyo. Shedding her backpack, Hayley dusted off a wide flat rock. She clambered onto it, then pulled out her sandwich and a pad and pencil. While she ate, she drew a rough map, sketching in significant trees and boulders and other pertinent features around the test holes, so she could find them again.

As she turned her attention farther afield, a splash of moving color caught her interest. Cattle. The undulations of rock-strewn arroyos were dotted with white-faced steers. Beyond them were square cultivated fields of hay. It seemed strange to see signs of human habitation interspersed with miles of palo verde, ocotillo, yucca and prickly pear. Near the edge of what Hayley judged to be her line of demarcation, were piles of volcanic rock, many with a green tint. Copper. Had her grandfather been drawn to this site by such blatant evidence of copper—before prices plummeted?

A horse and rider came into view over a grassy knoll. The glasses brought him to within seeming arm's length of Hayley. Her breath did a funny hitch. *Jacob Cooper.* He, too, had field glasses raised to his face. For a moment Hayley had the oddest feeling that they were staring at each other. But no, Cooper's head rotated downward. He'd zeroed in on a group of wandering steers. As she studied him, he dragged a pad from his shirt pocket, similar to the one fluttering on her lap. He withdrew a pencil from his pocket and made notations on his pad. Hayley watched until he returned the items to his pocket and let the binoculars swing free around his neck. He nudged the bay's flanks, and as quickly as he'd appeared, he rode out of sight. The collie trotted complacently at his side.

Only then did Hayley realize she'd been holding her breath. As she let it out, she had to acknowledge that he'd been a sight worth ogling.

Jacob Cooper's shoulders were wide. His torso tapered to lean hips that melded perfectly to his saddle. His butt was encased in denim so worn it seemed almost white in the brilliant sunlight. Having accidentally honed in on his long legs, Hayley realized why the worn denim hadn't made an impression before. He wore chaps to keep from being torn to pieces by cactus thorns. His chaps met scuffed and spurless boots. Hayley liked that. She'd always thought spurs were showy, and that the men who relied on them had little regard for the welfare of their horses.

A warm ripple ran up Hayley's spine when she realized Jake Cooper was exactly what he'd claimed to be. A rancher. She couldn't say why she'd felt any doubt before. Quite possibly because she was guilty of swallowing so many of Joe's lines. Hayley didn't think she'd ever be quite so trusting again.

She reminded herself that one good thing had come out of her brief sojourn with Joseph Ryan. A baby. The reminder brought her crashing back to the present—to her reason for sitting on a broad rock at the top of a dusty lonely hill. She'd come here to find the treasure her grandfather thought was somewhere in this desolate tract of land. She had no business wasting time salivating over Mr. Cooper's skinny butt, even if it *was* a nine and a half on a scale of ten.

Sighing, Hayley folded her empty sandwich bag and tucked it into her backpack to use another day. Telling herself she'd probably never see Jacob Cooper again, she took a long pull from her canteen, then started her down-hill climb.

JAKE HAD GLIMPSED Hayley Ryan seated on a flat rock at the very top of Yellow Jacket Hill. He'd been sur-prised to see she'd hiked so far since late morning, when he'd observed her scanning the hill from her camp. He'd been more surprised, though, to see her peering at him through binoculars. Jake didn't know whether she'd caught him giving her the once-over. He'd certainly made a show of counting steers to throw her off. His heart had yet to settle into a normal rhythm. Hayley Ryan made quite a picture framed by the rock, a ruff of trees and a cloudless blue sky.

Checking his watch, Jake discovered he'd better put some speed on. He still had to cross the pass into Hell's Gate, where he was meeting Dillon. It was past time he stopped obsessing over a woman he knew little about. One he'd very likely end up fighting with sooner or later.

But as he rode through the arid unfenced range land where the Cooper family had been raising cattle for four generations, Jake's thoughts remained on Hayley. He couldn't identify exactly what piqued his interest about her. He'd been fending off prettier women for years. Not that Mrs. Ryan was hard to look at, by any means. On the contrary, she was well put together. Small, but not so skinny you didn't know she was all woman.

And those eyes. Those changeable eyes that shifted from blue to the color of lavender to a deeper violet, almost purple. He'd never paid so much attention to any-one's eyes before. His own were light gray. Wouldn't it be an interesting experiment to see what color eyes their offspring would have?

"Whoa, dude!" Mojave dutifully stopped dead on the

trail. "Not you," Jacob laughed, bending forward to stroke the bay's neck. When Charcoal trotted back and sat staring up at him, Jake shook his head. "You, too, boy? Too bad you guys can't talk. You'd tell me soon enough how crazy I'm acting over a woman who'd like nothing better than to see my backside trucking down the trail. She may have warmed up after I pulled those veggies out of the bag, but if you noticed, she didn't request our return."

Jake let Mojave amble through the deer grass for a while before they crossed a dry wash and turned north. The sun beat down mercilessly. Jacob thought the humidity had climbed to seventy percent. He shucked off one leather glove, removed his hat and blotted sweat from his brow with the crook of his arm.

"Feels like monsoon weather," he muttered, settling the hat firm and low over his forehead. "I wonder if our Mrs. Ryan is prepared for the big rains that blow in here off the Baja. What do you think, Mojave?"

On hearing his name, the horse whinnied and swished his ears.

"I guess you're right," Jacob continued as if the gelding had spoken. "Better to keep my nose outta her business. She has Ben's truck and trailer. The old guy must've given her directions. If she was stabbing in the dark, she wouldn't have found her way to the Blue Cameo so easily."

The threesome covered another few miles before Jacob spoke again. "There's just something sad looking in the lady's eyes, don't you agree, guys?" Jake urged Mojave into a canter up a long steep incline over the ridge into the valley known as Hell's Gate. "But there's the matter of her calling herself Mrs. Ryan. Where do you suppose Mr. Ryan is? What kind of husband lets his wife prospect all by herself? Even more curious, why isn't she wearing her wedding ring?''

The horse blew out a long breath. Cresting the hill, Mojave automatically quickened his pace. Jake knew why. In the distance Dillon's horse, Wildfire, grazed on a picket. Dillon wasn't yet visible. Jake figured he'd holed up in the shade of a stand of black walnut trees. Likely he was whittling a car or a truck or some part of a train set from the ever-present hardwoods he carried in his saddlebags. Their granddad Cooper had taught both boys to whittle at an early age. Dillon was much more adept at it than Jake. As kids they'd played with wooden toys; now Dillon carved a batch each year, and Eden's church distributed them to needy children at Christmas.

In fact, that was how Dillon and Eden had met. She'd moved to Tubac from Albuquerque to open her own jewelry store, had joined a local church and dived right into community affairs. Small-town churches loved new blood. They'd put Eden to work collecting for the yearly toy drive. One October afternoon she'd arrived at the Triple C, all golden-hair and sweet smiles to beg for a donation of Dillon's toys. Jake recalled wishing he could carve as well as his brother did. Eden Priest was the most beautiful woman Santa Cruz county had seen in a decade. She was nice, too. And talented. Successful in her own right. Both brothers had thrown their hearts at her feet; it was Dillon's she'd picked up.

Jake grinned now, thinking about all the sneaky tricks he and Dillon had pulled trying to get into town without the other knowing. Some women would have strung them both along. It'd happened before. Eden wasn't that sort of woman. She chose Dillon fair and square. She

took Jake out for a cup of coffee at the local café and
let him down gently.

He remembered feeling lower than a worm's belly all
the way home. He hadn't planned to tell anyone in the
family. But his mom had either been perceptive or Eden
had told her. Nell Cooper arrived home from a long day
spent throwing pots to cook her youngest son's favorite
meal. Afterward she'd coaxed him into taking a moonlight walk with her, during which she convinced him
there'd be a woman in his future as wonderful as Eden.
Believing that, Jake had decided to shake Dillon's hand
and be happy for him. He vowed to find himself a
woman who had both Eden's qualities and his mom's.

It was going on two years now. There were times Jake
thought he'd set himself an impossible task.

His brother strode out from under the trees and raised
a hand in greeting, even though a half mile still separated
them. Unlike the volcanic terrain Jake had recently ridden though, this land was barren of all but an occasional
scrub brush or cactus. Distance was hard to measure. It
was why so many people who crossed the border illegally, seeking work in the larger Arizona cities, died of
exposure or of dehydration. On the desert floor temper-
atures in the summer and early fall soared upward of
115 degrees—exactly the reason Hayley Ryan's spring
was so important to the Triple C. There was precious
little hydration in the area. And not a drop of water to
spare.

Jacob covered the gap in short order.

"Yo, brother," Dillon called, holding his ground until
Jake had galloped all the way into his makeshift camp.
"Took your time getting here. I'd about decided we'd
got our wires crossed."

"Spoken like a man who's been forced to play the

hermit against his will. You haven't been gone from home a week. Couldn't be you're missing someone special, now could it?'' Jake laughed and jumped back from the teasing punch Dillon threw at his left shoulder.

"You damn well know I'm homesick as hell. How's everything at the Triple C?" In other words, how was Eden getting along without him?

"You know, Dillon," Jake said in a thoughtful voice, "I think Coronado misses you. Why, it's a crying shame how broke up that parrot's been this week."

"Very funny. You know the bird hates me." Dillon grasped Jake's shirtfront in both hands, nearly lifting him off the ground. Charcoal charged the men, baring his teeth and barking wildly. Dillon lost no time in releasing his brother.

"Tell me about Eden," he pleaded. "What did she send me? And don't hold out. She promised, and Eden never breaks a promise."

Jake knew when to back off and play it straight. He unbuckled Mojave's cinch, hauled the heavy saddle under the trees and dropped it beside Dillon's. Quickly he extracted a pink envelope from one saddlebag. So maybe he wasn't finished teasing. He passed the scented missive under Dillon's nose, then drew it back and pretended to take a deep whiff himself. "Mm-mm! I do believe she soaked this in pheromones. Better watch out, or every male in the animal kingdom will be swooping down on us."

"Give that to me." Dillon snatched his letter out of Jake's hand. He promptly put space between them, literally turning his back on his brother while his read it.

Grinning like a crazy man, Jake flopped down with his back against a tree trunk and uncorked his canteen to take a long swallow of the cool water. He'd give

Dillon time to read and reread his message from home. There was a limit to his pranks. But the darned thing was four pages long. Eden must have written a page for every night Dillon had been gone. Though he didn't want to, Jake suffered a stab of jealousy.

He supposed it was understandable. Growing up on an isolated ranch, he and Dillon had gone through all of the normal competitive stages that young boys and then young men developed. At times their poor mother had despaired of their surviving the sibling rivalry. But they had, and had emerged stronger men. They'd ultimately grown to be best friends. So what Jake felt now wasn't personal. He figured it was more that he'd reached the time in his life when the male in any species needed to find a mate and make a nest of his own.

The idea came so clearly that it surprised the heck out of him. He'd believed himself content to drift along, playing the field, so to speak.

He was concentrating on his thoughts and didn't hear Dillon at first.

His brother finished folding the letter and tucking it away. "Jacob, my man, what are you mooning about? Where's the sack of vegetables Eden says she sent me?"

"Oh, that." Jake knew he'd have to account for the missing produce. Suddenly he was reluctant to tell Dillon anything about Hayley Ryan. He didn't want his brother making a big deal over nothing.

"Hand it over, dude. I really don't know how the cowboys of old went for months eating out of cans. Call me spoiled, but I've gotten used to picking stuff out of the garden. Man, I can almost taste those beefsteak tomatoes."

Jake didn't see any way around it. He cleared his throat a couple of times. "Yeah," he muttered. "Well, don't get your mouth too set. I don't have the stuff Eden sent.''

''You left it at home?''

Jake supposed he could delay the inevitable by letting Dillon think he'd ridden off without the package. But he'd always been one to take his punishment rather than lie. It seemed pointless at any rate, since he'd told his dad he'd fill Dillon in on the situation at the spring. He opened his mouth and out poured the story of Ben O'Dell's demise—and Hayley Ryan's appearance.

''Let me get this straight. You and Dad just let that woman squat on the section of land Ben promised would be ours?''

''She isn't exactly squatting, Dillon. She filed legally. Instead of the claim being in Ben's name, now it's in hers.''

''Did she show you the papers?''

''No. But she has Ben's truck and trailer. Why would she lie?''

''Why wouldn't you ask to see proof?'' Dillon's eyes, a shade darker than his brother's, clouded as if heading into a storm.

Jake touched the still-swollen knot over his ear. ''She showed me all the proof I needed,'' he said wryly. ''The business end of a shotgun.'' Because it seemed almost funny now, Jacob spun that tale, too.

Laughing, Dillon slapped his knee. ''What I wouldn't have given to see that.''

''I'm sure. If you know what's good for you, you won't be spreading the story around. It was an accident. Could have happened to anyone. She aimed over my head and hit a damned branch.'' He gingerly fingered the lump on his head again.

''Maybe you won't mind telling me what insanity

possessed you to have a second go at her today. Why in heaven's name would you bring her food? *My* food,'' he said irritably.

"Regardless of the shotgun incident, she's a woman."

"Yeah, a woman sitting smack alongside the only fresh water for miles around."

"Exactly. Wild animals aren't my only concern. Granted, most illegals crossing the border aren't looking for trouble. But who's to say they'd consider a bitty woman trouble? Some might risk jail for her truck alone. Or a drifter might. Or the occasional homeless guy trying to live off the land."

"You have a point." Dillon ran a hand over his stubbled jaw. His hair wasn't as dark as Jake's. He'd inherited more of Nell Cooper's coppery highlights. When he did start to grow a beard, like now, it was redder still. "What did Dad say?" Dillon asked. "He's not going to let her stay, is he?"

"He and Mom went to Tombstone today. Dad's planning to find out if Ben mentioned our deal to anyone. Then the folks are going on to Tucson. Mom's been chafing to visit a new pottery-supply store she heard about. If Dad doesn't get answers in Tombstone, he said he'd pay a visit to the county recorder. To take a quick gander at the record of claims."

"Makes sense. If the woman's not savvy, she might have slipped up somewhere. Left a loophole or something."

"I wouldn't get my hopes up. She seems knowledgeable about filing issues."

"Well, hell. Did she happen to say what's so all-fired tempting about that twenty acres? Ben worked it for years and he never found diddly squat."

"We don't know that for sure. The old guy was pretty

closemouthed. Oh, he told some tall mining stories, but I can't recall him ever giving away anything personal.''

"He talked a lot about his silver mine. I had the idea it produced all right, didn't you? Why wouldn't that revenue be enough for his granddaughter?''

"Depends on what you mean by 'all right.' Don't you think if it'd been making good money, he'd have stayed home and enjoyed the fruits of his labor a little more?''

"Prospecting gets in some men's blood. It's a lot like gambling. A fellow always thinks his really big strike is over the next rise.''

"I found Ben more down-to-earth than that. I mean, if he had gold fever, he would have spent more than a couple of months a year on his claim. To me it seemed he treated it more like a vacation.''

"Maybe. Gold fever, huh? So you think he was hunting gold?''

"I haven't a clue. I just used that as an example.''

Dillon dug in his shirt pocket and pulled out a toothpick, which he stuck between his teeth. Modern cowboys, especially those who'd once smoked, had switched from tobacco to mint- or cinnamon-dipped toothpicks. Jake had never picked up the smoking habit. Dillon had, but quit at Eden's request. But during serious talks, he sometimes reverted to it. He shifted the toothpick from one side of his mouth to the other as he gazed toward the granite hills under discussion. "If communing with nature is all the yearly trek was to O'Dell, you gotta wonder why a woman snapped up the claim the minute the old guy cashed in his chips.''

"I don't know when he died. She just said he had. Don't tell me you're getting gold fever, Dillon.'' Jake sounded amused. "Strikes were never plentiful in this neck of the woods. The Blue Cameo is so remote, nuggets would have to be lying on top of the ground for anyone to convert the ore to cash. Hauling anything out of here over dirt roads takes money and guts.''

''It's not so far to hook up with Interstate 19. No one's ever found reason to lay out the money to improve the road, but that doesn't mean no one would if they turned up something worth big bucks.''

''I'd have to see it to believe it. It's not that I think a woman is less capable than a man of hacking into a ripe vein by accident. But I *am* skeptical of that woman being Hayley Ryan. If you could've seen her poring over elementary mineral and gem books, you'd agree. Plus, she's a flyweight.'' He shook his head. ''I think if we wait a while, she'll eventually give up and go home.''

''She might reach that conclusion faster, Jake, if you didn't supply her with fresh produce. My produce,'' Dillon reminded him.

''I know, I know. But if that was Eden camped there, would you turn your back and walk away, big brother?''

A sudden light dawned in Dillon's eyes. ''Are you saying you've fallen for this stranger?''

''No!'' Jake protested. A bit too fast and much too vociferously. ''We were raised to look out for women. So get off my back. You'd do the same—don't deny it.''

Dillon gazed at his brother narrowly. The staring match lasted only seconds. Dillon capitulated with a shrug. ''Then we'll leave it at that. What's your count of strays? I turned 1,010 head onto our leased grassland. Nine hundred and thirty to open range near Pena Blanca Lake. And twice as many near Hank and Yank's dry spring. By my figuring, we're down roughly five or six hundred head from the number Dad gave me.''

''I can account for roughly half of that in little knots of two or three strays. The missing might have merged with John Westin's herd. I'll ride past his spread and ask if he's seen any of our brand mixed with his.''

Dillon gave his brother a playful nudge in the ribs. ''This eagerness to volunteer to ride miles out of your way wouldn't have anything to do with Ginalyn Westin, would it? Like, give you a chance to ask her to the fall harvest dance?''

''And have Gordy White punch my lights out? Do I look like a man with a death wish?''

''Gordy's got no claim on Gina. If he did she'd be wearing his ring. But you're so obtuse maybe you haven't seen how the heir to the J & B pants after you, old son.''

''You won't catch me in the stampede to her doorstep. John and Bonnie have spoiled her rotten. Can you really see me licking John's boots and jumping through his hoops until he gets damn good and ready to hand over the ranch to his daughter? Her husband will always be a flunky. No, thank you.''

''Who mentioned marriage? I only asked if you were inviting her to the dance.''

Jake shot Dillon a quelling glance. ''Yeah? So sue me for reading between the lines.''

Dillon laughed. ''I'll concede Gina isn't your type. Hey, how about taking this Ryan woman? That way you can find out what she's really up to.''

Jake shook his hand. ''Oh, did I forget to say it's *Mrs.* Ryan?''

''I'm afraid you left out that crucial fact. Okay, I'll quit hassling you on that score. Too bad. Okay, go on. Ride out to the J & B. See if John can add to our steer count. You and I will touch base again on Saturday at the ranch. Until then, stay out of trouble.''

The brothers slapped each other on the back, saddled

up and rode their separate ways. On the dusty ride to the J & B, Jake couldn't seem to forget the idea of asking Hayley Ryan to the dance. But hell, it was still four months away. He was betting she'd be long gone and only a sweet memory by Labor Day.

# CHAPTER FOUR

IT WAS LATE AFTERNOON when Jake rode up the winding path to the Westin ranch. The house itself was far more elaborate than the Coopers' sprawling single-level home. John Westin had not been born into the cattle business as Wade Cooper had. Westin, who'd come from Virginia, was a latecomer to the Santa Cruz basin. A bankroll of family money, coupled with a desire to build an impressive spread, helped him forge a position into the elite establishment of cattle barons. Westin was brash and outspoken—traits that didn't seem to bother some in the valley. Jake, however, preferred his father's easygoing manner and willingness to look at all sides of an issue.

John walked out onto the veranda to light up one of the Cuban cigars he favored just as Jake clattered to a halt in the circular drive. Westin had laid gravel in the area for automobiles, but in deference to the business they were in, he also supplied a watering trough for horses and a hitching rail underneath a stand of shade trees.

"Jacob. Welcome." John puffed out a cloud of smoke. "What brings you to my humble abode?" He leaned negligently against a carved white pillar and guffawed. "As if I didn't know."

Jake glanced at the man's house. The three-storeyed structure looked for all the world like a plantation mansion from the nineteenth century. "'Humble' isn't exactly a word that comes to mind, John, when I see the J & B."

Westin rolled the cigar around his lips and his laughter deepened. "The place shows well at night. 'Course, my women don't give a damn about the cost of electricity. They turn on every chandelier in the house." He grinned. "I notice you evaded my point. You're here to see Ginalyn. Correct?"

"Nope, though I'll say hello if she's around. Dillon and I came up short on our steer count this week. Thought maybe some Triple C stock might have mixed in with J & B herds. If your hands run across our brand, give us a call, will you? I'll come cut them out."

"Will do. Grass is so dry all the stock's scattered. When's Wade going to wise up and toss that old fool miner off the spring property so we can divvy it up?"

"Dad and Mom are in Tombstone today. We heard Ben O'Dell died."

John's eyes lit. "Excellent. Couldn't happen at a better time. The valley's growing and changing. The Coalition needs free access to that water."

"I expect Dad will work out an equitable agreement if he's able to purchase the property." Jake didn't like the greedy gleam in John's eyes. Or maybe he was touchy about the subject because of the way Dillon had teased him about Hayley Ryan.

"What's to stop him? O'Dell promised Wade first right of option."

"Yeah, but it's come to our attention that someone's refiled Ben's claim."

"You don't say! Now that isn't right. Wade's been far too patient as it is. We ranchers need a show of strength. Did some big mining outfit move in?"

Jake shook his head. "Just a single prospector, like Ben." Jake couldn't say why he was reluctant to tell John more about Ben's granddaughter.

Fortunately he was saved the effort of evasion. The screen door opened and a pretty blond woman strolled out. Ginalyn Westin had her mother's classic beauty but was cursed with her father's arrogance. Though Jake had never seen her make a move that wasn't calculated to put herself in the spotlight, she was still a sight to behold. Shimmering straight blond hair, big blue eyes. She'd perfected the slow sultry drawl of her native Virginia and she had a definite, if practiced charm. Unless a man had seen how those fine attributes changed when things didn't go Ginalyn's way, he'd grovel at her dainty feet, which was what most sons of area ranchers did. Jake might be the only single male in a hundred-mile radius who kept his distance.

Which hadn't escaped the young woman's notice. "Why, I declare," she said, slipping a slender arm through her dad's sturdier one. "If it isn't Jacob Cooper. Let me guess. He's happened to ride in at suppertime, but before the evening's done, he'll get around to inviting me to the harvest dance." She managed to sound bored.

Jake, who'd whipped off his hat the moment she appeared, resettled it low on his brow. "Wrong on both counts, Ginalyn. My business was with your dad. We've concluded it, so now I'll get along home." Jake gave Mojave's cinch a yank. He whistled for Charcoal, who'd drunk his fill at the trough, and swung lithely into the saddle. Touching his hat brim with two fingers, he wheeled the gelding around and cantered down the lane. Not, however, before he heard Ginalyn's indignant sputter.

"Jacob Cooper, just for that I'll accept Gordon

White's invitation. And don't think I'll save you a dance, because I won't!''

Raking his boot heels lightly along Mojave's sides, Jake picked up the pace. He should go back and apologize. She was already complaining to her dad about Jake's rude behavior. The news would make its way to the Triple C. Wade would remind Jake that pretty eligible women didn't grow on trees. Eden and Nell, though more subtle, would find some other approach to get the same point across.

Ginalyn was a beauty and well educated. She just didn't happen to fit Jake's concept of an ideal partner and ranch wife. When his well-meaning family had asked him to spell out what he did want in a wife, he'd failed to put it into clear terms. As a result, the Coopers were exasperated with him. Hell, he was exasperated with himself.

He knew what he *didn't* want. He didn't want a wife whose focus was her looks, her clothes or the next big party. Nor did he want someone who'd set her sights on frequent trips to Phoenix. So many of the valley daughters were given a taste of the city at college, and they made no secret of wanting a man willing to help them escape the hard life.

Jake didn't think it was all that hard. Granted, the money was sometimes iffy and the weather could be the pits. By and large, the freedom a man felt when riding the range was worth far more than the disadvantages. The freedom to call his own shots and be his own man appealed to him.

He tried to understand the situation from a woman's perspective, a wife's, if you will. He certainly didn't object to women pursuing careers. His mother and Eden weren't tied to the ranch. What set them apart from women he'd dated was their ability to combine happiness at home with work. Jake couldn't explain it even to himself. He only knew he'd continue to hold out. No matter how tempting it was when winter rolled around to chuck ideals and simply find someone eager to warm his bed.

Lost in thought, Jake didn't realize he'd unconsciously detoured past the spring until the light from Hayley Ryan's campfire came into sight. It flickered and blinked in the distance, still far enough off that he could change course without her ever knowing he'd been there.

He still had plenty of time to skirt her encampment.

And he did kind of go around it for a few hundred yards. Then he dismounted and covered the remaining distance on foot. All the while his heart slammed against his ribs. For crying out loud, did he want her to shoot at him again—and aim truer this time?

Of course he didn't. He wanted to know if she'd found anything worthwhile in her trek over the hill today. Jake had walked to within shouting distance before he admitted that what he really wanted was to see that she'd made it safely back to camp.

Something shifted ever so slightly in his chest the moment he saw her kneeling next to a blazing fire pit.

"Hayley!" he called. "It's me, Jacob Cooper. I don't mean to scare you. I've been to the Westin ranch and thought I'd stop to say hello before I head home."

Hayley jerked and went white at the sound of a male voice. She'd been a million miles off in her mind, planning tomorrow's assault on the hillside she'd settled on to start her mineral explorations. Jacob Cooper was the last person she'd expected to see again today.

Yet his walking in on her with no warning sent shivers down her spine. He might have been anyone. She shouldn't drop her guard. Especially after the sun had set.

"Mr. Cooper," she said with a hint of unsteadiness in her tone. "Were you this much of a pest to my grandfather?"

Jake laughed as he looped Mojave's reins over a limb. "Ben always had a hot pot of coffee on the fire—and an occasional shot of rum." Thumbing back his hat, Jake moved closer. "If he thought I was a pest, his good manners kept him from mentioning it. I always had the notion that Ben got a kick out of my stopping to talk." Jake bent and patted the collie's heaving sides. He pulled a sack of kibble out of his saddlebag and, after sweeping a clear place on the ground, put out a handful.

Hayley dusted her hands along her thighs to wipe away the sweat dampening her palms. She didn't doubt that Cooper was telling the truth. Her grandfather, like most lonely prospectors, loved a captive audience. He didn't always waste time talking to her, though; he was a man's man. Hayley could well imagine him exploring a wide range of subjects with a local cowboy.

If she were to be honest, she'd admit that she, too, liked her long evenings broken up by lively conversation. Tonight might be the exception. Her stomach had felt queasy for a good part of the day. She'd brewed a pot of chamomile tea to go with her light evening meal, but she didn't know if this was because of the pregnancy or if something she'd eaten for breakfast hadn't set well. At any rate, she didn't feel much like entertaining. She particularly didn't feel like spending time with someone who might see more than she wanted him to see. Jacob Cooper struck her as a man who'd harbor strong opinions about what pregnant women should and should not do.

"You might want to start carrying a thermos, Mr. Cooper. I prefer herb tea to coffee." She slanted her gaze toward the pot sitting on the grate over her fire.

"Tea, huh?" Jake wasn't able to hide his disappointment. "My sister-in-law serves herb tea to her customers. Must be a woman thing." He stripped off his hat and raked a hand through his matted hair.

"Your sister-in-law runs a café?"

Jake shook his head. "She designs jewelry. In Tubac," he added, although he didn't know why. Hayley hadn't given him any reason to think her polite question had been an attempt to strike up a real conversation.

"I've never been there. To Tubac, I mean. Well," she said breezily, though she felt far from breezy as her stomach had begun mixing it up again, "don't let me stop you from going home to supper. I was about to douse my fire and turn in."

Jake's roving gaze lit on a nearly full plate of food she'd left on the small table that had earlier held her mineralogy books. He wasn't usually the type to stick around where he clearly wasn't wanted, but something perverse in him made him dig in his heels. Perhaps it was the tense look that brought an aura of fatigue to the Ryan woman's expressive face.

"Truth of the matter is, anything hot would go down well at this stage in the game. I hate to trouble you for a cup of that tea, but my animals could use a break. While you pour a neighbor a cup, I'll water Mojave and Charcoal at the spring."

Hayley opened her mouth to object. Then she bit back a sigh and reached for the pot, and the mug Jacob had drunk coffee from earlier. "You'll have to take it without milk or sugar. I'm short on some items."

"Plain is fine." Jake led his animals to the spring and

picked a spot where he could watch his reluctant hostess without seeming to. She'd told him she intended to spend several months working this claim. Why, at the outset, was she short on supplies? The story behind her being here intrigued Jake, as did that white strip of skin circling the third finger of her left hand. Maybe he'd do a little discreet probing concerning the whereabouts of Mr. Ryan before he finished that begrudgingly offered cup of tea.

After his first taste, it was all Jake could do to keep a straight face. The stuff was horrid. He didn't know how anyone could drink it for enjoyment.

Hayley must have detected his faint choking sound, or at least noticed the curl of his upper lip. "Something wrong with the tea, Mr. Cooper?" Eyeing him over the rim of her cup, she allowed a tiny smile.

"Uh. No. Say, didn't I ask you to call me Jake?"

She shrugged. "Don't think you have to finish the tea, Jake."

"It's different from what Eden fixes, is all. Mostly she serves stuff with a fruity flavor."

"Eden. What a pretty name. She probably sticks to the commercial berry teas. This one is chamomile—it relaxes."

"Relaxing's a good idea. Why don't we take a load off our feet?" Jake helped himself to one of the two lawn chairs, even though Hayley hadn't invited him to sit. "Go on, eat your supper. Anyone who climbed to the rim and back in one day needs nourishment."

"Have you been spying on me, Mr. Cooper?" Hayley's voice was flat, belying her alarm. As she sat opposite him, she recalled her earlier feeling of being watched.

"Jake," he reminded with laughter in his voice. "Not

spying, exactly,'' he said. ''Hunting strays day after day gets pretty boring.'' He waved a hand, indicating the field glasses slung over his saddle horn. ''About noon I spotted you at the top of the slope. I confess it's more tempting to track a pretty woman's progress than to keep after a bunch of cows. However, my dedication to work eventually won out.''

His candid acknowledgment and the fact that he'd called her pretty brought a surge of color to Hayley's cheeks. This type of casual flirting had never been her forte. Not to mention it had sucked her in and ultimately left her at the mercy of Joe Ryan. ''Some women might fall for flattery,'' she added hastily. ''I'm not one of them.''

Surprising Hayley, the dog loped over, placed a paw on her lap and gazed at her with soulful eyes. She found it disconcerting, but couldn't resist fondling his silky black ears.

''I've never considered it flattery to state a fact.'' Dragging his eyes away from his lucky dog, Jake forced himself to take another swallow of the abominable tea. He'd meant only to make small talk and ease some of the tension between them. His careless statement had obviously had the opposite effect. *Curious.* Jake thought she might be the only woman he'd ever met who took offense at being called pretty. But hell, she *was* pretty. Surely she saw that when she looked in the mirror. On second thought, observing the stiff way she now sat in her chair, Jake decided she might not. The absent husband could have done a real number on her. It made his blood boil to imagine such a thing.

''Eat,'' he said gently. ''I'll change the subject. You know, my mom's scolded me for years about getting too personal too fast. So don't be thinking she's some sort of bad person for not teaching me manners. Poor woman had to raise two irreverent boys. Did the best she could.''

Hayley let her guard slip a bit at that disclosure. ''This isn't the first mention you've made of your mother. She's important to you, I can tell. That's nice, Jake.'' Joe had so rarely mentioned his parents. The few times he had, his remarks hadn't been at all nice.

Jake latched on to a note of sadness he heard in Hayley's voice. ''I'm not an expert on the subject, by any means. It seems to me a mother has about the toughest job in the whole world.''

Hayley's stomach pitched. For a moment she panicked and worried that when her baby came she wouldn't have what it took to be a good mother. In fact, there probably wasn't a woman alive less equipped than she to step into that role.

''Are you all right?'' Jake's words came at her from a yawning distance. ''I seem to stick my foot in my big mouth every time I open it around you. Usually I'm much better at breaking the ice.''

''It's not you,'' she said, clutching her cup between restless fingers. ''I lost both of my parents when I was young. I grew up, well, unconventionally.''

So much was left unsaid, yet a whole range of emotions played across her face. Jake immediately wanted to know more, and at the same time it bothered him immensely that he'd unwittingly chosen yet another distressing topic.

Just how unconventional had her life been?

He took another slug of the tea, then made an inane remark about the brightness of the rising moon.

''More tea?'' Hayley asked, shaking out of an odd mood. She rarely wasted time wishing for things life hadn't seen fit to bestow on her. It wasn't good that a man, literally a stranger, could make her yearn for experiences she'd never known.

"I still have plenty," Jake said in a rush. He so quickly covered the cup with his hand, that they both laughed.

"You really don't have to drink it," Hayley said lightly. "I realize I didn't make you feel very welcome. But I can't help wondering why you'd go out of your way to drop in on me."

The question was direct. Jake saw there were many more unasked ones in her wary eyes. He felt unaccountably guilty and got out of the chair, tossing the contents of his cup on the ground. "It's a mystery to me, too. You've proved you can take care of yourself," he said, pointing ruefully at his head.

"I feel bad about that. I didn't mean—"

"Don't apologize. You have a perfect right to protect yourself."

She shivered and peered uneasily into the surrounding darkness. "I wish you'd stop making reference to vague dangers. I'm staying and that's final."

"Look. I'm not aiming to scare you." Jake set the cup down and jammed his hat on his head. "Water equals life around here. You're sitting next to the only good drinking water for miles. Ben recognized that. He allowed the Triple C and other local ranches to install the valve setup so we could water our herds."

Hayley crossed her arms, studying his suddenly rigid stance. "If that was a satisfactory deal, I can probably go along with it, too."

"It worked reasonably well," Jake said, shifting his gaze from her penetrating stare. "Thing is, there are plans waiting for implementation."

"What plans?"

"A real pumping station and a series of canals following the natural aquifers. The local cattlemen's association is waiting to start construction."

"Waiting for what?"

Jake backed away and unlooped Mojave's reins. "For Ben to relinquish his claim. Any of five other ranches besides the Triple C would give a lot to own this chunk of land. Not all are as community-minded as my dad. Ben picked right up on that. He promised to transfer water and mineral rights to the Triple C when his claim ran out."

"I see. My taking over his claim has thrown a wrench into everyone's plans."

"You could say that." Jake stepped into the stirrup and was soon gazing down on Hayley's worried moonlit face. "Some ranchers are tired of waiting."

"This is the twenty-first century. People don't jump claims anymore. Laws protect them."

"Along the border people write their own laws." Jake tugged on the brim of his hat.

"Are you threatening me?"

"Nope. I'm trying to make you understand the situation you've walked into."

"Are you suggesting... I mean, I said I'd stand by the old agreement."

"That'll help. I'll relay that to my dad. Even then, I hope you'll give this some added thought. The way our deal works is that whenever a rancher passes a herd near here, a vaquero rides in and opens one of the valves. You'd close it after a set time. Follow me. I'll show you how it works."

"That doesn't appear too difficult," she said after two demonstrations.

Jake puffed out a breath. "The men aren't always full-timers. Some are drifters. Ranchers don't ask a lot of personal questions before roundup. Sometimes we scrape the bottom of the barrel.''

Hayley had lived around the mines all her life. It was the same situation. Yet how much difference did any of that make? Her slick-talking husband, for instance, had been employed by a company that prided itself on doing employee background checks. She also had grave reservations about Tilford, the deputy sheriff who'd befriended Joe. ''I'll take my chances,'' she murmured. ''I'm working this claim.''

''All right. By the way, do you have a cell phone? Then you could call me for help if you needed to. I'll leave you my cell number and our number at the ranch.''

Hayley's face broke into a huge grin. ''I'm living on a shoestring. Sorry for laughing, but cell phones aren't in my limited budget.''

Jake walked the restless gelding around in a circle and stopped, facing Hayley again. ''Sometimes it pays to be safe rather than sorry.''

''Sometimes. But if I had extra money, I'd buy a few laying hens and maybe a cow. Tinned milk or recombined doesn't compare to fresh.''

A surge of empathy washed over Jake. Then he brightened. She'd just given him an excuse to keep tabs on her. ''I'll see if I can round up some hens. Cows are harder to come by. We're a long way from grocery stores. Folks tend to prize milk cows.''

''I doubt I can afford one, anyway.''

''If you don't object to my stopping by, I can bring you a quart of milk now and again.''

''I dislike being beholden.''

''No strings attached.'' Jake wanted to snatch back the words the minute they left his mouth. All favors came with strings. He wasn't exactly sure how that related to his confused feelings about this foolishly brave woman who seemed so pitifully alone standing there in the clearing. He only knew he'd find excuses to look in on her.

"In that case—" Hayley flashed another grin "—I'll try to be more gracious next time."

"I'll hold you to it. Well, I've got a ride ahead of me and you still haven't had your supper. Warm up that hash. It's not good for a hardworking woman to go to bed on an empty belly."

Automatically Hayley clutched a belly that was far from empty. Jacob Cooper's odd silver-gray eyes were far too penetrating—as if they could expose all her secrets. Not that she was ashamed of being pregnant. But it wasn't something she felt comfortable disclosing. Not trusting herself to speak, Hayley bent and petted his dog, then lifted her hand to toss Jake a casual wave.

"Take care." His words swirled around Hayley's head in the wake of his leaving. She stood next to the firelight for some time after the sound of hoofbeats had faded. The call of night birds and the singing of cicadas had resumed before Hayley finally took her eyes off the shadowy scrub brush through which Jacob had disappeared.

She didn't understand the wash of emptiness that assailed her whenever this man, a man she barely knew, rode out of her life. As a girl, and then as a woman, she'd spent untold hours left to her own devices. She didn't scare easily. At least, she'd never imagined bogeymen behind every little noise.

Hayley uttered a snort of disgust loud enough to still all the night creatures for a moment. Knowing she had to keep up her strength for the sake of the baby, she deliberately finished the plate of unappetizing hash. Then she banked the fire and went to bed—and pushed aside visions of Jacob Cooper to lay careful plans for her first dig the next morning.

JAKE SET A STRAIGHT COURSE for the Triple C. He felt as if he'd gained some ground with Hayley Ryan with respect to the spring. Now he was interested in finding out what, if anything, his parents had learned about her in Tombstone.

The house was brightly lit when he rode in. Eden's bright red Jeep Cherokee sat next to the front porch. That was good. He could deliver Dillon's message and apologize for having given away the food Eden had lovingly prepared for her husband. Jacob preferred face-to-face repentance to stammering over the telephone; besides, telephone apologies always sounded insincere.

He made short work of Mojave's evening care. Rushed he might be, but he never shirked caring for his horse. Besides, Jake had raised Mojave from a colt. The two had bonded as well as man and beast ever could.

Jake would have liked a shower next. He needed one after a long hot day on the dusty range. Afraid he'd miss Eden if he detoured past his quarters first, Jake marched straight to the kitchen.

Talk stopped. The three seated at the oak table greeted him with smiles.

"Well, it's about time." Eden got up from her chair and tossed back a fall of wheat-gold hair. "Did you see Dillon? Did you give him my letter and the tomatoes I picked? When's he coming home?"

Jake fit two knuckles over her upturned nose and pretended to twist. "Dillon and I met on schedule. He's coming home Saturday as planned. About that letter, my pocket still smells like roses. Poor Dillon had to air out the pages before he read them or risk an allergic reaction.''

''It was gardenia, you doofus. Not roses. No wonder you're still single. A woman likes a man to be able to distinguish between her favorite scent and that of all the other females around.''

Jake blinked, then buried his nose in her hair and sniffed. ''Mint, with a hint of rosemary. Am I right?''

His sister-in-law batted his nose away. ''Guess there's hope for you yet.''

Nell pulled a pot of stew off the back of the stove and ladled a generous portion into a bowl. Taking a pan of biscuits from the oven, she motioned her younger son into a chair, which he declined for the moment.

Wade tilted his own chair back and tucked his thumbs under his belt. ''How's the beef count coming, son? Do the numbers tally?''

After washing and drying his hands, Jake slid in next to his dad. ''We came up about five hundred short. Reason I'm late is that I rode over to the J & B to ask John to be on the lookout for strays. I've still got some territory to cover tomorrow, but not enough to make up for such a large discrepancy.''

Eden jammed an elbow in Jake's ribs and rolled her eyes. ''It makes a good excuse to visit little Miss Bright Eyes, doesn't it.''

Jake scowled. ''Lay off, Eden. Dillon gave me the same song and dance. I'm not interested in Ginalyn Westin, all right?''

His denial sounded so ferocious Eden reared back.

''Sorry for snapping,'' he muttered. ''Dillon got in his licks, too. It didn't set well. You'll probably hear in town how rude I was to Ginalyn.''

"Rude? Jacob Cooper? The rangeland Romeo who makes every unattached woman's heart go pitty-pat, pitty-pat with his special line of schmaltz?"

"Come on, Eden. It's been a long day."

She grinned devilishly, but did drop the teasing.

Jake tasted the stew, then broke and buttered a biscuit before he asked his father casually, "What did you and Mom find out about Ben O'Dell in Tombstone?"

"'Bout what we expected. He was a private old duffer. Died unexpectedly. The Ryan woman is his granddaughter."

"So why do you suppose he never mentioned her?" Jake stopped with the spoon halfway to his mouth.

"Could be because there was bad blood between Ben and the girl's husband," Wade said. "At least that would explain why he didn't say anything in the last year or two."

Nell poured coffee all around. "The town was full of her story."

"What *is* her story?" Jake tried to act nonchalant, but tension showed in the grip he maintained on his spoon.

Nell's gaze traveled the table before settling on her son. "Now, Jake, your father and I don't know how much is truth and how much was embellished for our benefit."

"Give it to me straight."

"Mrs. Ryan's husband sold Ben's silver mine and left town with another woman. That much folks agreed on. Whether or not Mrs. Ryan signed papers giving him the Silver Cloud mine was subject to conjecture. It was obvious she didn't tell anyone in Tombstone where she was going or what she planned to do when she left. According to the few people we asked, Hayley Ryan packed up all her worldly possessions one day and disappeared the next.''

''Well, I hope you didn't let on where she went.''

Wade held up a staying hand. ''Jacob, there's no call to snap at your mother. I don't recall anyone asking. But what difference does it make? We checked with the county recorder and she filed right and proper. Her claim to the Blue Cameo is legal.''

Jake would be hard-pressed to say why he felt so protective of a woman he barely knew. Perhaps it was the sadness he'd glimpsed in her eyes. Or the comment she'd let slip about losing her parents. Nor could he discount her being so alone—or the telltale white mark circling her ring finger. Jake did know he wouldn't stand by and let anyone harass her further. Which must have showed on his face when he cut Wade off with a stabbed spoon in the air. ''She's agreed to give us the same water privileges as you negotiated with Ben. You told me to handle it and I did. There's no reason for her to find out we've poked into her private affairs. No reason at all.''

Wade, Nell and Eden all stared at him in bewilderment. Nell was the first to react. She reached across the table and curved cool fingers around her son's taut wrist. ''That's fine news, Jacob. But remember, we still don't know much about Mrs. Ryan, other than that she's Ben's granddaughter.'' Casually tightening her fingers on Jake's arm, she turned to her husband. ''Wade, as head of the Triple C, you'd better ride out to the Blue Cameo tomorrow and firm up the deal Jake made.''

Jake recognized the steel in his mother's voice. It was a tone he'd heard her use for thirty-two years when she wanted things done her way. That same thirty-two years of experience told Jake when to back off and let her think she'd won.

"Sure 'nuff, Mom." He pulled away to help himself to more stew. "I'll be riding out at dawn, checking the draws between here and Ruby for strays. Thought I'd stop by and check on old Ted Mortimer. He's pretty much alone since he retired from ranching. I'll try and make it home in time for supper. This eating warmed-up food every night is getting old."

The tension he'd felt through Nell's fingertips a minute earlier, dissipated, as he'd known it would. A sixth sense made him hold his tongue with regard to the food he'd given Hayley Ryan. The same instinct advised him to skip sharing his idea of taking her a few of his mother's laying hens. Jake quietly finished his meal while Eden said her goodbyes. Shortly thereafter, he tuned into a conversation his mother had begun about finding a fantastic pottery-supply store in Tucson.

"I'm beat," he admitted around a giant yawn. "I'd like to see what you bought, but can you show me later?"

Nell chuckled. "Get off to bed with you. I don't have to be told twice that I'm boring."

Because he loved her very much and wouldn't hurt her for the world, Jacob leaned over and kissed her cheek soundly. "Never boring. I'm proud of you. It's why I'll be hunting until I find a woman like you. And why I lose patience with Dillon and Eden heckling me about the likes of Ginalyn Westin."

Nell exchanged bemused looks with her husband as their youngest son broke off abruptly and left the room.

"I told you to quit worrying about Jake and that Ryan woman," Wade growled. "Boy's got a good head on his shoulders. He's a chip off the old block."

## CHAPTER FIVE

THE SUN HADN'T YET RISEN above the mountain peaks when Jacob rode into Hayley's camp, a crate filled with squawking chickens balanced precariously across the broad rump of his mount. Instead of his bay gelding, Jake had chosen Paprika, a placid roan mare with a better disposition for serving as a pack animal. Her gait, however, wasn't nearly as smooth as Mojave's. Already Jake knew he'd pay dearly by nightfall. This trip had been a foolish decision.

"Foolish" was putting it mildly, Jake calculated as he reached the clearing and saw Hayley Ryan emerging from the spring. Though he was afforded little more than a flash of white limbs and womanly curves in the pale gray dawn, it was enough to send a hot corkscrew of blood to his gut. His knees, which gripped Paprika's sides, soon quivered with a different emotion. Anger at Hayley's carelessness replaced his initial masculine response.

"Are you insane?" he bellowed, shattering the serenity of the dawn. Birds flapped excitedly from the trees and a family of rabbits bounded toward previously unseen burrows.

Hayley, who'd wrapped herself in a short cotton robe and now vigorously toweled the ends of her long hair, froze in her tracks. Only the wild rolling of her eyes spoke of her true panic. Then she dived behind a tree trunk and came up holding a rifle, the gleaming barrel pointed at Jake's chest.

That cooled his anger and his ardor. For a moment, as they stared at each other through the hazy mist rising off the spring, Jacob saw his mistake in judging this woman vulnerable.

"Take it easy." He made his voice quiet and even. "It's Jake. I brought those laying hens we talked about last night."

With shaking hands and a disgusted look, Hayley let the gun barrel drop. Her heart still raced madly from the fright. Bending, she retrieved the towel that had fallen from her hair in her haste to protect herself. "Talk about insane," she said at last in barely disguised fury. "What brand of idiot sneaks up on a naked woman?"

"I wasn't sneaking, dammit! I rode straight in off the trail."

"On a strange horse and without your dog," Hayley said, standing the rifle against a tree while she swiftly fashioned a turban around her wet head.

Gritting his teeth, Jake swung down from the saddle. Didn't she know how revealing that damned robe became as the morning light filtered through the canopy of leaves? "You're dead right. I could've been anyone. A desperate man fleeing the border patrol. A deranged war vet wandering these hills trying to live off the land. Or even a no-account drifter riding from ranch to ranch looking for work. We've covered the possibilities before. Thank you for making my point. It's bad enough that you're bunking out here alone. It's pure stupid to be hopping around naked."

"I was not hopping. Well, maybe when I first got out. When you're wet, the air feels cold." She stopped to collect a shell-shaped dish that contained a bar of soap, then stalked over and stoked a bed of coals. "I suppose you'd prefer I slink out in the dead of night to bathe and be eaten by the wild animals you said come here to drink."

Jake untied the ropes holding the cache of chickens to the saddle. He caught the crate seconds before it crashed to the ground. "In my opinion, you shouldn't be bathing at all."

At that, Hayley faced him and arched an amused brow.

He felt a suffusion of heat streak up his neck and into his cheeks. "I mean, not out here in front of God and everyone. Can't you wash up in the trailer?"

"I plan to wash my clothes out here, too. And dry them on that rope I strung between these two trees. Would *you* settle for spit baths if you had this lovely waterfall within reach?"

Still scowling, Jake unwound a roll of wire mesh, took a staple gun out of his saddlebag, and set about stringing the mesh into a reasonable pen for the chickens.

"Well, would you?" Hayley demanded, when the silence stretched out.

"I hardly think it's the same. Even the orneriest scalawag would hesitate before tangling with me. You, on the other hand, are an open invitation." He gestured at the trailer. "Don't let me keep you from going inside to dress."

Hayley, who rarely got her dander up enough to raise her voice, shouted, "Are you accusing me of trying to be provocative?"

"Stop putting words in my mouth. I never said that. But when a man happens on another man skinny-dipping in a wilderness stream, it's no big deal. Let him stumble across a woman in the same situation and…well, there's a lotta guys who'd take advantage.''

The fight went out of Hayley. He was right of course. If she'd been Ben's grandson and not his granddaughter, Joe Ryan would still be peddling mining supplies in the back of beyond. And she'd be unmarried, still living in Tombstone. But then, she wouldn't be looking forward to having a child. A baby of her own.

Holding in thoughts and emotions she couldn't share with anyone, Hayley took a deep breath and gathered her robe tightly under her chin. Then she turned and stomped into the trailer.

Jake had watched the various expressions that crossed her face, including reluctant resignation. He disliked being the one to open her eyes to the harsh realities attached to her present venture. But better him than some guy who thought women had only one role in life—to serve men's baser needs. While most cowboys held women in high regard, he'd met some who didn't. There were men who'd take advantage of rural women who had no sophistication. He didn't know Hayley Ryan well enough to place her in that category. Yet she didn't strike him as particularly worldly.

He released the chickens into the makeshift pen and then dawdled, breaking apart the crate and stacking it carefully near the fire to be used as kindling. The longer it took for Hayley to reappear, the more Jake considered mounting up and leaving her to sulk. After all, he faced a hard day's ride. Why stick around? He'd done his duty, and had even delivered a lecture that would've made his mother proud. What Hayley chose to do with the information wasn't his problem.

Nevertheless, Jake was glad that the door to her trailer

popped open and she stepped out before he could sling a leg over the roan's broad back.

Clean shiny hair curled over delicate shoulders covered in a form-fitting khaki blouse. She'd tied the blouse at the waist of form-hugging denims, worn white in spots from frequent washing.

Jake's breath whooshed out as if he'd been sucker-punched. In a way, maybe he had. His brain backpedaled furiously. It was difficult to know what transformation he'd expected to see. Certainly not this look of innocence, this utter lack of guile. Or the engaging sunny smile she flashed him.

"I'm glad you didn't ride off before I could thank you for bringing me the hens. I started thinking you must consider me the most ungrateful wretch who ever lived."

"Not at all. We got off on the wrong foot today. My fault," Jake mumbled. "For riding in unannounced. For calling on you so early."

A self-conscious laugh fell from her lips. "That's okay. Much later, and I'd have been out digging." She tugged a few loose bills and some change from a tight jeans pocket. "How much do I owe you for the chickens? I'll have to trust you to set a fair price. So far, the only fowl I've ever brought came wrapped in plastic."

Jake grinned at that. "Well, now." He stroked his chin in an exaggerated manner. "I could pad the bill and try to make my day's wages. Then I could skip hunting strays and goof off all day."

Hayley played along. "You could. But I recall you telling me your family owned the ranch. So wouldn't that hurt your profits, too?"

"Smart lady. In any event, I'd be wise to charge you enough to keep me solvent while I hunt for a new job.

I've got a feeling blood won't count for much when my mom discovers I swiped her private stock.''

Hayley's smile disappeared. ''You're selling me stolen chickens?''

''Nope. I'm giving them to you. I do have some scruples.''

She looked aghast. ''And what do I say if anyone else from your ranch wanders past and happens to recognize these birds?''

Jake laughed. He gathered Paprika's reins in his left hand and swung up into the saddle. Gazing down at Hayley's puckered brow, he knew he should assure her of his mom's generosity. He should make her understand that Nell Cooper would give a neighbor her last dime if need be. But Jacob felt a sudden unexplained need to dig a deep boundary between his home, his family and this woman. He sobered and dropped all pretense of joking. ''Give them hens a few days to see if they lay eggs for you. If they do, I'll stop by and collect ten bucks for the lot. I'll even write you up a bill of sale.''

''All right.'' Hayley, who understood that something in their give-and-take had shifted, folded her money and tucked it back in her pocket. ''Goodbye until then,'' she said.

Jake, who'd hardened his resolve, who'd argued internally that he couldn't keep riding out of his way to check up on this woman, gave a curt nod. He jerked the mare's reins sharply to the right. The surprised horse wheeled and bolted up the trail. It was all Jacob could do not to turn back and offer a friendly wave, but he kept his shoulders square to the saddle and let the momentum carry him out of sight.

Hayley lifted a hand. Once she realized he wasn't going to return her wave, she curled all four fingers into her palm. She didn't try to gauge how long she stood there smarting at his slight. Longer than she should have, she acknowledged with a grimace. Who was Jacob Cooper to make her feel like an insignificant bug? He was nobody, that was who.

The day she'd filed for divorce from Joe, she'd seen pity on the face of the clerk as she read what Hayley had written: *for reasons of abandonment.* Hayley had promised on the spot that no man would ever make her feel pitiable again. Certainly not an arrogant cowboy. For all she knew, he might be feeding her a line about his relationship to the owner of the Triple C. He could be any old saddle bum.

She would have collected her gear and stomped off into the hills at that moment, if not for the fact that her stomach decided to act finicky again. Very likely because she hadn't eaten breakfast. Hayley chose to place the blame on Cooper's effrontery. "I'll give him back his damned chickens." She fumed aloud as, with jerky movements and roiling insides, she filled a pot of water to heat for tea. After hurrying into the bushes to empty her stomach twice, Hayley dug out the booklet Dr. Gerrard's nurse had given her, outlining what she could expect over the ensuing months of pregnancy. Without the book, she'd probably have panicked over the sudden bout of weakness and flulike symptoms.

Fortunately she'd read the booklet cover to cover before heading into the wilds. Now she had to hope one of the book's recipes—a tincture of horehound, peppermint, ginger and fennel, which she'd bought at a health-food store—would have the promised calming effect on a stomach gone amuck.

The booklet also indicated that staying calm tended to ease many problems associated with pregnancy. Her seeming inability to do so was something else she laid at Jacob Cooper's door. "Insufferable man," she grumbled, sitting down to drink the concoction she'd brewed. As she glared at his morning gift, one of the hens spread her wings and flapped them frantically, then squawked and made gross noises as she burrowed into a pile of dead leaves. When she stood, a pristine white egg lay atop the heap.

Grinning like a fool, Hayley ran to the pen and plucked up the egg. "So, girl," she said, adding a soothing layer to her voice to disarm the bird. "It's high time your new mistress learns to think before she shoots off her mouth. After all, the man went to considerable trouble to cart you ladies here. Maybe I shouldn't be so hasty about throwing you all back in his face."

She promptly soft-boiled the egg, layered it between two halves of a toasted biscuit and ate every morsel. By the time she'd polished off the meal, her nausea had disappeared. With an improved disposition, Hayley gathered her mining tools and set off to coax the rocky hillside into giving up its secrets.

IT WAS STRAIGHT UP NOON when Jake reached the Mortimer ranch that abutted the fenced perimeter of the old ghost town of Ruby. He'd turned up another hundred head of Triple C stock. They looked fat, sassy and content, so he jotted their approximate location in his log; he'd let the wranglers flush them out during roundup.

Ruby was a once-prosperous mining town that had been abandoned for nearly three decades. Its location discouraged all but the most avid ghost-town enthusiasts. Along with other local boys, Jake and Dillon had loved exploring the old buildings, which were still in surprisingly good condition. The mine, originally named Montana Camp, had at one time yielded lead, silver, gold, zinc and copper. Somehow, shortly after Arizona received its statehood, the town's name had changed. According to the story Jake had heard, the owner of the general store and post office had named it after his wife. Currently the town was privately owned. Jake knew the owners hoped to restore Ruby and open it to tourists. But area residents liked the tranquillity its anonymity afforded them. Locals, and Jake included himself, would be happy to see Ruby maintain its status quo.

Ted Mortimer's house overlooked the remains of Ruby. He'd quit ranching after his wife died, but couldn't bring himself to leave the old homestead.

It was time for lunch, and Jake always preferred sharing a meal to eating alone. Besides, catching Ted up on area events would take Jake's mind off Hayley Ryan. He'd meant to forget her after he left her camp. So far it hadn't happened. Visions of her intruded on him all too frequently. He found his mind wandering in her direction when he should have been paying attention to business.

"Yo, the house," Jake called, sliding out of the saddle.

A man appeared from behind a clapboard house. "Well, bless my bones, Jacob. Welcome." He grasped Jake's right hand and squeezed it hard. "Hope you have time to sit a spell. It's been a coon's age since anybody stopped by."

"Isn't Pima College still running field trips to Ruby?"

"Yeah, but them professors and kids have got their own agenda. Between you and me, I think they pity me."

"Pity you? Why?" Jake loosened Paprika's cinch, dropped the saddle on the porch and led the mare to a metal tub brimming with water. Shading his eyes, he gazed over the rolling hills, taking in a hawk soaring against the cloudless sky.

"I get the feeling all those folks from town believe I'm an outcast forced to reside next to a ghost town as punishment."

Jake laughed and followed the man to a shaded side of the porch, where he helped himself to a seat on the soft cushions of a swing glider. "'Course, you don't set 'em straight, do you?"

"You've got my number, boy. But I don't lie. I tell them this is the closest a man gets to paradise without dying. Still, that don't mean I'm a damned recluse. I hope you've got time for a glass of lemonade and a corned-beef sandwich."

Leaning back, Jake swept off his hat. "You know my weakness for corned beef. And lemonade would go down easy. Anything I can do to help?"

"It's ready. I saw you cross over the loop a couple hours ago. You're right on schedule." The man's words were cut off by the bang of a screen door as he went inside. He emerged from the house moments later with a tray of glasses, thick sandwiches on homemade bread and a frosty pitcher of lemonade. Silence settled comfortably around them as the men dug into their lunch. Suddenly the one-time rancher wiped his mouth and said, sounding miffed, "When you see Ben O'Dell next, tell him I'm plenty p.o.'d that he flew past here without bothering to stop by and say howdy. He must be getting close to bringing in a payload to be in such an all-fired hurry."

The corned beef stuck in Jake's throat. When he finally managed to swallow it, he took a big swig of lemonade. "Ben died," he said, rubbing idly at the moisture beading the outside of the glass. "That was Ben's grand-daughter you saw driving his rig. The girl's filed to work his claim."

"A girl miner? Well, don't that beat all!"

Jake saw Hayley Ryan as she'd looked in the early-morning light. "I should have said woman," he corrected himself. "I don't know her age, but I'd guess she's in her twenties."

"When you get to be my age, sonny, any woman under forty-five falls into the category of 'girl.' Tell me about Ben. He stopped here on his way home last fall. Looked hale and hearty then."

"I don't know a lot. All I've heard is that it was pretty sudden. My folks went to Tombstone to check out the girl's story. It isn't any secret that Ben agreed to give us first option on the land. That spring has been the topic of conversation all year at the Cattlemen's Association meetings."

"So now this gal shows up out of the blue with clear claim to your ranch's main water supply. I think I see how the wind blows."

"Well, she said she'd give us the same deal we had with Ben. If she doesn't renege on the bargain, the Triple C, the J & B and probably the Rocking R—that's owned by Marshall Rogers—will still be able to meet the water needs of our summer stock."

"Do I hear a *but* at the end of that statement?"

Jake gave the swing a lazy push with his boot heels. "No. Nothing I can put my finger on."

"I think I understand. This woman's a new unknown player in the game. She could get fed up with digging her fingers bloody in the dirt. If she flies the coop without telling anyone, or if she up and turns loose of her claim, any Tom, Dick or Harry could snap up the land. Including the water and mineral rights.''

''You've got that right enough to ruin my lunch.'' Jake stopped swinging. ''I hadn't got around to putting my fears into words. You summed them up nicely.''

''Is she a looker?''

''Wh-what?'' Jake stammered.

''The woman. Is she pretty? If she is, you might want to marry her. Won't give you automatic rights to her claim. But damn, boy, you'd be in a position to keep tabs on the situation.''

Jake's first inclination was to laugh. Somehow the laugh never materialized. ''She's already married,'' he muttered, lavishing an inordinate amount of attention on the uneaten portion of his sandwich. ''Or she could be in the process of divorce. According to rumors floating around Tombstone, Mrs. Ryan's hubby took off with another woman after selling Ben's silver mine out from under her.''

''Then you wouldn't want to get tangled up with her if she's already a loser.''

''I wouldn't classify her as a loser.'' Jake didn't realize he'd betrayed his interest in Hayley, until his companion let out a cheeky laugh, winked and jabbed Jake's ribs.

''So, the thought of corralling this filly has already crossed your mind.''

''If you want the continued pleasure of my company, old man, stop deviling me. I get enough of that from Dillon. There's ways to keep tabs on the lady without going to such extremes. I've devised any number of reasons that'll take me past her campsite on a regular basis till roundup starts. If she sticks around that long,'' he added.

"You've got a point there, son. Ben had the know-how and the patience to work a claim. Most folks get discouraged if they don't see any monetary gain. To my knowledge, Ben never took a dime out of the Blue Cameo. Still and all, he seemed mighty sure she'd pay off one day."

"Did he ever mention what he expected to turn up?"

The iron-haired man rocked back in his chair and contemplated. "Can't say that he did. Last year when he stopped by, I thought he seemed reluctant to go back to Tombstone. Hinted about being close to a payload. Hell, I've never met a prospector who isn't just a shovelful of dirt away from riches. I'll think about our last visit. If I remember anything more, I'll give you a jingle at the ranch."

"I'd appreciate that. Frankly I hope there isn't anything. All we need is a big gold strike to bring every hopeful miner from both sides of the border converging on us. Can't think of anything worse." Jake grimaced.

"Ben was right to play his cards close to the vest. Sometimes all it takes is the rumor of a find." He shuddered. "I remember my pa saying that happened once at Lynx Creek. Before scuttlebutt was proved wrong, the rush of miners leached the area clean, destroyed the vegetation and eventually dried up the creek. That area's a wasteland now."

Jake nodded. "Thanks for the warning. I believe I'll mosey back by Mrs. Ryan's camp on my way home and press upon her the need for secrecy."

"Telling a woman not to blab is like waving a red flag at a bull. When you've lived as long as I have, you'll understand the female species makes a point of doing whatever a man tells her not to."

Jake stood and shook hands with his friend before

settling his hat on his head. "Not all women gossip. My mother and Dillon's wife detest the practice."

"I only met your brother's wife at the wedding. Your mother, now, is a rare lady."

"She is at that." In fact, the biggest thing standing in the way of Jake's burgeoning feelings for Hayley Ryan was the reservations his mother seemed to have.

The old man followed Jake and watched him saddle the mare. "One last bit of advice, Jacob. A woman always takes suggestions better from another woman. You might make more headway if you could get Nell to visit your Mrs. Ryan."

Jake made a face as he climbed on the broad-backed horse. "She's not *my* Mrs. Ryan. I hope you remember that. Especially if you cross paths with anyone who works for the Triple C. Or for that matter, the J & B."

"Don't tell me you're sniffing after Westin's little honeybee?"

"I thought you knew me better than that."

"Glad to hear you confirm it. I like John Westin all right. It's a damn shame he's so blind when it comes to his kid."

"People all have their own ways of raising kids. I'm afraid I can't render an opinion until I get some experience. Which isn't likely to be soon." Jake waved goodbye to the man on the porch—whose laughter followed him up the trail. That, as nothing else had, changed his mind about looking in on Hayley Ryan again.

As the mare walked carefully through the brush, flushing a covey of brightly plumed Gambel's quail, Jake's thoughts returned to what he might be like as a father. He'd always assumed he'd have kids someday. Most of his friends in the area, guys he'd gone to school with, were married and had started their families. Bob Verner and his wife had recently had number three.

Link Thompson and his wife, Bev, had four girls. *Four.* Link was two years younger than Jake. Oddly, Jacob found that unsettling. At least Dillon and Eden weren't expecting yet. Jake wondered if they sat around home at night and talked about optimal timing.

"Nah," he said aloud, shaking his head and setting the mare into a trot. "Dillon lives moment to moment. He's not big on long-range plans." Eden, now, was a different story. She organized, saved and kept meticulous books. Building and furnishing the house on Dillon's hundred acres had been her doing. Nesting. Jake would bet Eden did have a baby plotted into her chart somewhere.

It shouldn't matter to him what plans they made. So why did the picture of them sitting around the family Christmas tree, bouncing a laughing infant, stick in his craw?

At that moment Jake spotted a group of steers feeding in a ravine. All wore the Triple C brand. Stopping to take an exact count and write it in his logbook returned his brain to work mode. Not that he considered this *hard* work. Riding the range, even on the back of a horse as uncomfortable as Paprika, hardly fell under the heading of work at all to Jake. His dad used to say he'd been born in the saddle. Ranching was in his blood. Even in the winter when the wind froze a man's nose and any other body part he was unlucky enough to expose, other cowboys bitched and moaned. Jake rarely uttered a complaint. He truly did not understand why so many of his contemporaries couldn't wait to trade the red dust of the Santa Cruz valley for the sizzling concrete of Arizona's cities. Jacob didn't mind wearing white shirts and ties to funerals and weddings. The thought of having to don that getup with regularity sent chills down his spine.

Most women of his generation fawned over jokers wearing suits. Jake saw it at the dances and the singles' bars he frequented when he went to Kansas, Wyoming or Texas to the bull sales. Plenty of women flirted with cowboys. Few committed themselves for the long haul once they had a taste of what it took to carve a home out of earth and rock.

For many of his cowboy buddies who'd gotten married were single again, and looking. Jake would admit cowboying could make a man lonely, and it sure resulted in a few aching muscles. Which was why curling up at night next to a woman's softer body held such appeal. But not just any body, dammit.

When Jake left the Mortimer ranch, he'd set his course for the Triple C. It was a shock to suddenly wake up out of his fog and find himself staring down through a waning sun at Hayley Ryan's camp. *Again...*

He sucked in a huge gulp of air. After all, he'd reversed his decision to pay her a visit. Yet because he was here, he raised his field glasses and scanned the clearing. Just checking to see that all was well. Once satisfied, he'd ride on without her ever being wiser.

Her campfire danced brightly. The chickens Jake had penned earlier scratched contentedly. Her truck and trailer sat untouched. Letting the glasses fall to the end of their strap, Jake gathered Paprika's reins in his left hand, preparing to skirt Hayley's camp. In two seconds he would have been gone. But he happened to catch sight of her. She leapt from her chair beside the fire, bent low, clutching her stomach with crossed arms and made a beeline for the trees.

Jake fumbled with the binoculars again. Sweat popped

out on his own brow when he finally brought her into focus again. She looked close enough for him to touch. And touching was what she needed. Her face had turned a ghastly white. Perspiration dampened the fine dark hair that framed her oval face. It hurt Jake physically to see her cling to a sapling and retch violently.

Never giving thought to her wanting or needing privacy at a time like this, Jake snapped the mare into high gear and galloped full tilt into Hayley's camp. He dismounted on the fly and ran to her side.

"What's wrong?" he demanded, sweeping her up and into his arms. He babbled the whole time he ran, carrying her to the spring. "Did you catch a flu bug? Or food poisoning?" Stripping off his dusty neck scarf, Jake dipped it in the cool water and began to bathe her face. He forgot to wring out the material and soon soaked both their shirts.

"Stop," Hayley sputtered. "Where did you come from? You scared the daylights out of me." Struggling to get off his lap and out of his arms, she felt her stomach drop and heave. Only the worry on his face eased her struggles.

"I...I...didn't know anyone was around," she managed. Embarrassment gripped her tongue. She couldn't tell this man that she was apparently one of the unlucky women who suffered morning sickness twice a day. According to the book, one in four women endured nausea both morning and evening. One in ten, the booklet said, were sick all day. Hayley had counted her blessings to falling into the one in four category. However, being tenderly ministered to while languishing by a man not responsible for her condition, Hayley didn't feel lucky at all. In fact, she felt about as miserable as she imagined a woman could feel. She did the only thing she could do to save face; she forced her roiling stomach into submission, and she lied.

"Thank you for your concern. I wor…worked my claim all day. Got a tad too much sun, I guess." Hayley did separate herself from his muscular arms this time.

Jake's racing heart put on the brakes at last. Now he felt like a fool watching her untie the tail of her blouse and mop at the water he'd all but drowned her with.

"Heatstroke is serious. Didn't you wear a hat?" For some reason he found it easier to sound tough rather than to give in to his desire to gather her in his arms again. She'd fit into the crook of his elbow just fine. Her hair hadn't smelled like that of a woman who'd toiled all day in the sun. A light floral fragrance had tickled his nose, reminding him of the flower shop in town.

Hayley turned away, carefully spreading her laced fingers across her still-shaky stomach. "I wore a hat. A baseball cap. I do have a floppy ghastly straw hat with a big brim. It makes me look like Mother Goose." She would have gone on, but choked and turned clammy when she realized he might get suspicious at her reference to a child's storybook character—or was she totally overreacting. *Damn, damn, damn.* Why didn't Jacob Cooper go away and keep his nose out of her life?

"Women." He expelled the word along with a massive sigh. "You won't find a man letting fashion rule over his good sense."

"You have some nerve." Hayley found the strength to muster indignity. Already the wave of nausea was passing. "You don't know anything about me. Nothing at all."

"Is that so?" Jake let hostility cover his emotions. "You say you're married, but I know your husband really left Tombstone with another woman. Maybe you should ask yourself if she was less vain, less concerned with looks and more mindful of good health.''

The minute the shock registered in her wide eyes, Jake wanted to retract his cruel words. Dishonest words.

''Leave!'' she said through quivering lips. ''I'm going into the trailer to change into dry things. I want you gone when I come out again.''

Jake called himself a million and one foul names as Hayley darted across the clearing and jerked open the trailer's door. The pitifully tiny place she called home. Of course she wasn't vain. He ought to be ashamed.

He was ashamed.

He hung around the fire for twenty minutes, wanting an opportunity to apologize. Jake gazed vacantly at various-size samples of ore she had sitting around in boxes. If she'd dug all of those samples today, no wonder she had a touch of sun fever. Some blue slabs glittered in the firelight. He didn't know enough about rock and minerals to know if she'd found anything worthwhile.

He hoped she had. Jake felt like a rat. Lower than a rat.

After ten more minutes of silence, it became apparent that Hayley wouldn't come out again until he left. He had no doubt that she never wanted to see him again. Shame overwhelmed him and ultimately convinced him to bow to her wishes.

He climbed slowly into Paprika's saddle and then trotted the horse as close to the small side window in the trailer as he could get. ''You can come out,'' he called. ''I'm leaving.''

Waiting, he listened, fully expecting to hear sounds of weeping, which would make him feel terrible—exactly what he deserved. Only silence greeted him. In a way it was worse than tears.

He rode off, keeping one eye trained over his shoulder. If she emerged before he lost sight of her camp, he'd turn back and beg her forgiveness tonight. As she kept stubbornly to herself, Jake knew he'd be riding this trail again in the morning. He only hoped that between now and then, he'd figure out some way to make it up to her.

# CHAPTER SIX

WADE COOPER intercepted Jake as he tried to sneak into the house without going through the kitchen, where his parents were sure to be. He was still in a foul mood after the way he'd left things with Hayley. Tonight, food and family chitchat had fallen off his list of priorities.

"You've put in some long days in the saddle lately, son." Wade placed a broad hand on Jake's shoulder and turned him from the dark hallway toward the bright light spilling from the kitchen.

"Yeah," Jake grunted. "I'm bushed. Tell Mom a shower and sleep takes precedence over whatever she might have saved in the oven tonight."

"Oh. Sorry to hear it." Wade looked glum. "We're on our own. Nell is firing kilns tonight. She and Eden are spending the night in town. I waited dinner. Thought you and I could throw together a batch of nachos. I already iced a six-pack of beer."

Jake wavered at the threshold. His dad was so transparent. Since his accident, he wandered the ranch like a lost puppy. The whole family tried to look out for him—keep him occupied so he wouldn't feel useless and start to overdo things. It surprised Jake that his mom had abandoned her shift. He said as much.

"It's the new clay she bought in Tucson. She'd have stayed home, but I know how badly she itched to get her fingers in the new slip. I convinced her I was meeting

John and some of the other ranchers to talk about water.''

"Is that how you spent the day?" Jake's curiosity carried him into the room. He saw that Wade had already grated cheese and cut up jalapeños, tomatoes, and onions; there was a bowl of black beans, as well as olives and a bag of large corn chips.

The elder Cooper twisted off the caps from two long-necked brews. He handed one to Jake, then set the other aside while he prepared the chips and popped them into the microwave. "John doesn't want to wait for the Ryan woman to get bored. Pearce and Lowell would accept the original agreement if John and Marshall weren't pressuring them to take action."

"Action? What action?" Jake turned off the buzzer, grabbed an oven mitt and set the steaming plate between them on a thick pot holder. "Ben's granddaughter filed legally. You checked. As long as she works the claim, we can't force her to sell."

"No. But John says there's nothing stopping us from giving her money to abandon her claim."

Jake bit into a jalapeño that made his eyes water. The chili pepper wasn't all that burned. What John Westin proposed sounded like a cheap underhand trick to Jake. "How does John suggest you set fair compensation when no one knows the value of what Hayley's prospecting?"

"Hayley? Pretty familiar aren't you? But then, I suppose a woman might get friendly fast with a guy who took her five laying hens."

Jake choked on his swig of beer. He should have known his dad would notice. The man had always had a sixth sense when it came to his boys.

"I hoped you planned to tell your mother. Soon as

she figures out those hens are gone, she'll be claiming the gray wolves Fish and Game released last winter got 'em. The way you stood up to the neighbors and backed that release program, I'm sure you don't want to be responsible for its demise. Nell raised that flock from chicks, you know. John's not the only one in the valley who can incite people to riot.''

''You've made your point. I'll talk to Mom soon. And to be clear on another thing, Dad, nothing's going on between me and Hayley. I'm just...well, concerned about her situation. Fool woman's oblivious to what can happen along the border.''

''Then John's plan should appeal to you. Take up a collection and help her move back to Tombstone posthaste.''

It did sound reasonable, Jake allowed. At least it did until he considered how stubborn Hayley was, how intent on self-reliance. ''I don't think she'll go for the idea.''

''Why not? Surely she can't enjoy toiling in the sun day after day, digging through rock until her hands bleed. Breaking her back for zip.''

''She's got Ben's pride and more.'' The minute he said it, Jake realized he was making a judgment call. He didn't really know Hayley Ryan, as she'd pointed out tonight. She might well take the money and run. The notion left a bad taste in his mouth. Or maybe it was the beer. He pushed the half-full bottle aside.

Wade licked cheese off his fingers and narrowed his eyes at Jake before he fumbled a napkin from the holder. ''O'Dell wouldn't even come to our house for dinner. Said he didn't take handouts. Unlike his granddaughter, he'd never have accepted those chickens.''

Guilty color splashed across Jake's angular cheekbones. "I told her if they produce eggs, she could pay me. Ten dollars for the lot."

Wade choked. "Those prize chicks cost Nell twenty bucks apiece."

Jake didn't respond. He didn't have to. The seed had been planted, and he didn't even know if he should have stuck his neck out. But it was too late. Wade was weighing what he'd do if that was Eden or his wife dug in at the spring. Enough had been said. Unless there was a majority vote to buy Hayley out, Jake bet his dad would vote to leave her be.

Jake rose, rummaged in the fridge, then added slices of roast chicken to the next batch of nachos. He let the hum of the microwave fill the silence.

Both men tucked into the newest platter with gusto. Talk gradually resumed and turned to the beef count and the upcoming roundup. Though Hayley's name didn't surface again, Jake's mind conjured her up. He wondered if he should forewarn her of Westin's plan.

Even though Jake told himself repeatedly that he'd done his part and should keep his nose out of it, he lay in bed that night and worried about the doggedness of the other ranchers. Westin hadn't built an empire by avoiding land grabs. He'd been known to undercut neighbors. People didn't dwell on it, but the truth was there if anyone cared to examine it. Jake had a hunch most partners in the coalition wanted the Triple C to possess the land surrounding the spring rather than letting Westin get his hands on it.

Jake already had his reasons for visiting Hayley in the morning. Technically he didn't owe her anything but an apology, but as sleep continued to evade him, he mulled over ways to put her on guard. What could he say, though, that wouldn't place all the ranchers in a bad light? Including the Coopers. After all, he'd been the first to approach her about leaving her claim—and then about sharing the spring.

By the time the milk cows began to low and the song-birds awakened, Jake had wrestled the problem every which way from Sunday—to no avail. He decided to deliver his apology and ignore the water issue. It was possible nothing would come of John's proposal. Even if it did, Jake needn't be involved. He'd already made up his mind that after today, Hayley Ryan was on her own. He had a job to do for the Triple C, and it didn't include riding herd on a headstrong female.

Decision made, Jake would be hard-pressed to say what prompted him to fill two jugs with fresh milk before he saddled up, whistled Charcoal to heel and then set a straight course for the Blue Cameo mine.

HAYLEY HAD SPENT a sleepless night. By midnight not so much as a breath of wind wafted through her window screens. She'd spent the night thinking about her baby. About how she'd support a child if the mine didn't produce. By law, Joe should pay support. But if he did, maybe he'd demand visitation rights. She couldn't bear the thought of him having even the slightest influence over her child—or her. Support of any kind would make her beholden. By three in the morning she'd decided her only choice was to see that the Blue Cameo gave up its secret cache, whatever that might be.

This morning the air was quite humid and heavy, which added to Hayley's exhaustion. She wondered if it was going to rain.

Jacob Cooper rode into her camp and dismounted in a cloud of red dust as she was trying to decide whether or not to haul yesterday's ore samples inside. Hayley hated to admit she'd kept one eye on the trailhead, expecting, hoping, Jake would appear.

Though it annoyed her no end, her spirits lifted magically when he did.

She was pathetic. Really pathetic. Last night he'd insulted her. Desperate to hide feelings that made no sense, she opened her arms to the black-and-white dog and pretended to ignore his master.

"Morning." Jake had had twelve hours to polish his apology. Hearing Hayley's low alluring laughter, watching his dog lick her face, wiped away any trace of polite conversation. It was all Jake could do to lift down the milk jugs and thrust them wordlessly into her hands. He'd never wanted to kiss any woman as badly as he wanted to kiss Hayley Ryan.

"Milk. So fresh it's still warm," she exclaimed. Her delight over his thoughtful gift blurred any lingering ambivalence. "Of everything I can't pick up daily at the grocery anymore, it's fresh milk I miss the most. Thank you, Jake."

He took the jugs back as he fought the effect of her smile on parts of his body over which he normally had better control. "I'll suspend these under the waterfall so the milk can cool. I hope a few glasses will settle your stomach."

"My stomach?" Hayley went still and grabbed her middle.

Jake had started for the spring. Pausing, he glanced with surprise into her frightened eyes. There was no other word to describe the turbulence he saw there. "The heat, you know. You said it caused you to…well, throw up. I'm sure it's not a pleasant memory. A steady diet of camp food can cause indigestion. Milk soothes the stomach. You can't be sure it was the weather that made you sick,'' he ended lamely.

"Oh. Sure." Realizing how silly she must look holding on to her stomach, Hayley dropped her hands.

She was doing it again, looking fragile and...and soft. Shaken, Jake felt the need to say, "I had no right to lay into you last night. For all I know, you kicked your husband out. And he probably deserved it. Anyway, I'm sorry I upset you and then rode off like a jerk without apologizing."

His contrition was so surprising and complete, Hayley felt as if she'd been thrust backward through a knothole. During their brief marriage, Joe had done a lot of things he should have said he was sorry for. The word hadn't been in his vocabulary. Gramps, too, came from the old school where men lived their lives to suit themselves. Women fit in and adapted, or they lumped it. Jacob Cooper would very likely be shocked to know he'd just atoned for all the men in Hayley's life. She hadn't realized how badly she needed to hear that men could feel regret for the hurt they so often caused women.

She sank into one of the lawn chairs and ran her fingers through the collie's soft fur. "Joe, that's my husband, er, ex. He...he...did leave town with another woman. Which doesn't give me license to take my feelings of inadequacy out on you."

Jake had met a lot of divorced women. In his experience, a few were willing to share blame for the breakup of their marriages. Most placed the culpability squarely on the man. Hayley's unvarnished statement of fact told Jacob a lot about her character. "Look, I don't want you to think I went out of my way to be nosy. My mom and dad were in Tombstone the day after I met you. They heard all that stuff."

"Gossip is the lifeblood of mining towns."

"Ranch towns, too."

"I'm sure. How did my name happen to come up? Why?"

Her straightforward questions made Jake uncomfortable. "It wasn't that we doubted you had a good claim. But...well, Dad hoped Ben had told someone about his deal with the Triple C. We should have known if he'd told anyone, it'd be his next of kin."

Hayley's fingers clutched convulsively in the dog's fur. "There you go, making assumptions again. Gramps's poker partner knew this claim existed. I didn't."

"Wh-where did you think he went for months at a time every year?"

"Prospecting. When I was little, he took me along. After I reached school age, he left me with a friend who taught me sewing, cooking and such."

"He wandered off for months on end and left you alone? That must have been rough."

"I'm not complaining," she said lightly. Too lightly.

"So if you weren't aware the Blue Cameo existed, I guess you really don't know what Ben was after." Jake started to wave a hand and realized he still hadn't submerged the milk in the water. Worried that he was prying again, he told her she didn't owe him an answer. He hurried to the spring.

Wanting to make amends, Hayley stood up and brushed the dog hair from her hands. "Are you any good at reading streak plates?"

Jake made a half hitch in the rope he'd threaded through the jug handles. "Excuse me?"

"You know. The color of powder left behind when any given mineral is rubbed over the cut edge of an unfinished tile or unglazed porcelain streak plate defines what's been found." It sounded as if she was reciting a definition from a textbook. Which, essentially, she was.

"Is that all there is to prospecting for, say, diamonds or gold?"

"There's the Moh scale, too," she said matter-of-factly. When Jake shrugged, she went into a little detail. "For hardness. The scale indicates what mineral scratches another mineral. Talc is number one. Diamond is number ten. Gypsum, calcite, feldspar, quartz and topaz and corundum are a few that fall in between. The Moh is a novice prospector's Bible. Someone experienced, like Gramps, identifies minerals from the way they break. I have to run all the tests." She sighed. "These are the samples I dug yesterday."

"Sounds like a lot of work for maybe no reward," Jake ventured.

Her chin shot up to the angle he'd begun to recognize as determination. "There'll be a big reward," she insisted.

Jake tucked his hands in his back pockets and headed for his horse. He'd ridden Mojave again today, and the bay gelding looked up with interest and began to move toward him. Freeing a hand, Jake grabbed the reins. "I wish you luck, Hayley. I'll try to stay out of your hair from now on. Next week we start roundup. From time to time we'll send a man to open the valves to the ditches." He pulled a piece of paper out of his shirt pocket. "These are the brands you'll deal with from now to November. If a horse carries any of these brands, please don't shoot the rider." His eyes teased as he handed her the list.

"This sounds like goodbye." Hayley almost dropped the paper.

Gazing at a spot beyond her right shoulder, he removed and resettled his hat a couple of times. "Busy time of year for the Triple C. About the only socializing I'll do for the next few months is with ornery cows."

Hayley's chest felt suddenly hollow. A few months sounded interminable. By then, her pregnancy would show. Because she didn't know how to introduce that subject, she donned a bright smile instead. "I trust you'll spread the word that anyone showing up on a horse *without* these brands is courting danger."

"I surely will. I showed you how to close the valves to the various ditches. To keep traffic in your camp to a minimum, let the water flow for six hours, then shut her down."

"Right. I'm not planning on going anywhere. Oh...unless I need to replenish supplies. So if my truck isn't here, I've gone to Tubac. I assume the water system will do its thing if I'm gone. I don't foresee ever spending a night away from camp."

"Does that pickup have a radio? The road between here and the highway can turn into a quagmire during our August monsoons. Sometimes a road washes out. Usually we fix it within a day or so, but you need to stay alert."

"I have a portable radio and cases of batteries. The truck also has a radio."

"Good. Then I guess you're set. I took the liberty of drawing a map to the Triple C on the back of that paper showing the brands. If you need anything, anything at all, someone will most likely be around our place or Dillon's. I marked his house on the map, too."

"Thanks. Don't worry that I'll wear out my welcome. I've got a lot of ground to cover right here. Anyway, I'm not a big mingler."

It was on the tip of Jake's tongue to ask if she liked to dance. What Dillon had said about inviting her to the Harvest Dance ricocheted inside his skull. But the decision he'd made before he left the house—to keep his distance from Hayley Ryan—loomed larger. Jake tipped his hat, whistled for Charcoal and climbed into the saddle.

Hayley moved beside his shifting horse. "It's really humid today. I don't have to worry about storms yet, do I? Because July isn't over?"

Jake squinted at the sky. Clouds had rolled in and covered the sun without his noticing. That showed how much this woman confused him. He was dead right to cut the self-imposed ties and go on about his business. "We've had gully washers in July before and we've been a spell without rain." He took some time to study her camp. "You're laid out the same way Ben used to be. He weathered a few humdingers. I expect this'll blow over, but if the spring should fill and overflow, open the valve marked *one* for a while."

"Thanks. Well, I won't keep you." This time the smile she pasted on didn't feel so bright. It must have fooled Jake. He galloped off without a wave.

Hayley didn't budge until an attack of nausea drove her into the bushes to empty her stomach of breakfast. Darn, this couldn't be good for the baby. Not even if the book said it was fairly normal.

Alone, lonely and vaguely out of sorts, Hayley grouped her ore samples around the fire pit. Telling herself that she didn't need anyone's company but her own, that she was happy to be rid of Jacob Cooper and his constant interruptions, Hayley hunched over her boxes doing streak-plate tests until her fingers bled. Eventually the roll of thunder and the crack of lightning drove her inside. At least she could blame her wet cheeks on the rain that had begun to spit.

HUDDLED IN A NARROW CAVE with a wet smelly horse and dog, Jake stared out at the storm he'd wrongly told Hayley would blow over. Since the clouds started dumping, he'd wager two inches of rain had hit the ground. Arroyos filled and there were tumbling rivers where hours ago none existed.

But Hayley Ryan wasn't his problem.

*What if she forgets how to open the valve? What if it sticks?*

Against his better judgment, Jake nudged Mojave into the downpour. He simply wouldn't draw an easy breath until he was satisfied Hayley's camp hadn't washed away. That didn't mean he planned to let her know he was checking up, however.

At the same vantage point he'd used the other day, Jake lay spread-eagle in the wet saw grass. He scanned the clearing below, gnashing his teeth until he could determine that she was snug in her tin can of a trailer and that water flowed through the valve merrily, keeping the spring at an acceptable level.

Two days later Jake came down with a doozy of a summer cold. For three days after that, when the high desert heat had once again set in, he was grumpy as a rank bull. Everyone but his mother maintained a discreet distance. She brought soup to his room. *Chicken* soup. And casually mentioned her missing hens.

"I planned to tell you," Jake mumbled. "It slipped my mind. So I guess Dad ratted."

Nell Cooper met the challenging gaze of her handsome personable tenderhearted youngest son. "What sort of woman has a man thieving from his own family?

You're sick because of her, too," she accused. She held up a palm when Jake's head came off the pillow and his eyes blazed. "Don't deny it. A mother knows these things."

"Mom, no. I played good neighbor a time or two. That's the extent of it. She's out there digging her damned rocks. Soon as I'm well, I'll be joining the roundup on the north range."

Nell hesitated at the door. "Since Dillon and Eden's wedding, I've watched you change, grow restless. The right woman will come along, I know it. Someone as nice as Eden."

Jake sneezed four times. Dropping his chin to his chest, he muttered, "My soup's getting cold."

"So eat. I'll have my say and then I'll leave. This phase will pass. You don't have to settle for a...a divorced nomad, Jacob."

He rallied to Hayley Ryan's defense. Too late. His mother had said her piece and gone, slamming his bedroom door. Well, hell! He didn't plan on seeing Hayley again, anyhow.

Still, his mother's words grated. He was a grown man. One capable of making his own decisions where women were concerned. His mom loved him and meant well. But she was a potter, not a damned psychologist.

By the middle of the following week his cold had cleared up, but Jake was still angry when he rode off to the roundup. The crew sensed his mood and left him to his own devices. They probably figured hard work and the elements would take it out of him soon enough.

And they were right. A blistering sun rolled up every morning, soon drying every trace of that one brief monsoon. The few pockets of water that remained after the sandy soil had sucked in the excess simply evaporated as the earth baked to a hard clay. Slowly plodding steers kicked up clouds of dust. Jake ate his share. Yet every night, when the majority of the wranglers knocked off for dinner break, he'd take a fresh mount and ride out to check on Hayley. He did that for several weeks.

The first day that Dillon let the herd rest for a full twenty-four hours, Jake cut a small surefooted pinto from the remuda, saddled her and presented her to Hayley.

"I can't take such an elaborate gift." She had, by chance, cooked extra macaroni and cheese, and handed Jake a full plate. "What makes you think I can even ride?"

"Can you?"

"Yes." Her cheeks burned as she glanced away.

"I heard your pickup stalled twice on your drive into town to replenish supplies. Graze the mare regularly and she won't break down."

Hayley laughed. Jacob couldn't know that the gift of his visit meant more to her than anything tangible. Including the chickens and the rock sled he'd sent last week with the man who'd opened the valve. The sled helped make removal of the ore she blasted out much easier. She'd had the wrangler take a look at her pickup's engine while he was there, as well. He must have been the one who told Jacob about its stalling.

"Jake. This morning two men, ranchers, came to visit me."

His fork stilled. "Who? What did they want? I hope you showed them your shotgun."

"No. They were gentlemen. Checking on the spring." She unfolded the sheet of brands and tapped a skinned finger with a broken nail on the intertwined J & B.

"Westin and his foreman, Gordy White," Jake breathed after she'd finished describing the two.

"The older man tried to give me five thousand dollars to quit what I'm doing here. Before he left he was up to fifteen thousand."

Jake made mush of the steaming macaroni. He tensed, prepared to hear, but hoping he wouldn't, she'd accepted John's offer.

A frown settled between her brows. "I expected you to act surprised. I thought they were trying to pull a fast one on your family. You know, go behind your back and buy this parcel out from under you. But I can see you knew about it," she said, sounding hurt.

"I'd heard rumors. John's the Cattlemen's Association president. Almanac predictions that we're heading into a long drought probably spooked him. He owns a huge thirsty herd."

"Well, I'm not dropping my claim."

"Look at your hands," Jake said gently. "Do you really think whatever's under the quartz and granite hill is worth killing yourself for?"

"I thought you were in my corner, Jacob." Her eyes, suddenly sad and serious, seemed to assess him.

"I think you're crazy," he muttered, heaving himself up to scrape his plate into the fire. She kept it burning even though the heat was almost 110, even this late in the day. Earlier, when they'd been talking, she'd confessed to having seen mangy coyotes and several rooting families of javelina at the spring. The Southwest pigs were ugly razor-backed animals. Jake had seen them turn nasty; he worried they might attack Hayley if the drought got really bad.

"Thank you." Now her eyes snapped. "Thank you so much for the vote of confidence. I didn't ask you to hang around. And I don't need any of your sneaky bribes. Take back your chickens and the mare. Stop plying me with vegetables and milk." This last fell reluctantly from her lips. But he'd called her crazy, and that hurt. Jacob Cooper had sneaked past her defenses, reminding her acutely of how swiftly and easily she'd been duped by Joe Ryan, too.

"Hayley, dang it! I'm not part of that extortion party."

"Can't prove it by me. Go, Jacob Cooper. I can take care of myself."

Without another word, Jake gathered Mojave's reins, mounted smoothly and left, taking the pinto with him. He felt frustrated by her attitude. And darn, he'd hated watching Hayley's complexion go from lightly tanned to sunburned to scaly brown. His mother's hands and Eden's, too, bore the calluses of their work. Neither had cracked skin and horribly broken fingernails the way Hayley did. If, on occasion, Eden burned a finger with her jewelry soldering iron, a Band-Aid took care of the problem. Jake doubted a normal first-aid kit contained enough bandages for Hayley's cuts and scrapes.

Once again, as he covered the punishing miles back to the roundup, Jacob vowed that Hayley Ryan wasn't his problem. Let her mummify, for all he cared.

He managed to stick to his guns for the rest of August—three weeks spent branding and moving a third of the herd to the rail cars. Then he rejoined the crew. The first afternoon back, he had occasion to object to the wrangler Dillon had chosen to send to Hayley's camp to open the valves.

"Send Julio, instead," Jake barked, indicating a wrangler with nearly white hair.

"It's my decision." Dillon rounded on Jake. "If I ask

Ray, you want Alonzo. Miguel, instead of Orleans. What in hell is wrong with sending Emilio?''

"He's new. What do we really know about him?''

"That he gives us a full day's work for a day's pay.''

"You're always riding point so you don't hear the men talk like I do. The others joke about him being a ladies' man.''

"Exactly what half the valley says about you.''

Jake crowded Mojave close to Dillon's mount. "I've never forced myself on a woman. Besides, you feed into that hype, and you damn well know it.''

Dillon studied Jake's smoldering eyes and cocked jaw. Backing his big black gelding up a couple of steps, Dillon placed two fingers between his lips and issued an earsplitting whistle. "Hold up, Emilio,'' he shouted. "Take a load off your horse and go get some chow. Jake'll go open the valves tonight.''

The young stud, Emilio, galloped up to his boss. It was obvious he was too disciplined and too in need of the job to argue. But the mockery brimming in his dark eyes let Jake and Dillon both know he'd figured out the score.

When Emilio wheeled his tired piebald mare around and proceeded to ride to the chuck wagon as he'd been ordered, Dillon curled a hand around his brother's hard forearm. "Maybe I should go. Honestly, dude, I've never seen you in this state over a woman.''

"I'm not in any state. That punk Emilio thinks he's hot stuff. The Triple C doesn't need the reputation of hiring guys who can't keep a lock on their zippers.''

"Sounds as if what you've got in mind is the same thing you're accusing him of.''

"Bull puckey! I'll be glad to let you bust *your* butt making the round trip to release the water.''

Dillon laid an arm across his saddle horn while his horse nibbled the sparse dry grass. "Maybe you're far too willing at that. I guess the hots you had for the Ryan woman have cooled. Hope you don't mind if I relay that bit of news to Mom and Eden. They've had their heads together, plotting to import a woman the two of them met at the last craft show. A quilter. Mom's gung ho, but Eden thinks the woman's too old for you. She's thirty-nine," Dillon said slyly.

The smile Jake forced more closely resembled a grimace, but he knew what Dillon was trying to do. Shake him up and make him admit he still had a yen for Hayley Ryan. "I've dated older women," he said, determined to keep his brother guessing.

Dillon stroked his stubbled jaw. "You trust the judgment of those two in picking you a woman? If I were you, I'd hurry up and ask someone to the harvest dance."

For the first time in a lot of years, Jake considered skipping the dance. He wasn't fool enough to tell Dillon. He'd never hear the end of the razzing.

"The older you get, Jacob, the slimmer the pickings in the valley. Ask Dad to let you attend more stock shows. I hear there's an abundance of pretty, well-heeled ranch widows looking to find second husbands there."

"Or I'll just build my house and live out my days as a bachelor. What's it going to be, Dillon? Are you riding out to open the valves or am I?"

"Aw, go on. Seniority has its privilege. I'm happy to let you get saddle sore."

In answer, Jake whistled for Charcoal. He nudged Mojave forward and let him pick his way around the herd. The minute they cleared the hill, out of sight of Dillon, Jake urged the gelding into a gallop. Damn, he didn't want his mom and Eden importing some designing woman. He'd ask Hayley Ryan to the dance. It'd serve those sneaky matchmakers right.

Jake rode at a steady clip, eager to see her. He wondered if the weeks had passed as slowly for her as they had for him. It made no earthly sense, but he'd missed sparring with her—and missed other tings about her, too.

He couldn't resist spying on her camp when he landed within field-glass range. Not that he'd see her if she wasn't seated by her campfire. The days had grown shorter. Ten minutes ago the sun had dropped behind Bella Vista Point.

Raising the binoculars, he fiddled with the central focus. Suddenly Hayley's camp loomed right beyond the tips of Mojave's ears. "What in blazes?" Jake kneed the horse forward. Was the woman having a party?

*No!* A hiss escaped Jake's strangled lungs. Two men, a woman holding a baby and four other kids were sitting cross-legged near her fire. She wove between them, scooping food out of a metal pot. Every one of the ragtag group seemed nervous and ill at ease. "Damn! She's got herself visitors from across the border."

His heart leapt half out of his chest. Were they armed? If Jake hadn't been so panic-stricken, he might have watched longer and thought through his actions a little more clearly. All he could imagine was Hayley lying bloodied and battered, her meager possessions appropriated by the crooks who promised to guide illegals through the desert.

He let out a rebel yell guaranteed to raise the dead. And he rode Mojave hell-bent for election into her camp, sliding the shocked horse to his haunches a foot from the crackling fire. Ashes scattered, and so did Hayley's visitors.

Charcoal, loving the unexpected chase, ran hither and yon, setting up a din that drove every animal in the countryside wild.

Within seconds of Jake's making his grand entrance, all that remained of the wanderers was six cracked plates and an unholy silence. Even the animals who'd been drinking from the stream went quickly to ground.

"Jacob Cooper, are you drunk?" Hayley braced her hands on her hips. Hips that had broadened an inch or two since the last time he'd seen her. In fact, there were other changes in her appearance. Her hair had grown. It now swirled about her waist. Instead of the ever-present blue jeans, she wore a long loose print jumper over a round-necked T-shirt. In the center of her jumper, below where her waist should be, Jake noticed a bulge—like a misplaced pillow.

His eyes nearly popped out of his head. Hayley Ryan was pregnant, or Jacob Barrett Cooper had not been raised on a ranch where the procreation of God's creatures was a cyclic fact of life.

Hayley stopped yelling at him the minute she saw where Jake's eyes were trained. Nervously she smoothed a hand over the secret she'd kept from him. Then she caught herself and carefully shook her jumper loose so that nothing showed. As if she believed that, once hidden from prying eyes, her condition no longer existed.

Jake went hot, then cold, then hot again. He stumbled over two of the plates dropped by the fleeing family. As the night creatures began to stir, he slumped heavily into the closest lawn chair. Instantly the webbed seating gave way with a loud rip, dumping Jake in the dirt. But his pain and humiliation seemed minor compared to the turmoil in his gut. *Pregnant. The woman he hankered after was going to have some other man's baby.*

## CHAPTER SEVEN

"MY STARS, JACOB! Are you hurt?" Hayley ran to his
side and extended a hand to help him up from the tangle
of metal tubing that had been a chair. "This belonged
to Gramps. I knew the webbing was frayed. Honestly, I
never dreamed it would give way," she babbled, hov-
ering over him anxiously.

Almost in a daze, Jake watched Hayley's cotton
jumper flow from her shoulders, draping the tops of her
boots in a shapeless mass. He wondered if he'd imagined
her condition. Yes. The light from the fire pit must have
been playing tricks. Her face hadn't changed. It was the
same narrow oval. Her arms were still slender, although
darkly tanned now from her work in the sun. The wind
must have billowed out her dress. After all, he was used
to seeing her in jeans.

Clambering to his feet—with the only real injury to
his pride—Jake dismissed what he thought he'd seen.
Instead, he tackled the subject that had brought him roaring into her camp. "Those people you were feeding. I
hope you knew them."

"We didn't get around to exchanging names. The
children...the entire family was hungry. You barged in
here like some demented warrior and scared them wit-
less." She walked to the outer edge of the clearing and
peered into the darkness. "It's all right," she called

softly in Spanish. "He's a friend. Please come back and eat. The baby didn't finish his milk."

"Hayley, for God's sake." Jake vaulted the dog to reach her. Gripping her shoulders, he yanked her out of the shadows. "It's okay if they milk our cows at the Triple C or butcher an occasional steer. There are men around to handle anything that might get out of hand. But you're alone, for crying out loud. I guarantee one guy in that outfit is being paid a lot of money to illegally get those folks into Arizona. It's a huge racket. A dangerous one for the families and for you. You simply can't put out the welcome mat. You're damn lucky I arrived when I did. The instigator might have stolen everything you owned, or worse, left you dead in the process."

"You are so cynical, Jacob Cooper. They were polite and appreciative. Down on their luck, but since when is that a crime? Oh, I'm wasting my breath. I doubt you've ever not known where your next meal is coming from."

"I understand the problems. We hire as many family men with temporary work permits as we possibly can. The people who traffic in humans for money are bastards. Con men. They charge exorbitant fees and as often as not dump *la familia* in a blistering desert without resources of any kind. It's less the family I'm trying to warn you about than the guy in the Panama hat who was with them. He's probably a ringleader."

Hayley released a sigh of resignation. "*Abuelo,* the little boy called him. Grandfather. The mother's younger than me. Her dream is to provide a better life for her kids. Is that so wrong?"

She spoke with such passion while unconsciously cradling her stomach that Jake's heart collided with his own churning stomach. His first impression had been correct.

He had no notion how far along she was, but Hayley Ryan was definitely going to have a baby. That made it a thousand times more foolish for her to be out here. "You're pregnant," he said simply. "Why didn't you tell me that right off the bat? It puts a different spin on everything. You can't stay here. When's the baby due, anyway?"

Hayley, who'd hoped Jake had missed her new rounder shape, wheeled away from him and extended shaking hands toward the fire. She felt suddenly cold. Not stay here? She *had* to. The makeup of ore she'd dug the past few days had changed dramatically. She wasn't altogether sure what the changes meant, but felt in her bones that she was on the verge of discovering something that would make a difference in her baby's life. "It's for me to say what I do, Jacob," she said with renewed ferocity. "Go away and leave me alone."

"Damn, Hayley. I worried when I thought it was just you." Jake flung an arm wide. Mojave shied and Charcoal paced between the two humans, whining as he looked at each. "But you and a baby... It's craziness for a pregnant woman to be this far from a good road. You need to be close to town, where there's adequate medical care and decent doctors."

"Thank you very much for your flattering opinion of my capabilities. I've seen a doctor. He gave me a book describing all the stages of pregnancy. I plan to be out of here and back in Tombstone long before it's time to deliver my baby. Anyway, I don't answer to you. It's my baby. My responsibility. My decision." Her eyes flared as she crossed her arms protectively over the gentle slope of her abdomen.

"Oh? So the kid doesn't have a father? I'll bet he'd

have plenty to say about how you're jeopardizing his child's life."

Hayley's face crumpled. Her lips trembled and her eyes filled with pain. Long seconds ticked by before she seemed to get a grip on her emotions. "You're wrong. Joe didn't care about me. He's not the type to be a husband or father. Besides, he forfeited all rights when he walked out on me."

"I didn't mean to open old wounds. It's just…if it was me, I'd want to know I had a baby in the works. A man deserves a chance to do right by his child."

A haunting smile came and went. "Not all men have your sense of responsibility, Jake. Believe me, the last thing Joe Ryan wants is to be tied down."

"He married you. I'd say that represents a tying down of sorts."

A harsh broken sound emerged from her throat. "You don't know the facts."

"So tell me." He walked over and shackled Hayley's restless fingers in his larger hands. "I want to understand why you're willing to take such risks."

Hayley kept her eyes averted. A second sound, this one more like a sob, worked its way to the surface. No words or explanations followed.

Jake felt the pain that obviously racked her body. Releasing her wrists, he gathered her against his chest. It was impossible not to notice the slight framework of her bones. Hell, her head didn't even reach his chin. Despite everything Jake knew about her tenacity, her determination to tough it out on her own, she seemed fragile enough to break.

He wasn't in the habit of kissing women to comfort them. Especially not women who were pregnant with another man's child. But something about the stoic way

Hayley tried to hold back tears suggested she believed this pregnancy was solely *her* obligation. Jake didn't know why her husband had chosen to leave with another woman. He didn't care, except that Hayley had clearly decided it was because she wasn't desirable. Which was hogwash. Outwardly, though, she put on a good show. Inside, she was like a raft breaking apart in high seas. She needed to be shown there was nothing wrong with her in the desirability department.

He could tell her in so many words, but Jake didn't think she'd listen. Or if she did listen, she wouldn't believe him.

Kisses were harder to dispute. And kissing Hayley Ryan was far from a hardship.

Yet he didn't want to scare her. He took care to slide his hands to the nape of her neck. Tunneling his fingers beneath her heavy hair, he slowly tilted her face toward his. He lowered his lips even more slowly, leaving a decorous space between their bodies, making sure, however, to meet her eyes. He didn't want her mistaking his intentions. No way did he want her misconstruing this as a pity kiss. He had to be honest—he was doing this for him as much as for her. Kissing Hayley had been on his mind for some time. And damned if he didn't intend to do it right.

The campfire popped and shot sparks. Hayley's heart cartwheeled, and she gave a start—a move plastering her to Jake's body. Even with her belly slightly rounded, she felt, and instantly recognized, the hard ridge pressing against her from behind his jeans zipper. She was assailed first by panic and then shock as his lips covered hers. But as his kiss grew more demanding, she felt herself responding. Her eyes drifted closed, and soon she ceased to think at all. She let the human contact soothe a desperately lonely ache that resided deep inside her. An ache Joe Ryan had done nothing to assuage.

Jake's mouth was soft, mobile. His tongue warm and coaxing. His body hard and urgent. Everything around her receded. The campfire, her trailer, his animals. Vanished, as did the night noises beyond the perimeter of the dancing flames. Scary sounds that too often pulled Hayley from sleep and set her heart pounding in fright—the way it did now.

*No, it wasn't the same.* She felt nothing of the dread that inevitably followed the sudden stark awakenings. Those black moments of pure terror that forced her to face facts. She had only herself to rely on now.

She was all the tiny life inside her had, too.

Yet…in holding her close, in kissing her, Jacob Cooper offered solace. Solace and something more. He offered hope.

*Hope for what?* Some part of Hayley's befogged brain struggled to make sense of why she stood here, her lips locked to a virtual stranger's. A series of flutter kicks low in her stomach served as a potent reminder. She was pathetic. This wasn't the first time she'd been blinded by that lonely vacant feeling. A need to be held, comforted and loved. The very need that had confused her and made her fall for Joe's lies.

He'd never wanted her. Not really. He'd only wanted the easy profits from the Silver Cloud mine. And Joe had been unscrupulous enough to walk her down the aisle to get them.

*What did Jacob Cooper want?*

Hayley's baby kicked again, a sobering reminder. The Blue Cameo. Of course. Or rather, the water—the natural spring that was on this site. For a second Hayley was sorely tempted to grab whatever fleeting comfort she could derive from Jake's kisses and the strong arms in which he cocooned her—until she remembered that *fleeting* wasn't what she wanted for the child growing inside her. In a hailstorm of regret, she began shutting down her senses and started to withdraw.

Jake was vaguely aware of faint movements beating feebly against him. At first he was too engrossed in the pleasure of kissing Hayley to realize he was feeling her baby. When she arched her back to gain leverage to push him away, it dawned on him how tightly their lower bodies fit together. That flutter he'd felt was a tiny human being.

Sensations raced through him. Awe, mixed with heat and lust and outright possessiveness. As he paused to catch his breath and stroke his thumbs lightly over Hayley's kiss-dampened lips, he was suffused with a blinding desire to safeguard something precious. Hayley and her unborn child.

Shaken by such intense feelings he let her go and took a stumbling step backward.

Freedom from the threat of Jake's closeness was what Hayley wanted. And yet she reeled from their sudden separation. But when he reached out a hand to support her, she shrank away, telegraphing a touch-me-not warning. She hauled in the next breath, her breasts rising and falling rapidly, then clutched her stomach and began retching. "Just…leave," she choked out, moments before she lurched into a nearby thicket.

"Like hell!" Jake shouted, not fully understanding her rapid transformation. "I'm taking you to the Triple C. Go sit by the fire while I hitch up your truck and trailer."

Hayley poked a white face out from a network of shrubs. "Don't you dare lay a finger on anything that belongs to me.'' Racked by the nausea that chose indiscriminate times to strike, she bent double into the bushes again, and this time emptied the meager contents of her stomach.

Darn, but she hated having Jake see this. Over the past three or four weeks, she'd discovered that her morning sickness, which had gotten a late start according to the pregnancy-advice booklet, descended at any time of day or night.

"Hayley…'' Jake's tentative voice battered her ringing ears. The bouts were always followed by cold sweats. She clung to a sapling, waiting for the waves to pass. And pass they always did.

Jake stripped off the neck scarf he wore to protect his face from the dust kicked up by plodding steers. He ran to the spring, wet the material thoroughly and, though his knees weren't steady, bulldozed his way to Hayley's side. "Here,'' he said gruffly. "Let me wipe your face. Do you have a cup out there? I'll get you some water.''

"Go away,'' she said weakly. "I'm fine.''

"Yeah, you sound fine. Just great. How long has this been going on?''

She pressed her face into the cool fabric of his bandanna, willing him to leave her to her misery. Even in the darkness afforded her by the trees, Hayley felt his concern. From what little she knew of Jake, she doubted he'd walk off and abandon her in this condition. But maybe she could shake him with a lie.

"I have an aversion to being grabbed and kissed,'' she said, trying to sound angry and disgusted, instead of merely weak. "That's why I'm sick. I'm sure it's not a reaction you're used to getting, since you probably have your choice of women in this valley. Collect your horse and ride out. Forget me, Jake.''

His brows shot up. Dammit, he'd *felt* her react with desire to that kiss. Not for one minute did he buy into this claim that kissing her made her sick. However, a lot had happened in the past few minutes and he saw the need to give them both some space. "I reckon we can set aside this contest of wills while I deal with the business at hand. Make yourself comfortable in your remaining chair while I turn on the water."

Sometimes Hayley could will the bouts of nausea away. She tried now, taking deep breaths as she patted the damp cloth to her face and neck. "There," she breathed. "All better." That was an out-and-out fib she thought as she led the way out of the thicket on wobbly legs. The booklet said it was rare for vomiting to stretch beyond three months. On the other hand, at the end of each discussion of possible side effects were exceptions to the rule. Hayley figured she was exception number four. Four being her unlucky number. After all, she'd married Joe Ryan on the fourth day of the fourth month. A double whammy if ever she'd encountered one. And exception number four in the booklet said a few women experienced nausea and vomiting for all nine months of their pregnancy.

Falling into step with her, Jake slid a supporting arm around her thickening waistline.

If she hadn't felt so rocky, she'd have never allowed his help. "Really, these spells pass quickly," she said in a matter-of-fact voice. "It's common for pregnant women to suffer some vomiting. Stress adds to the frequency."

"Mm," he said noncommittally. He saw her firmly seated before he left to open the valves. "I'll bet you all four of those women live within a ten-minute drive of their doctors," he muttered.

Starting to shrug, Hayley looked guilty, instead. But she wasn't going to let him draw her into an argument over something that wasn't his business. She clamped down on her tongue just in time. The minute he was out of sight, she got up and put on the kettle to heat water for tea. Peppermint generally calmed her stomach.

Jake hadn't missed the stubborn light that flicked on inside Hayley's eyes. And it made him worry that he wouldn't be able to persuade her to leave the Blue Cameo's site. Well, first things first. Going out into the desert with Charcoal, he rounded up her family of strays. He spoke to them in fluent Spanish and quickly determined they weren't part of a larger illegal ring. Best of all, the men possessed work permits. He made them understand that he lived on the Triple C, and that if the two men in the unit knew cows, they were hired for roundup.

He led them back to the campfire, and they resumed their meal with many expressions of gratitude. Then Jake gave them directions and told them about another migrant family living in the valley who would give the wife and kids temporary shelter.

Hayley thanked him quietly and fervently.

Only later, after he'd collected and washed the dishes left by her visitors and he'd again broached the subject of towing her trailer to the Triple C, did Jake accept that her refusal didn't mean *maybe*. She had every intention of remaining right in this spot.

"Look, you *can't* stay here," he said, stomping angrily around the fire for about the hundredth time in the past hour.

If she hadn't been so weary of going over the same ground, Hayley might have smiled at his seriousness. Setting aside her now-cold cup of peppermint tea, she formed her fingers into a tent in front of her chin. "You warn me not to take in strays. Yet it's precisely what you'd be asking your family to do. Not only wouldn't they appreciate you dragging home a pregnant stranger, Jacob, it doesn't sound to me as if the Triple C is all that much closer to town. Anyway, it's irrelevant. I'm not going."

Frustrated by her logic, Jake raked a hand through his hair. "I'll admit this is a busy period for us. Right now is when my mother and Eden replenish their stock—you know, for their shop. Mom's a potter and Eden makes jewelry. And it's roundup, which keeps Dillon and me hopping. But you'd have access to phones at the ranch. A telephone could make all the difference if something went wrong."

Jake carefully avoided making any comment about his family welcoming her. He thought they would. Or rather, he thought that, given time, he could talk them into it— although he suspected his mother might object to his taking a more-than-neighborly interest in a pregnant woman.

Be that as it may, he couldn't tolerate the thought that Hayley might be risking her safety and her baby's if she stayed here. Her stubbornness exasperated him beyond belief. "Look," he shouted, pushing his face close to hers, "I don't have time for this. I have to get back to help with the herd."

"Then go. Who's stopping you?" Hayley bolted upright, clenching her fists. "I survived without a man before. I certainly don't need one calling the shots now."

Jake let his anger drain. "This isn't about me ordering you around because you're a woman and I'm a man."

"No? Then what is it about?"

Jake's thoughts and feelings were so jumbled he

couldn't honestly answer her. In a lot of ways he barely knew her—as his family kept telling him. He certainly didn't know her well enough to stake any claim. Yet he felt in his soul this was about more than principle. More than the chivalrous values his parents had instilled in him. He hesitated and finally stuttered, "It's because I'm worried about you. I can't completely explain it. The baby, I guess. And I admit that what you said earlier is true—I'd never have questioned Ben's decision to stay out here alone."

For a minute there Hayley thought Jake was going to blurt out something more personal. Her breath had even stalled in her throat as he wrestled with his words. In that teetering moment she realized she'd have capitulated and followed him like a pitiful puppy if he'd offered so much as a token reason suggesting that she might, in any way, be special to him.

The moment passed for both of them. Jake felt flushed and ineffective.

Hayley's resolve doubled right before his eyes. She built a bulwark of strength around her. Nevertheless, he made one last stab. "I'll leave Charcoal with you. If you need me for any reason, tell him to find me."

"That's very kind," Hayley said in a brittle voice. "But I can't…won't accept. He's a cow dog. He deserves to do what he's trained for. Besides, what if he wandered off or got hurt? No. You take him."

As Jake tightened the girth on his saddle and prepared to mount, he searched for reasons to stick around longer. Clearly, though, Hayley was anxious for him to go. "You're sure…" he began once his knees gripped the leather.

"I'm positive." Hayley plastered a confident smile on her lips. It remained in place until he was gone and there was no way the occluding darkness would allow him to see it slip.

Jake rode slowly and methodically away from the clearing. Away from Hayley. Many times he hauled on the reins and stopped. Half of those times he turned Mojave and almost went back. He did send Charcoal in his stead, continuing on his way to rejoin Dillon only after he'd verified from a vantage point on the ridge that Hayley had emerged from her trailer and discovered the dog. Though not as satisfactory as having Hayley parked at the ranch, he guessed it'd do until he found a way to change her mind.

"YO, LITTLE BROTHER." Dillon rode out to meet Jacob ahead of the meandering herd. "What's happening up at the spring? Is she going dry?"

Jake reined in sharply.

Dillon snapped his fingers in Jake's face. "Earth to Jacob. Did that woman chase you off with a shotgun again?"

Jake finally sorted through his brother's barrage of questions. "I released the water. It ran a couple of hours. Should have filled the ditch."

"Made a thin stream of red mud, is all. Half the herd went without a taste. We've pushed them hard since yesterday. Their tongues are hanging out. If they don't get more water by morning, we could be in trouble."

"I didn't follow the ditch back to the stream. It must be blocked somewhere." Jake shifted in his saddle, making the leather creak. "I suppose I'd better ride back and find the problem area. I sent two men to see you. Did they get here?"

"Yes. I took 'em on. And Dad showed up an hour ago. He says the doctor cleared him to help us finish roundup. You know he'll overdo it if he takes it into his head to beat the arroyos for strays. And I need a break. So Dad and I will check the route to the spring. We'll meet up with you at Lark's Meadow tomorrow.''

"Sure." Jake stripped off the high-powered binoculars that hung around his neck. "I doubt you'll have to ride all the way into Mrs. Ryan's camp to find the blockage." He paused. "There are several places where you'll overlook her camp. Would you mind making sure she's all right?''

Dillon gave his brother the once-over out of lazy-lidded eyes.

Jake tightened his jaw. "Just do it, all right? A woman's got no business digging rock. It's plain damn foolish for her to be out there doing it alone—as I told her.''

"I take it she didn't appreciate your opinion. Guess I haven't taught you anything about handling women, eh, Jake? You gotta sweet-talk 'em. You can't just throw out orders.''

Jake snorted. He recalled vividly the feel of Hayley's lips under his. He'd always thought kissing worked better than sweet talk, and he'd never needed Dillon's instructions when it came to dealing with women.

Wade Cooper rode up on a brown-and-white pinto gelding. His appearance effectively put an end to Dillon's teasing. Talk turned to water, or the lack thereof. "Dammit, we need full control of that spring," Wade fumed. "I'll bet Ben's grandkid hasn't found a nickel's worth of assayable ore. You were there, Jake. Did she show any signs of capitulating?''

Jake shook his head. Personally, knowing her condition, he figured she'd have to stop sooner than later. He kept her secret, though. She'd seemed so desperate to stay in spite of being pregnant. And he'd seen her boxes of rocks. She hadn't sat idle. If there was something valuable in that claim, Jake wanted Hayley to find it. He shook himself out of a stupor to hear his father talking again.

"John Westin's pressing the co-op to use their collective muscle to commandeer that plot. I'd feel a whole lot better if he'd shut up."

Dillon leaned an arm across his saddle horn. "Me, too. Westin's been growing too fast. Eden heard rumors in town that he's overgrazed his fields. He's leased to the maximum on government range."

"Yeah," Wade put in. "Yesterday I heard even more disturbing news. Link Thompson said John bought Ginalyn the old Naylor spread out on Cougar Flats. He's leased from there to the Arivaca junction in her name. Link said if anyone thinks Ginalyn's going to be out there punching cows, he has some swampland to sell them."

Dillon swore. "The only water for Cougar Flats would have to come from our spring."

"Except," Wade pointed out, "it isn't ours."

"Ain't that the truth," Dillon said. "Hey, Jacob. Where's Charcoal?" he asked suddenly, shading his eyes to gaze around.

"I, uh…" Jake stuttered. "I left him with Hayley." When Wade lifted a brow, Jake explained again about the illegals Hayley had fed.

"I hope you don't mind if we mosey on into her camp and pick up your dog," Wade said. "The object here is to get her to abandon that mine, not facilitate her stay."

"I do mind," Jake growled. His comment drew surprised glances from both Dillon and Wade. "Hayley's determined to work that claim, even though it's not safe.''

Dillon laughed as Wade continued looking troubled. ''Come on, Dad. I think it's high time we took a gander at this woman who's got the valley's most eligible bachelor dancing at the end of a short rope.''

''I'm not dancing on anybody's rope!'' Jake shouted. ''Mom used to send pickles and bread to Ben,'' he said more quietly. ''Tell me how this is any big-deal different?''

Grinning lecherously, Dillon appeared ready to try. Wade called a halt by glowering at both his sons. ''Jake, take the herd on to the Triple C. Dillon and I will ride ahead and set up the grain feeders and the branding pens when we finish inspecting the stream. I figure we'll all be too busy over the next week or so to worry about acting neighborly.''

His statement severed any further conversation about Hayley Ryan. Jake recognized his father's method of manipulation. As far back as Jake could remember, his dad had piled on the chores to keep his two sons walking the straight-and-narrow path he'd decided they ought to take. Never before had Jake felt the resentment he experienced now in watching Wade ride off, complacent that his edict would be obeyed.

Jake's anger flared. He was no longer a boy. He didn't appreciate his father's heavyhanded tactics. He'd choose what women to date. And he'd fit them into his work schedule. *Not them, her. Hayley Ryan.* If he wanted to see her badly enough to give up his sleep time, he damn well would.

But Jake hadn't allowed for his father's breakneck pace. The first twelve days of September passed in a blur of hard work before he found time to do more than stare at the dusty horizon, wondering how Hayley was doing. On the thirteenth day, after the whole weary crew packed the last beef into the cattle train headed for market, Wade gave everyone two days off before starting the entire process again on the south range.

Jake, who'd ridden into Tubac with Dillon that morning, saw a woman on the street whose hair color reminded him of Hayley. He was struck by an acute need to visit her. "Hey, Dillon. I've got better things to do than hang out in town. If you're going to stick around and bug your wife, I'll take the truck home and let you snag a ride with her."

"What do you have to do that's so all-fired important?"

Jake grinned disarmingly. "Catch up on my sleep. Dad's a slavedriver. I liked it better when the doc made him stay off a horse."

"I hear you." Mistakenly Jake assumed Dillon had bought his story. He dismissed that notion when Dillon punched his arm and said, "When you drop my pickup at the house, go on inside. There's a package of soup bones on the second shelf of the fridge. Charcoal will be right happy to get one."

Jake swung around, his guilty gaze colliding with Dillon's mischievous grin.

"You never could lie worth shit, little brother. Frankly, the Ryan woman didn't strike me as anything to write home about. But deny a man access and he'll never find that out for himself."

Jake bristled, then rotated his shoulders and sighed. "I can't explain the attraction myself, Dillon. It won't do me any good to try defending it to you."

Dillon pulled up next to the curb outside Eden's jewelry store. He left the pickup running as he climbed out.

"It's only fair to tell you that your lady ran Dad and me off at shotgun point. Dad was apoplectic all the way home. He's definitely going to need time before he greets your friend with open arms."

"What made Hayley go for her gun? Never mind." Jake slid under the wheel and released the parking brake. "I want to hear her version first." He slammed the door on whatever Dillon had to say.

HAYLEY BENT HIS EAR plenty when he rode into her camp and interrupted her as she washed screen-bottomed trays filled with some blue-streaked stone.

"I don't need you bringing me bribes, Jacob Cooper. Much as I liked having Charcoal here for company, you can take him home, too. Tell your father and brother I *have* discovered something worthwhile." She gestured at an array of oddly lustrous rocks.

"Doesn't look like precious metal to me," Jake said, going on one knee to examine the collection more closely. "What is it? And why should it make any difference to my dad and Dillon?"

"Ha!" She loomed over him, hands on her hips. "As if you didn't know they stormed in here the day after you left and gave me an ultimatum. They said if I didn't discover something of value in two weeks, they'd file a petition with the state recorder's office to have my claim revoked. Well, I've found an opal deposit!"

Jake didn't hear her at first. He was furious to think that a man of his father's gentle nature would bully any woman, let alone one so obviously pregnant. For Hayley was no longer able to hide her condition in the folds of her loose jumper. The roundness of her stomach was quite prominent now.

"I guess you're speechless, huh?" she demanded.

"On second thought," she said, wagging a finger in his face, "I'd rather you didn't spread the news around town. I don't want a stampede of gem-hunters crowding me."

"Gem-hunters?" Jake shifted his eyes from her stomach to stare blankly at her flushed face.

"Honestly! Haven't you heard a word I said?" she asked as he rose to his feet. Too happy not to share her joy with somebody, Hayley flung her arms around Jake's neck. "I hit a vein of opal! I'm not sure of the grade, but I've positively identified my find. A lower grade only means the difference between my baby and me surviving and being comfortably rich." Her delighted laughter was muffled against Jake's chest as she tightened her arms and buried her face in his shirtfront.

He didn't even realize that his heart had kicked into overdrive or that he'd flattened his palms across her narrow back. Once again Jake felt the wriggle of new life when Hayley's stomach pressed tight to his. "I've missed you," he said simply, bringing her against him. "Missed you a lot. Now that you've made your discovery, you can hire someone to dig this stuff. You can supervise from the Triple C." He unwound her arms and held her at arm's length, then yanked her close to hug her again. "I can't explain what's going on inside my head—and my heart," he said, raining kisses on the top of her head. "I only know I want you where I can take care of you and your baby."

"What are you talking about?" She freed an arm and then wrenched out of his grasp. "I can't leave my claim. I have to stay here and dig as much ore as I can. Enough to sell and tide us over until my baby's old enough to bring here with me. "I can't afford a crew, Jake. Even if I could, I wouldn't trust them not to steal me blind.

Please, if you want to do what's best for me, go home and forget what I've found.'' Her voice broke with emotion. "I shouldn't have told anyone."

Jake didn't like to hear her beg. "I won't tell," he promised gruffly, feeling sick inside as he clasped her hands and found them chapped and bleeding. "Just because I've agreed to go along with your harebrained scheme doesn't mean I'm giving up trying to get you to leave. If I have to ride out here every night after roundup and help you dig this stuff by moonlight until you have what you consider *enough,* then that's what I'll do.''

She looked at him oddly. "I'm not sharing this find."

"Who asked you to?" He sounded as annoyed as hell.

"I just wanted to be clear up front. Joe walked away with the proceeds from Gramps's silver mine. He also stole a blue cameo that belonged to my mom. The only thing I had of hers. I was gullible once. I won't be twice."

"Hey—not every man is a scumbucket like your crummy ex.'' Jake could see from the distrust in her eyes that Hayley didn't believe him. *Too bad.* He didn't like being painted with the same brush as the jerk who'd let her and his baby go.

Striding to his horse, Jake yanked the cinch tight. Climbing on, he whistled for Charcoal to heel. "If you ever wake up and discover that people are worth more than money, you can find me at the Triple C.''

She looked very small and alone standing in the middle of those rock trays she wanted so fiercely to protect. Jake figured she must not have heard that opals were supposed to be bad-luck gems. However, that wasn't something he'd ever mention, since it would only diminish her delight in her find.

The bottom-line truth—he might be peeved enough to

leave her to her stubborn pride for now, but he would never do anything to hurt her.

He hadn't ridden far before he gained control over his anger. He'd been unwilling to admit to Dillon or anyone—not even himself—that Hayley had gotten under his skin. He could no longer deny that she had. She was entrenched good and deep. At the moment he didn't know how to go about convincing her of that. It nagged at him the entire ride home.

## CHAPTER EIGHT

WHEN JAKE ARRIVED home, he discovered that his mother had left work early to barbecue for the family. "To celebrate midpoint in the fall roundup," she informed him as she urged him to hurry and unsaddle Mojave. His dad, brother and sister-in-law were already gathered outside around the barbecue pit.

"I see you got Charcoal back," Dillon observed after Jake had showered, changed clothes and joined his family.

Jake, who'd stewed all the way home about the shabby way his dad and Dillon had treated Hayley, grabbed his brother by the shirtfront. "I'm sorry my dog didn't bite you at Hayley's camp, you sorry son of a bitch. Those bully tactics you guys used on her don't set well with me."

Ever the self-righteous older brother, Dillon roughly broke Jake's hold. "Watch it. This is a new shirt Eden bought me."

"Boys! What in heaven's name is wrong?" Nell's gaze skipped from her older son to her younger. "Stop squabbling this instant."

"We're not boys," Jake snapped, never taking his eyes off Dillon. "And men don't run roughshod over women."

Looking confused, Nell sent a silent appeal for help to her husband.

He popped the lids off two beers and shoved one into each of his son's hands. "Cool off, Jacob. That was Triple C business and I handled it as tactfully as possible. So happens, it's just as well I did. Westin formed a committee to go meet with the governor. If he endorses their proposal to seize the land, I foresee bigger problems than we have now. John talks a good game, but he's splitting the co-op. I have some pull with state environmentalists, and I'll call on them if necessary. I thought it only fair to give Ben's granddaughter a neighborly warning."

"She said you gave her a two-week ultimatum to come up with a strike or else. That sounds stronger than a neighborly warning."

Wade shrugged, but he denied nothing as Nell stuck a long-handled fork in his hand and asked him to turn the steaks. "Could we forget about water and mining claims for tonight and enjoy one another's company? You men are heading into phase two of the roundup, and by next week, Eden and I will be inundated at the shop with the start of tourist season. Who knows when we'll get time together again?"

Eden slipped her arm through Dillon's. Smiling at Jake, she edged her husband toward the screened porch that held a table set for six.

Dillon poked Jake. "Looks like these sneaky women have found you a date for tonight," he chortled. "Who'll it be, I wonder? My money is on the unknown quilter."

"Mom!" Jake counted the table settings twice before he strode toward his mother.

Eden gave Dillon a rap on his arm. "It's nothing, Jacob. Lisa Clover is someone Nell and I met and liked.

She's in town for the arts-and-crafts fair. We wanted to show her some Southwestern hospitality, that's all.''

"Uh-huh!" Jake didn't buy into Eden's too-pat explanation. But it was too late to beg off. Twin headlights turned into the lane, slicing through the gathering dusk.

"Be nice," cautioned Nell as she and Eden headed around the house to greet their guest.

"You're in for it now, brother." Snickering, Dillon ducked the foamy beer bath Jake attempted to douse him with from a well-shaken bottle.

The women returned. Nell introduced her friend. Lisa had shoulder-length auburn hair and direct blue eyes. She wore layers of loose clothing—obviously an artsy type. She'd brought a cold twelve-pack of beer and a set of handmade coasters for Nell. Cleverly quilted ranch scenes. A thoughtful gesture, Jake decided. But he wouldn't have sat next to her at the table if the choosing had been up to him. Eden had handled seating arrangements, and Jake didn't feel like making a fuss that would hurt her or their guest.

As it turned out, Lisa was easy to talk to. Partway through the meal, though, Jake started to think about Hayley spending the evening alone at her camp. At least he *hoped* she was alone and that she wasn't entertaining iffy visitors. He grew quiet once he'd dispensed with the usual opening subjects. He found himself picturing Hayley in place of Lisa at tonight's gathering. She wouldn't be nearly as confident or as chatty.

The others at the table began to notice his one-word responses. Nell and Eden shot puzzled looks his way. Nell finally rose and tapped him on the shoulder.

"Come help me serve up the apple pie and coffee, Jake.''

Eden and Lisa both offered to lend a hand. "No, no.''

Nell stayed them with a glance. "I haven't seen Jacob lately. We'll get in a few private words while we're preparing dessert plates."

Dillon waggled his eyebrows, announcing at large, "Uh-oh. Jake's in for it now. Mom's about to deliver lecture number 199 on company etiquette." Eden silenced him with a kick under the table, but not before their guest followed Jake's departure with bewildered eyes.

Inside the kitchen Jake waited for the lecture to begin. He knew he'd dropped the ball out there. All his mother and Eden had expected of him was that he'd make this friend of theirs feel welcome. It wasn't that there was anything wrong with Lisa Clover; it was just that his mind happened to be stuck on another woman.

Nell moved the pies to the table, found a knife and plates. Jake had played out this routine enough times in his life to automatically cut slices of cheddar for the top of each pie slice. That accomplished, he counted out forks.

"Lisa is considering renting the vacant shop next to ours permanently after the craft fair."

"So she said." Jake popped the first two pie wedges in the microwave and turned it on low, long enough to soften the cheese.

Nell sighed loudly. "She's nice, don't you think?"

Jake turned and caught her looking exasperated. "You and Eden must've already determined that or you wouldn't have invited her to dinner."

"Jacob Cooper, why are you being so obstinate?"

"I'll give our guest the first piece of pie." Jake whipped the two plates out of the microwave, added forks and hurried out to the patio. His mother was slapping slices of pie on the remaining plates when he returned for another batch.

"You know perfectly well I wasn't talking about your company manners, Jacob."

"Maybe you ought to quit pussyfooting around and spell out what you mean, Ma."

"All right. Lisa is bright and funny and talented. She'd settle here with a bit of encouragement. And don't call me Ma. You know I detest it."

Jake didn't say anything. He delivered the next two pieces of pie. As he made his way back, his mother busily covered the leftovers in the pie tins with foil. Their two slices sat awaiting cheese. Clearly he hadn't heard everything she had on her mind.

"Dillon said you haven't asked anyone to the harvest dance yet. Lisa happened to tell Eden that she loves to dance."

"I haven't asked anyone, but I have someone picked out."

"Who?" Nell wouldn't be put off. "Eden and I hear all the gossip in town. All the single girls are already spoken for."

Jake turned his back. He studied the number pad on the microwave as the carousel went around. "I'm going to ask Hayley Ryan."

"A stranger? Why, Jacob? She's frustrating your father and the others in the co-op over her silly mining claim."

Jake leveled a glare over his shoulder. "What she's digging out there isn't silly to her. It's important. She has no family left, Mom. And...and...Hayley's pregnant."

Nell stifled a tiny gasp. "Pregnant? Where's her husband?"

"He walked out on her, remember?" Jake's jaw tightened. "She shouldn't be there alone in her condition. Near as I can tell, she hasn't got a thing for the baby. I intended to ask you to visit her. She claims she's consulted a doctor in Tombstone and is following the advice in some booklet he gave her. I thought you might talk to her. Find out if she's overdoing things, what she needs—you know."

The carousel had stopped rotating, but neither Nell nor Jake made a move to retrieve the pie. Nell's throat worked. At last she croaked out, "Jake...I...you...we really shouldn't get involved. We don't know anything about this woman."

Jake hooked his thumbs in his belt, his stance belligerent. "I'm not hungry for pie, after all. See if Dillon wants an extra piece. I'm hitting the sack early."

He was crossing the living room by the time Nell rallied. She stepped to the center of the arch and called out, "Jake, this is foolish, arguing over an outsider like this. Think about what you're doing. Ben worked that claim every summer. He never found anything of value. Besides, Hayley Ryan will leave at the first frost. Jake, you're opening yourself up to get hurt."

"I just asked you to be neighborly. *She's* the one who's hurt. Good Lord, her ex even stole the one thing she loved most, a blue cameo that belonged to her mother. And you're wrong. Hayley's made a strike. She doesn't want it spread around, but she found opals."

Nell digested that as he disappeared and the door behind her opened.

Eden joined her mother-in-law. "We're almost finished with our dessert. What's keeping you and Jake? Why were you two shouting? And who found opals? Are they jewelry quality?"

Pursing her lips, Nell spun and plucked the last pie wedges from the microwave. "That woman at the spring has apparently led Jake to believe she's unearthed something at Ben's old claim."

"Jake's so gullible. I've never heard of opals being mined in Arizona."

Nell gazed toward the door through which Jake had escaped. Her eyes went soft. "Maybe not. But I've suddenly decided I want to meet this Hayley Ryan. You don't know Jake like I do, Eden. For years I've watched girls and women chase him. This is the first time I've detected more than a superficial interest on his part. Since he and Dillon fought over you, that is," she added with an affectionate grin. "Because I tend to see both my boys through a mother's prejudiced eyes, I'd welcome a second opinion. What do you say? If we can break away early one day, would you run out to the spring with me to check out the Ryan woman?"

"Certainly. If for no other reason than to debunk her phony claim. Although there *have* been veins of opal found in Mexico," Eden mused thoughtfully.

"Jake said to keep the news under wraps. I know you share everything with Dillon. But until we know for sure what we're talking about, I'd like to respect Jake's wishes and keep this between us. I have a feeling Wade would try to talk me out of going."

"Sure. Okay, I have no problem honoring Jake's request for secrecy. And, Nell—I didn't mean any disrespect in calling him gullible."

"I know. I prefer to think of him as tenderhearted. In this case, however, gullible just might be a better word. Eden, he told me Hayley Ryan is going to have a baby."

"What? Not his?"

"No. She's Mrs. Ryan, but her husband took a powder."

"Wow. This is heavy-duty stuff. Is she looking for a sucker, you think?"

"I don't know. At this point I'm willing to give her the benefit of the doubt. From what Wade's said, Jake's invited her to the ranch and she's refused to leave her mine. That doesn't sound like someone trying to take advantage."

Eden swiveled toward the door as Dillon pushed it open. "Hey, ladies. What's the holdup? Your guest is making noises about going home." He withdrew, leaving Nell and Eden to exchange frowns.

"I'd planned to suggest Lisa spend the night," Eden murmured. "Probably pointless, huh, given how we've struck out with Jake?"

"Seems like it. However, she doesn't know the roads and they can be quite confusing at night. I do feel responsible for her."

"Dillon and I'll lead her out. We can stay at the shop tonight. He might be late for the second phase of roundup is all." Eden's eyes turned sensual.

Nell smiled. "Then Jake will have to oversee things until Dillon puts in an appearance. It'll do him good. Maybe take his mind off Mrs. Ryan. I might put a bug in Wade's ear about giving Jake more work to keep him occupied, too."

"Roadblocks, Nell? Did you do stuff like that to slow down Dillon's romance with me?"

"Not at all. The way he and Jacob quarreled, I knew one way or the other you'd end up in the family. In fact, I counted on it."

"Jake was never serious," Eden said.

"No, but he thought he was. Which is why I'm sticking my nose into this Ryan situation. Jake's getting antsy about living under our roof. He's going to build on his acreage. When a man's that ready to settle down, he doesn't always make his choices with a clear mind. And he sure seems obsessed with this Mrs. Ryan.''

"Darn. Lisa would have been so perfect. You with your pots, me with my jewelry, and her making quilts.'' She sighed. "You're right. We need to find time soon to visit Mrs. Ryan. If Jake's in the nesting mode, he'll completely forget about family compatibility.''

"My fear exactly.'' Nell collected the two plates. "So it's set. Next week we scope out the enemy camp.''

MONDAY, AFTER DILLON had left the shop and headed for the ranch, Nell announced to Eden that she was going to knit a baby blanket before they called on Jake's pregnant nomad.

"Aren't you afraid that'll give her the wrong idea? I thought you wanted to discourage her involvement with Jake.''

"I don't know what's gotten into me, Eden. I woke up in the middle of the night thinking how Jake said she didn't have a thing for her baby. I remembered some of the stuff we learned about her when Wade and I went to Tombstone. She lost both her parents at an early age. Ben took her in, but he was gone prospecting a lot. And her husband absconded with her inheritance. Knitting her one blanket is not like I'm giving her a key to the ranch or anything. Call it a goodwill gesture. I think I can finish one by Friday, if I knit while my kilns are firing.''

"I'll keep Friday afternoon open. I hope we don't run into Jake while we're there. What if he rides in off the range to pay her a visit?''

"He won't. Wade put him in charge of branding strays. The south range is a catacomb of arroyos. He'll be tied up well into September finding them. I intend to get a handle on this woman way before then."

Eden nodded and started back through the connecting door into her shop. "So is the baby a boy or a girl?"

"I don't have any idea. If Jacob knew, he didn't say. I plan to buy a soft pastel-green yarn. Why are you asking?"

"I love buying baby gifts. I can never resist those cute outfits. Maybe I'll pick up a couple of terry sleepers."

Nell smiled. "Now who's a softie?"

"Actually there's method to my madness. If she really did discover some decent opals—and granted, that's a big if—I wouldn't mind having first crack at buying them."

"Yes—she'd need an outlet. But don't get your hopes up, Eden. She may have been trying to buy time. You know Wade and Dillon issued an ultimatum. Either she strikes a vein worth further exploration or they'd petition the state claims agent to force her to trade this site for another."

"In that case maybe we should ride in waving a white flag of truce."

"The thought has crossed my mind. I'm not forgetting she took a shot at Jake and brandished a shotgun at Wade. Of course, Jake did blunder into her camp at sunset. We'll go in daylight and carry our gifts in plain sight."

"You know," Eden said, "add up all we know about this woman and she doesn't sound very appealing. What do you suppose Jake sees in her?"

"That, my dear Watson, we won't know till Friday. Let's go early, shall we?"

NELL STOPPED her four-wheel-drive Range Rover outside Eden's house at the time they'd agreed on. A gaily wrapped package lay on the back seat. In a box on the floor behind the seat sat a hot crock filled with a mild tortilla soup.

Before Nell could climb out and go to the door, it opened and Eden came out juggling a wrapped gift, another foil-wrapped package and a small covered dish.

"What's that you're bringing?" Nell asked, hurrying around the car's hood to take one of the items so that Eden could lock her house.

"I baked bread last night. And churned butter. I get domestic when Dillon's gone."

"Ah," Nell said. "You couldn't sleep, huh?"

Eden, who would never admit such a weakness to her mother-in-law, denied it. "Actually I started thinking it wouldn't hurt to butter up the Ryan woman." She giggled. "So to speak."

Nell chuckled. "I stayed up and cooked up a batch of Grandmother Cooper's tortilla soup. I craved that stuff when I was carrying Dillon."

"No wonder he cajoles me into making it whenever he can. But isn't it too spicy for someone who's pregnant?"

"I used chicken and the mild chilies I grow to pickle and make into relish. She must be in fair health if she's out there chopping holes in the hills."

Eden set her things on the back seat, climbed into the passenger side and buckled her seat belt. "Makes sense. Of course, we don't know if she'll break bread with us or not. We're assuming a lot."

As Nell eased into the lane that led up and over a ridge that cut the ranch off from Hayley Ryan's camp, she looked doubtful for a moment. Then she said, "I owe it to Jake to go once. He's worried about her pregnancy and asked me to pay her a call. Men think having babies is something to worry about, although most are too embarrassed to broach the topic.''

''Aren't ranchers matter-of-fact about life and death? At least, Dillon acts like our getting pregnant is an inevitable evolutionary process.''

Nell's face erupted in a smile. ''Are you two…well, are Wade and I going to be grandparents?''

Eden blanched. ''Uh…no. Sorry, Nell. I shouldn't talk behind Dillon's back, but having a baby is the only thing we've argued about. To him, it's no big deal. I *want* it to be a big deal, dammit. I want my carrying his baby to be special.''

Patting Eden's tightly fisted hand, Nell said gently, ''It will be. Wade is ten times more pragmatic than either of his sons. But with both of my pregnancies, he was a basket case from the minute I started to show.''

''He always treats you like a queen.''

''Yeah, but that didn't come without a lot of reminders that I wasn't just part of the stock.''

''You're kidding?'' Eden gave a little laugh. ''Dillon's not as unromantic as that.''

''He'd better not be. I hope I raised both my sons to be caring men. I expect them to remember birthdays and anniversaries. Their father was notoriously lax the first few years of our married life. When he forgot our third anniversary in a row, I ordered myself the biggest bouquet the florist could stuff in one vase and had the flowers delivered all the way out here from town. I also had the credit-card statement sent to Wade, so he opened it along with the feed bills.''

''What did he do?''

''He's never forgotten another special date.''

"I feel guilty for complaining about Dillon," Eden said. "He's forever buying me little gifts." She donned a complacent smile and wore it all the way to Hayley Ryan's camp.

Hayley was in the clearing washing rocks when the dusty vehicle bounced to a stop next to her pickup. Her jumper was streaked with water, her boots caked with mud. She wore an out-of-shape khaki bush hat to hide her tangled hair. Even though she hadn't talked to another human being for more than a week, she was wary enough to retrieve the shotgun braced against a nearby log.

Expecting men to emerge from the range vehicle, Hayley let her mouth fall agape when two women climbed out, instead. She was even more surprised to see their hands filled with what looked like wrapped packages and food containers. Both women wore fashionable boots, jeans and pretty blouses tucked under leather belts that spanned narrow waists. Hayley felt dowdy by comparison—and a little intimidated. For that reason, she didn't offer a welcome. Not even when the older of the two women—and they both looked energetically young to Hayley—greeted her with a winsome, somehow familiar smile. Hayley was quite certain she'd never met either woman before. They weren't the forgettable type.

"Hello. I'm Nell Cooper and this is Eden." Nell inclined her head toward her daughter-in-law, never taking her eyes off the restless fingers clamped around the shotgun. "You've met my husband, Wade and Eden's husband, Dillon. But it was my son Jake who suggested you might enjoy a woman's company. Sorry if we've come at an awkward time. We know how it is to have your work interrupted. I throw pots and Eden designs jewelry.

Neither of us likes to leave in the middle of tasks. We did bring lunch on the off chance you'd take a midday break. If it's not convenient, we can leave soup, bread and fresh butter. Oh, and a couple of things for the baby. Jacob mentioned that you were expecting.''

Hayley ran a tongue over lips gone suddenly dry. ''You brought things for my baby?'' Letting the gun slide through her fingers, Hayley blinked rapidly in an effort to halt the tears that fell without warning.

Nell quickly covered the ground separating her from the crying woman. ''Oh, my dear, you haven't lost the baby, have you?'' It was impossible to tell, given the shapeless cotton jumper Hayley wore.

''No,'' Hayley said through chattering teeth. Her bottom lip quivered badly. ''I...I...I don't know what to say. Food and gifts. I...well, Jake and I argued last time he was here. He even took Charcoal with him. Not a day's gone by that I haven't regretted my words. Lord, I should be used to my own company. But the days get long and the nights even longer when a body has only squirrels to talk to.''

''And chickens,'' Nell said, her attention drawn to the pen filled with her fat laying hens. She set the things she carried on the small table next to a single lawn chair and slid her arms around Hayley. ''I shouldn't kid, you poor thing. Solitude is great up to a point, but no one can survive a steady diet of it. Come, sit down and open your presents while Eden and I heat up the soup and slice the bread.''

Hayley pulled away and ran her hands nervously over the front of her jumper. ''You shouldn't touch me. I'm a mess. I've been working. Did I get your nice clothes dirty?''

''I'm not afraid of a little dirt. Neither is Eden. We

work up to our elbows in clay and silver dust. I don't think either of us buys clothing that isn't washable. Relax.''

Hayley tried to blot her eyes. She didn't know why she was crying when her heart felt lighter than it had in days. "I...I can't seem to stop these pesky tears," she admitted, burying her face in the crook of her arm.

"It's part and parcel of being pregnant. Weeping over nothing comes with the territory." Nell ran a soothing hand over Hayley's hunched shoulders. She felt the sharp outline of a narrow backbone. Something shifted inside Nell's breast. Her heart went out to this waif her son had befriended. She was probably working too hard and not eating right. At least not eating regular meals.

Hayley's teary eyes widened and locked with Nell's. "The booklet my doctor gave me mentions mood swings. But not crying jags. This past week I've found myself sobbing over nothing. You're saying that's normal?" She let her unsure gaze drift toward the younger woman, Eden, as if wanting her concurrence.

Eden placed her offering on the seat of the lawn chair. "I've never had the PG experience. Too newly married," she said with a shrug. "But my best friend cried from about the sixth month on if anyone so much as looked at her cross-eyed. She was weepy up until her baby was a month old. So if she's any example of what's normal..."

"That's often the way it goes," Nell agreed. "Would you prefer we heat this soup inside your trailer or out here over the open fire?"

"It's like an oven during the day in my trailer," Hayley said, again acting uncomfortable in the presence of strangers. "I live pretty primitively. Jake probably told you he disapproves. We had words over him wanting me to move my trailer to the Triple C.''

"He didn't say that, no," Nell admitted. "However, it sounds like something I'd expect of him. Of the Cooper men in general. You'll find they speak their minds."

"That's certainly true of your husband and hers, Mrs. Cooper," Hayley said, her expression suddenly cool. "Is that what's really at the bottom of this visit? Did they send you to softsoap me into giving up my claim?"

"Goodness, no! And call me, Nell. When Eden and I are together, it's too hard to figure out which Mrs. Cooper a person means. Anyway, I doubt Wade and Dillon will follow up on what they said last week. It depended on your failure to find anything of value. According to Jacob, you've made a significant find."

Hayley dusted her hands. "I haven't had a formal chemical or mineral assay done yet," she said as if afraid to predict good things.

Eden went down on one knee next to a tray of robin's-egg-blue rocks. "You've done preliminary testing, haven't you? These samples look like tectosilicate."

Hayley used a toe to push the tray out of Eden's reach. "Nothing's official."

Nell clasped Eden under the arm and raised her to her feet. "Why don't we sample the goodies we brought? Talking business on a full stomach is more palatable, don't you think?"

"So this *isn't* a social visit?" Now Hayley's eyes turned positively flinty.

"It *is* a social visit," Nell insisted. "Eden sets her silver designs with local turquoise, citrine and tourmaline. Her antennae went on alert when she heard Jake mention opal to me. But I insist we table any work-related discussion until after we've eaten and you've opened your presents. The soup will only take a few minutes to heat. Eden, I'll hang this crock over the fire. Why don't you slice the bread? Hayley, if I may call you that, have a seat. We'll put this together in a jiffy.''

"Oh, but I only have one chair!" Hayley exclaimed, once again worried about her ability to play hostess.

"Not a problem," Nell assured. "I have two or three folding stools in my Range Rover. I use them at craft fairs."

"I'll get them." Eden headed to the vehicle immediately.

Nell bustled about. She hung the soup crock over the fire, brought water from the spring and poured it into a washbasin Hayley already had sitting on a stand. "The spring is getting low. We could do with another rain. Rainstorms have bypassed us this season."

Hayley squinted at the blue skies overhead. "It won't hurt my feelings if the rain holds off another month or two." She clasped her hands over her stomach. "I don't have any idea how much rock I need to earn enough to pay for the delivery and then get the baby and me through until next summer, when I can dig again. I figure I'll need to spend every day until the end of my eighth month just digging ore."

"How far along are you?" Eden asked as she opened the two stools she'd carried over and set them next to the chair.

"I'm due around Christmas."

Nell looked concerned. "Have you allowed time to close up here, get out and still buy the supplies you'll need once the baby's born? You certainly don't want to risk hauling heavy rock and bringing on premature labor."

"I don't want to, no. This is just what I have to do."
Hayley lifted her chin.

"Of course. I didn't mean to meddle." Nell bent and
stirred the soup a bit more vigorously than necessary.

"That sure smells good." Hayley had finished washing her hands and now sniffed the air. "I appreciate your
thoughtfulness. I've been hungrier than normal lately,
and I've got to make my supplies last."

"Nell and I both have gardens," Eden said. "The
veggies are spoiling on the vines faster than I can pick
them. You're welcome to come get all you'd like. It'll
be the end of them soon. Or Jake can bring by a sackful.
But he might not be free until roundup's over. That
could be three or four weeks yet."

"Since no one's come to open the valves recently, I
assumed roundup was over."

Eden shook her head. "Only the north range. They're
working the south sections now. Here," she said, thrust-
ing two packages into Hayley's hands. "Open these. I
don't know how you've resisted. I can't stand to let
wrapped packages alone."

Hayley hugged the gifts a moment before she sat and
patiently untied the bow on the gift from Nell.

"You can rip the paper," Eden said dryly. "Honestly,
I'd have torn it apart by now." She'd no more than said
it than Hayley parted the outer paper, then the tissue.

"Oh!" she cried. "This is beautiful. Did you...? It
looks handmade."

Nell shrugged it off as nothing.

Hayley lifted the soft folds, then jumped up and ran
to wash her hands again. She washed twice before she
was satisfied her hands and fingernails were clean of the
red clay. All the while, tears rolled unchecked down her

cheeks, leaving the other two women at a loss as to what to do.

"This is so beautiful," she crooned over and over. "Mint-green is my favorite color. Oh, but I can't let it touch my dress. I need to go change. My jumper is gritty with ore." She carefully set the blanket on the chair and ran to her trailer.

Eden paced the clearing. "Will she be gone long enough for me to get a look at those stones? I'm not an expert on opal, but blue ones are rare. If the stone doesn't shatter when it's scratched, she may have stumbled on a real find. I'd pay her a fair price. A good price. Do you think she'd trust me to do that?"

"I don't know, Eden," Nell said impatiently. "How can you focus on rock when what we need to do is talk her into getting good prenatal care? Think how much effort it takes to dig this much rock." She gestured at the ore Hayley had spread out. It's backbreaking labor. And speaking of labor, what if she's out here alone when her labor starts?"

Eden shook her head. "There's enough Coopers to keep tabs on her. She sounded pretty adamant to me about staying and following this through." She shrugged. "It is her life, after all."

Hayley returned then to open her other package. Eden fell silent, letting Hayley exclaim over the sleepers and cap and sweater she'd purchased at a local baby store.

"You don't even know me, and look what you've done! My baby will come home from the hospital in style. Thank you both so much. Jake said nice things about you two. I think he understated the case." Hayley seemed reluctant to put the baby gifts aside and accept the bowl of fragrant soup Nell handed her.

Hayley had her teeth sunk in a thick buttered slice of

bread when Eden again brought up the subject of her gems. "If these samples are opal, Hayley, I can do more for you than a few baby items are worth. Should it cut, polish and set well, I'd be willing to buy all the raw material you can provide. Even discarding the potch or matrix to get to the usable stone, I'd like to purchase what you have here." Eden figured in her head a moment and came up with an amount.

Hayley gasped. "So much? I...thought maybe half that amount...in my wildest dreams."

"That's conservative, depending on the grade. If you'd trust me with a slab to take back to my shop, I'd know better by the end of next week. Are you familiar with how consignment works? If the ore is high-grade, I'd advance more as my jewelry sells."

"And," Nell broke in, "to keep tabs on what she's doing, you could come and spend a few weeks at the Triple C, Hayley."

"Now I *know* you're related to Jake." Hayley smiled, but she kept shaking her head. "If the ore isn't high-grade, I'll have to dig twice as much. I appreciate your wanting to help, but I'm not going anywhere. Take a sample or two, Eden. All I ask is that you don't let anyone know where you got it."

"That's the least I can do," Eden murmured. "A good jewelry designer never reveals the source of his or her materials. I'd like to nail down an exclusive contract, but in all fairness, I have to tell you that you're free to sell to any market."

"To save us all a major disappointment," Hayley said, "Why don't we wait for the assay results?"

"Fair enough." Eden stood and collected the soup bowls. "I don't want to rush you, Nell, but you know how I am when I face the prospect of working with a new stone.''

"Yes. You're as obsessed as I am when I discover a new clay or dye. Are you sure you won't reconsider, Hayley? We'd make you comfortable at the ranch.''

"Thanks, but no. Maybe I'll drive over at the end of next week for those vegetables. And if you could spare a gallon of milk—I'll buy one,'' she added quickly.

"Nonsense. It's a gift. That's settled, then,'' Nell said, clasping Hayley's work-roughened hands between her own callused palms. "If I see Jacob in the interim, shall I tell him you've had a change of heart and would welcome Charcoal back?''

"Would I ever.'' Hayley's eyes brimmed again. Because she wasn't used to so much kindness, she hugged each of the women awkwardly, then stepped back and waved while they climbed into the Range Rover. Her campsite seemed twice as lonely after they'd gone. Yet Hayley knew her decision to stay and extract additional ore was the right one.

A memory of Jake's kiss taunted her. She wondered if his mother would be so chummy if she knew about that—and the way he'd touched her.

## CHAPTER NINE

JAKE DIDN'T KNOW about his mother and sister-in-law's visit to Hayley when he rode in on Wednesday of the next week to turn water into the southern ditches. He arrived at approximately four in the afternoon and found Hayley up to her knees in mud as she washed ore. Piles of blue-streaked rock, some boxed and some not, all sorted by size, made it difficult for him to navigate the clearing on horseback.

Charcoal ran through the piles, sniffing each one. He barked and wagged his tail enthusiastically when he finally reached Hayley. She let him lick her face, but tried not to pet him with her muddy hands. The blood coursing through her veins gushed like water through a broken dam the moment she'd identified Jake. Darn it, she didn't want to admit how much she'd missed his visits. She did her best to appear nonchalant.

Frankly, she was surprised to see him after what Eden had said concerning the timetable for roundup. Content to watch the easy way he sat a horse, Hayley stopped work and waited for Jake to speak first. He said nothing, only swung from the saddle, inspecting her from the top of her wind-tousled hair to the muddy soles of her boots. She returned the favor, shading her eyes with a dirty forearm. "You look exhausted," she said, shocked to see that it was true. "There's no coffee made, but I'll fix a pot. Give me a minute to wash up." She got to her feet, and at her first step, tripped on a large speckled rock.

Jake vaulted two rock heaps in succession to steady her. "I don't look half as tired as you do," he growled. "Sit. I'll fix the coffee."

"You haven't been here five minutes and already you're bossing me around." It made her nervous the way Jake zeroed in on every tiny detail. Gazing into his hungry eyes, she felt an urgent need to keep him at arm's length. "I'll knock off when these samples are clean. Anyway, I'm not drinking coffee, remember? Caffeine isn't good for babies." She thought a reminder wouldn't hurt, in case he'd forgotten her condition. Although he could hardly miss the changes in her body. This week she'd begun to feel as if she waddled rather than walked. Straightening, Hayley rubbed the heel of her palm on a spot that had ached constantly since she'd started hauling ore by hand again.

Jake thought she'd been doing that a lot—rubbing a place low on her spine. Mud caked the back pleats of a jumper that appeared sun-streaked from frequent laundering. She'd worn a T-shirt under the jumper the last time he'd seen her, but today her brown arms were bare and coated in dust. She also had dirt streaks on the brim of her hat and on her forehead, where she'd wiped away perspiration. It was hot. A hundred and five. It'd been that temperature for more than a week, and it felt twice that in the rocky canyons Jake had explored to hunt for strays. It must be worse digging ore from a hillside with the sun blistering down. "Now that we've agreed we both pretty much look like hell," he said, removing his hat and hanging it on a limb, "let's see what a hug will do to improve our sorry state of affairs." Giving her no time to object, Jake enfolded her in his arms. The minute he felt her warmth, it was as if his tiredness disappeared.

Hayley's hat tumbled from her head during a brief struggle for release. Then as Jake's hands slid to the base of her spine and began to massage away the dull ache lodged there, she relaxed against his chest and sighed. While her head told her she shouldn't let him touch her so intimately, her body dissolved under the motion of his hands. Almost before she knew it, her fingers had curved over his shoulders and she began to stroke his tight shoulder muscles.

Closing his eyes, he practically purred. They both did. And no words passed between them as they gave and took pleasure from the simplest touches. Jake didn't know when his body passed the basic need for comfort and slammed sexual desire through him, instead. It hadn't been his intent when he reached for her. Or maybe it had. She'd been on his mind constantly, day and night. At night, as he lay looking up at the same starry sky that covered her, his thoughts had been quite graphic.

Touching her ceased being enough. He wanted to taste her and watch the change in her eyes as he slowly worked up to burying himself deep inside her.

Hayley felt his transformation at about the same time as he recognized exactly where they were headed. Jake had started at the neck of her jumper, unbuttoning the long row of buttons that traversed the length. Though her cheeks grew hot, Hayley tried to ease from his hold without making a big deal of it. ''You have magic hands,'' she murmured, catching them before he exposed her breasts. Breasts swollen and more tender in recent weeks. She'd had to dispense with wearing bras.

Jake brought her scraped fingers to his lips. He tasted

his way up the inside of her arm, pausing at the elbow. "I saw you rubbing your back. Come stand under the waterfall with me. The water's warm and it'll help me do a better job of getting the kinks out. I'll lend a hand washing your hair, too," he said, swishing her long braid around to the front where she could see the bits of dried mud clinging to the ends. A chunk fell off and went down the open front of her jumper.

She pulled back, wadding the gaping edges of material into one hand. "We can't get naked together, Jake."

"Mind telling me why not?" His liquid gaze heated another trail up her body.

"Because…because it's still daylight, for one thing," she sputtered.

"Yeah. So…?" He smiled crookedly as he ran his index finger down her cherry-red cheek and over the indignant quiver of her lower lip. Bending, he let his tongue trace the path his finger had taken. "A guy kind of likes to see the woman he loves looking the way nature made her," he said huskily, his breath tickling her skin.

Hayley sucked in a hot puff of air so fast she choked as it seared her lungs. "Have you…have you been drinking?" she asked in a strangled voice.

"You're the one acting weird." Frowning, he thumped her solidly on the back.

Indeed, she probably was, Hayley thought as her head reeled and spun, and her legs went rubbery, forcing her to flop into the lawn chair. "You might have heatstroke," she muttered under her breath. "Or else you accidentally chewed locoweed."

Jake knelt in front of her and spanned her hips with both hands. "It just dawned on me what I said. I swear I'm not in the habit of tossing the *L*-word around, Hayley. I wouldn't say it just to get you out of your clothes. You've gotta believe me, it's what I feel. I want to go to bed with you at night, yes, and wake up with you in the morning. Now, and when you're eighty. But that's only part of it. Damn, I'm not good with words.''

She scooted her chair out of his reach. With fingers that shook, she tried restoring her buttons.

One look at the pale cleavage, creamier by far than her exposed suntanned skin, made Jake hard again. It didn't seem to matter—to him, anyway—that he obviously had stronger feelings for Hayley than she had for him. He must be in love or he wouldn't have made that declaration she'd refuted. He'd lusted after other women. Never had he mistaken those feelings for love. Jake was reasonably sure this was the real thing.

A thought struck him as he watched her fumble with the button just below her breasts. Scrambling closer on his knees, he batted her fingers away and slipped the button carefully through the buttonhole. ''Is it the baby?'' he asked earnestly.

''Is what the baby?'' Hayley shivered, although sweat popped out on her forehead. She wished he'd stop this assault on her senses.

''I can love another man's baby. It won't make any difference, I swear. I know I didn't mention the baby when I said I wanted to be with you. I assumed you'd understand it went without saying that I want you both.'' As if to prove the point, Jake caressed her stomach and kissed it. He was surprised to discover how much the bulge had expanded in the weeks he'd been away. As he marveled, a tiny foot or elbow smacked him in the nose. Amazement spread through them both, bringing them closer for a moment. They stared at each other and enjoyed the interlude, neither remembering that four buttons of Hayley's jumper remained open.

Which wouldn't have made a difference if Eden Cooper hadn't wheeled into the clearing in her gleaming Cherokee and hopped out in a cloud of dust. Her precipitous appearance caught them disheveled and flustered.

She skirted boxes and jumped over piles of stone, breathing fast when she finally arrived at their side. "What happened? Did Hayley faint? Oh, God, she hasn't gone into early labor, has she?"

By the time his sister-in-law loomed over them, Jake and Hayley had sprung apart. Their faces had gone pale. It wasn't until a minute later, when no one jumped in with answers, that Eden recognized the expressions they wore as guilt. She slapped a flat palm to her forehead. "I, ah, I'm interrupting, aren't I?"

Jake saw a blushing Hayley fumbling to fix her jumper. He rose and quickly placed himself between the two women, allowing Hayley her privacy. "What in hell are you doing here, Eden? Has something gone wrong at the ranch? Did Dad get hurt again?" he thundered.

"No. Didn't Hayley tell you about Nell's and my visit? Or that I took some of her ore samples to have them assayed?"

He acted as if she was speaking a foreign language. Eden snapped her fingers in front of his face. "Hel-lo. Nell said you asked her to visit Hayley. I realize I wasn't part of the equation." Her lips twitched in a grin. "I heard you mention opals before you made your grand exit the night of the barbecue. You should know it's like waving a red flag at a bull. I had to see her discovery for myself."

Hayley struggled to rise from the low-slung chair.

"This is only Wednesday. We'd set Friday as the day you might have news. I planned to drive over to the Triple C in the afternoon. You have bad news, don't you?" She looked stricken. Accepting Jake's help, she'd finally managed to stand, but her pinched lips reflected her disappointment.

"Not bad news at all," Eden declared, reaching to grip Hayley's arm. "The news is good. Great, in fact. All the tests show the opal to be a good grade. The most important test was one I had to farm out to a geologist I know—which is why I'm here early. He knew from the makeup of the dirt and surrounding rock attached to the sample that the ore was mined locally. I'm afraid he'll stir up interest among local gem-hunters, even though I asked him not to say anything. It might only be a process of elimination before someone connects these opals to your recorded site."

"Why should it matter?" Jake and Hayley asked in unison.

"Hayley needs to go to the recorder's office and list the discovery of valuable mineral deposits on her claim. Then if anyone accidentally or purposely crosses her vein, she can legally prosecute them." She turned to Hayley. "You don't have to use the term *opal*. Call it cristobalite. It's a term for opals rarely used outside of Australia. A person would have to be a seasoned opal hunter to recognize what you had."

Hayley sat again, hard, and feeling dazed, she looped her arms around the dog's neck. She remained mute until he bathed her cheek with his rough tongue. "I can't seem to comprehend anything beyond the fact that you verified the legitimacy of my find. I hate to sound mercenary, but I have to think about feeding and clothing my baby this winter. Is my opal worth anywhere near the amount you mentioned during your last visit?'' An outflung arm encompassed her collection of rocks.

''More.'' A smiling Eden leaned down so she could meet Hayley's eyes. ''The stone is so high-grade that even if you sell only to me and come here to dig once a year, you and your baby will be able to live comfortably for years. Probably until the field plays out. As opals typically form over quite a large radius in areas that were once basin lakes, it might behoove you to do some research and extend your claim.''

''Great!'' Jake yanked Eden upright. ''The Cattlemen's Association is hunting ways to kick her off this land, and you're recommending she encroach on Westin's leased range.''

Eden presented a stubborn jaw. ''He's leasing the land for grazing, not mining. But if word gets out before Hayley files the appropriate changes, I wouldn't put it past Westin to file his own mineral claim.''

''It doesn't matter,'' Hayley broke in. ''To make a trip to the recorder's, I'd have to leave what I'm doing. Someone could jump my claim while I'm gone.''

Jake's brows drew together. ''I wasn't suggesting you not protect what's already yours. I just don't want you to face off against guys like Westin and maybe get yourself hurt. Hell, I'll stay here and guard the place. Let Eden drive you to the courthouse in the morning. Fast as she drives, you ought to be back before noon.''

''Are you insinuating I have a lead foot?'' Eden punched his arm.

''Dillon's the one who told me you have a drawerful of speeding tickets and you got a letter from Motor Vehicles asking you to come to Phoenix to review your driving record.''

''That was a long time ago. Right after I got my

driver's license. My dad, bless his heart, felt that if Dillon was going to marry me, he deserved to know all my faults. Of course, he'll tell you he was trying to scare Dillon off.''

"Could be true. As I recall, your dad wasn't keen on your dating cowboys.''

"The very same man who griped about me graduating with an art degree. He insisted that all artists starve.''

Jake turned to Hayley. "Did I tell you Eden has jewelers all over the world fighting to sell her designs? You couldn't have found a better outlet for your opals.''

"You're the one who made it all possible. Heaven only knows how long it would've taken me to find a market if you hadn't asked your mom to drop by. Why did you, by the way?'' She gave him a blank stare.

"Because I...well, you wouldn't listen when I said you shouldn't be out here by yourself. I thought she might be more convincing. Boy, was I wrong. She and Eden set you on a breakneck course to become a millionaire.'' He glared at his sister-in-law.

She arched a brow and smiled wickedly. "So what were *you* offering her, Jacob?''

His eyes glittered darkly. "What do you mean, what was I offering her?''

Eden inspected a polished fingernail. "A little bird told me you're pressing Wade about building a house on your acreage. It occurs to me that a woman and baby need a solid roof over their heads.''

Jake knew very well that Eden was trying to provoke him into revealing the extent of his involvement with Hayley. Even though the idea of marriage had planted itself in his mind, he hadn't reached the point of discussing it with her. Jake would be damned if he'd let her learn something so important secondhand—or in front of an audience.

"You're on a fishing expedition, Mrs. Nosybody, and it'll get you nowhere. I hate to think what label you'd paste on me if I didn't show a little concern for a woman stuck out on her own here. More than once I suggested she use the ranch as home base. Ask her what she thought of *that* idea."

Hayley wrinkled her nose. "Don't argue, you two." It was plain that Eden assumed she and Jake had a romantic relationship. And equally plain that Jake was backpedaling for all he was worth. Hayley felt a yawning pit opening in the bottom of her stomach. She shouldn't let it affect her, she'd known Jake hadn't meant it when he said he loved her. How could he mean it? He barely knew her. Besides, it'd be a few months before her divorce from Joe was final. Hadn't jumping into that marriage been the lesson of a lifetime for her?

Jake stood by silently and watched steely resolve replace the vulnerability in Hayley's beautiful eyes. He felt helpless to try to rectify her misconceptions here in front of his sister-in-law. For one thing, he wasn't that sure of himself around Hayley. She'd rebuffed all his offers so far. Even if she seemed to fall under his spell when he kissed her, she got over it quickly enough when the kissing ended. While there was a lot to be said for physical compatibility, Jake didn't fool himself into thinking it could hold a marriage together. A good marriage needed more substantial glue, like friendship and respect, as well as good sex.

"You ladies go ahead and take off," he said. "Spend the night in Tubac and hit the recorder's office in Nogales tomorrow. Eden, if you wouldn't mind swinging past the ranch, would you roust Dillon on the mobile

phone? Tell him what's going on. I promised I'd turn
the water into the spillway, then scour Vulture's Roost
for strays tomorrow morning. Tell him it'll be afternoon.''

"It'd be better if you went with Hayley,'' Eden told
him. "I'll ride Mojave to the ranch. Bright and early
tomorrow I'll get Nell to bring me back. The two of us
can load the bed of her Range Rover with this ore. That
way, if anyone does chance by, there'll be nothing to
show you've found anything worthwhile. I'll weigh it at
the shop and write Hayley a check. Then I can start
cutting and polishing. Which is what I really want to
do.''

Jake deferred to Hayley. "It's your call.'' Seeing Hayley hesitate, Jake pulled her aside and lowered his voice.
"Is Eden moving too fast? She has a tendency to run in
high gear, especially in matters related to her jewelry
designs.''

Eden, who'd overheard her brother-in-law, looked
chagrined for all of two seconds. "We're approaching
the main tourist season. The sooner I get some opal
pieces on the market, the sooner we'll know if I'm right
about this venture making a profit for both Hayley and
me. But if you don't trust me to weigh this without
you—''

"It's not that.'' Hayley cut her off. "I wondered if I
could help polish the stones. My grandfather left some
lapidary equipment with a friend. If whoever takes me
will circle through Tombstone, I could collect the tumbler. If I dug ore during the day and polished stones at
night, it'd speed up the process.''

Eden paced among the piles of ore, inspecting indi-
vidual pieces here and there. "I'd need to run a few
additional tests. The early samples stood up well and

didn't fracture or crumble. But opal's delicate. Some jewelry-makers fill the cracks with a type of silicone. That reduces the value of a piece. And it won't stand up under the scrutiny of a well-trained appraiser. I'd never use fill. My signature on a piece means quality. If this opal is touchy, I'll have to handle the polishing phase myself.''

"Of course." Hayley linked her hands and dropped her gaze. "I wasn't suggesting that we cut corners. Forget I said anything.''

Eden swung round. "No, don't apologize. I'm amenable to your offer. In fact, I've been considering hiring an apprentice, someone I'd teach cutting and polishing. My time is better spent designing and working with the silver and platinum settings. If you decide to stay around here, Hayley, you may fit the bill.''

"Stay around here, how? You mean live in Tubac? I don't know—I've heard it's a really expensive place to rent or buy property. Tombstone or Bisbee would be less expensive"

Eden wasn't subtle about jamming her elbow in Jake's ribs. "I meant…like settle on the Triple C.''

Hayley's face colored. So did Jake's. He recovered first and hissed, "Mind your own business, Eden.''

Jumpier than a frog on a hot skillet, Hayley set about dousing her campfire. "It's getting late. Hadn't we better go, Eden? I don't know anyone who'd put us up for the night, and motels in Tombstone fill up fast this time of year. Oh, if we're making the circle trip, would you mind swinging by Dr. Gerrard's office?'' Her gaze remained on Eden.

"Is something wrong?" Jake and Eden asked together.

"Not that I know of," Hayley mumbled. "If it's too much trouble, I'll skip it."

"No, you won't." Jake made the decision and then, declared he'd be the one escorting Hayley. "Eden, tell Dillon I'm taking the whole day off. The doctor will need to work Hayley in."

"Gerrard's winding down his practice," Hayley said. "He's never that busy. Old-timers in the area still go to him. Newcomers prefer the younger doctors. Dr. Gerrard delivered me—and my mother. He knew Tombstone in its heyday."

"Is he competent?" Jake asked.

"What? You think he bounced me on my head?" Hayley laughed.

"Very funny. Not all deliveries are routine. Ask me," Jake said. "I've run into some dicey situations during calving season."

Hayley flexed her arm. "I'm healthier than a horse."

"And more stubborn than a mule," Jake said wryly. "Come on, grab a change of clothes and climb into Eden's rig. Let's get this show on the road. Eden, you'll feed Mojave and Charcoal, I presume?"

She nodded on her way to adjust the stirrups.

The minute they buckled in and drove off, Hayley felt tongue-tied. Where bantering had seemed easy around the campfire, now Jake was too close and seemed far too male. She cast about for a safe subject. "The Cooper men must be so proud of Eden and your mom."

"Why is that?" Jake asked, unexpectedly ejected from thoughts centering on the woman seated beside him. He enjoyed the feel of them driving off together— as if they were already a married couple.

"Are you kidding? They're talented and intelligent and beautiful."

"So are you."

Jake glanced up from the washboard tracks he was doing his best to take slowly. "You sound as though you think they're something you're not."

Her eyes met his ever so briefly, then she paid an inordinate amount of interest to the passing scenery, shadowed by the lowering sun. "I appreciate your trying to bolster my ego, Jake. But I'm nowhere near their league."

"Hogwash!"

Hayley shook her head. "As nice as your mother was to come visit and knit me a gorgeous baby blanket, she'd just as soon I disappeared. Please assure her I have no intention of inveigling my way into the Cooper family circle."

"Did my mom hurt your feelings? It was about the harvest dance, wasn't it? She wants me to take that quilter, Lisa. I said I was inviting you. It's a big event, weekend before Thanksgiving. To celebrate cutting the winter wheat. Say you'll go with me."

"I don't dance. I never learned how." Hayley was embarrassed to admit it. "That's what I'm trying to tell you, Jake. I have no talent. I barely finished high school. Look at the way I dress, compared to your mom and Eden. I'd never fit into their crowd. Or yours. Ask someone to the dance who does."

Her jaw was so tense Jake knew arguing served no purpose. They talked little after that. It was quite late by the time they reached Tombstone.

When he'd first thought about accompanying her, Jake had imagined them sharing a room. He stopped at the first motel with a vacancy sign and without asking booked them each a single. She thanked him and refused his offer to take her out for a meal. "I'm exhausted," was her excuse.

"Dammit," he growled. "You need nourishment."

"I was tired before we left. Bracing myself against that unpaved road sapped any energy I had. Let's meet for breakfast at seven. We'll go to the café where Dr. Gerrard eats every morning. That way, we'll know early if he can see me, and when."

Jake didn't like her edict, but she did look weary and he hadn't the heart to make a fuss. He skipped eating, too. And slept poorly, thanks to all the thoughts that kept running through his head.

Nor was he in the best of moods when they met in the lobby the next morning and he discovered Hayley had canceled his credit card for her room. "Why?" he demanded. "It's no crime to be short of cash. If you feel you have to pay me back, by the time the bill comes, you'll have money from your mine."

"Shh." She put a finger to her lips as the motel clerk stopped what he was doing and cocked an ear.

Jake gave the clerk a dirty look before he led Hayley out to the car. He thought she seemed more rested today—and really pretty in a violet maternity jumper he'd never seen her wear. It brought out the lavender flecks in her eyes. He was on the verge of complimenting her, but the moment passed as she scolded him for mentioning her mine.

Clamming up, Jake drove the few blocks to the café. Their entry into the establishment stopped talk. Hayley paused beside Dr. Gerrard, who was seated at the counter. She got her appointment—and some unwelcome news.

The doctor wadded his napkin as he spoke in hushed tones. "Joe blew back into town last week." The old doctor trained suspicious eyes on Jake, who hovered near Hayley, a proprietary hand settled low on her back.

He felt the ripple of alarm that shook Hayley. Jake thought for a minute that she was going to bolt. Instead, she took a deep breath and let it out slowly. She seemed calmer after Jake had moved his hand to her shoulder and squeezed.

"Joe's whereabouts don't concern me," she told Gerrard. "Our divorce will be final soon." Catching Jake's hand, she led him to the center of the room, to the only open table. But in a few minutes the buzz of normal conversation resumed around them and he relaxed.

The waitress added to the news about Ryan when she took their orders. "You'd probably like to know what I heard on good authority—Cindy Trent fleeced Joe after she hooked up with some guy she knew from Vegas. Joe showed up here, figuring you'd take him back. Ha! As if you would, considering what he did." The woman flashed Jake an admiring grin. "Looks like you've done all right, honey," she said, nudging Hayley. "Serves Joe right. But you take care. That man's trouble. He's hanging out with Deputy Dawg again. You know who I mean, Shad Tilford." The waitress ripped the order off her pad and started away. Suddenly her steps faltered. "Speak of the devil and his sidekick. Look who walked in and lowered the caliber of our clientele."

Jake, who sat facing the door, saw two men threading their way through the tables. One had greasy black hair and beady eyes. He wore a badge and a holstered weapon. The other had blond hair. His unshaven upper lip needed more hair to pass as a mustache. In Jake's estimation, Ryan could use a beard to hide a weak chin.

His stomach took a drop when Hayley turned, spotted

the duo, and looked as if she'd faint. "Steady," he murmured, holding one of her hands tightly.

It was Joe who hitched up his pants and swaggered over to confront Hayley. "Well, well. Rafferty over at the Holiday Inn said you'd found yourself a new stud. What's this about another mine?" The pale blue eyes were nasty. "That kid they say you're carrying can't be mine. Hell, I didn't hardly snap my fingers and you fell into my bed. But by law, babe, we're still married. If ol' Ben left you another mine, half belongs to me."

Jake would have punched Joe Ryan before he finished spreading his bullshit if he hadn't wanted to know more about the bastard's plans concerning Hayley. But he felt bad for waiting, because Hayley gave a low keening sound, like a wounded animal.

Leaping from his chair, Jake's knuckles crunched against the sparse hairs of Joe's mustache, meeting resistance at feral white teeth.

Hayley screamed and slumped forward as Joe went airborne and landed two feet away, crumpled at the feet of a fast-stepping waitress who dropped two orders of eggs and one of pancakes over the felled man.

Shad Tilford lunged for Jake but crashed to the floor as he tripped over a size-twelve boot someone slid across his path. Spitting and fuming, he made dire threats about arresting Jake for assault. "I'll throw your ass in jail!" he bellowed.

Dr. Gerrard moved fast for an old man. He sidestepped Joe's prone form and in a low authoritative voice ordered Jake to bring Hayley to his office. Her friends in the room cleared a pathway to the door. Jake wasn't sure if it was by accident or design that patrons formed a body blockade to keep the furious deputy inside the café.

In the doctor's waiting room, Jake paced. Gerrard's receptionist, Esther, provided Jake with the whole story of the Ryan courtship and subsequent marriage, and Joe's infidelity with the woman from the nail-painting place. What could Jake do but listen?

Esther hinted that Joe was responsible for Ben O'Dell's early demise. Even then, she wasn't quite finished. ''That no-good Joe Ryan wouldn't have found out a thing about Hayley's new mine if that snake, Shad Tilford, hadn't strong-armed good folks in town to notify him if she ever showed up. Since Joe's return, he and Shad have been thick as thieves. Too bad you brought Hayley to town, young man. Might be best if you skedaddled out the back way. Shad's watching the front. I doubt he knows the clinic has a back exit. I'll call a couple of miners who used to work for Ben. They'll create a diversion long enough for me to pull your Cherokee into the alley.''

Jake declined her offer. It tasted like cowardice. Slinking off with his tail tucked between his legs wasn't how he operated. But one look at Hayley's wan face and huge eyes bruised with pain, and he changed his mind. He gave Esther the okay. Within twenty minutes he and Hayley were burning up the highway out of town.

Hayley sat so quiet and withdrawn Jake felt a shiver of apprehension. ''The doctor didn't find anything wrong with the baby, did he?''

She idly smoothed a hand over her stomach. ''The doctor said everything's on track.''

''That's good. Why aren't you happier?''

Fear choked the life from Hayley's eyes. ''Someone provided Dr. Gerrard with a running commentary on what Joe said after he came to. He's going to sue me for half the mine. If he files before our divorce is final, all my work will be in vain. I'll just get shafted again.''

''I won't let that happen!'' Jake exploded. ''It's my fault for mentioning it at the motel. Anyway, he's got to find the Blue Cameo first. That ought to give us time to bleed the damned vein dry. I'll skip the rest of roundup and help you dig.''

''Like your dad'll let you do that. He already wants me gone. I wouldn't put it past him and your brother to lead Joe straight to me so they can make a deal with him for the land.''

''I guarantee that they wouldn't. Not that it matters, since the claim is solely in your name. In the eyes of the state, there's not a damn thing that asshole you married can do about it. Free claims transfer to family by different rules than mines on land a person actually owns.''

She sat for a minute and studied the rhythmic flexing of Jake's stubborn jaw. ''I'll fight my own battles, Jake. I want you to stay out of it.''

A numbness invaded his chest. Eden's Cherokee weaved from side to side as he left the two-lane highway and merged onto the freeway.

''Slow down, Jake! My life may not be the best, but I'm not ready to die.''

''Can't prove it by me,'' Jake snapped, mostly because she'd hurt him with her curt reply. ''The danger you're in—staying out in the middle of nowhere all alone—hasn't changed.''

''I *am* alone,'' she raged back.

''You don't have to be. I said I want to be there for you, Hayley.''

Her resolve wavered for a second. Not long enough to give Jake hope. In a gritty passionate voice, she lashed out, "I trusted a man's promises once. They turned out to be silver-plated lies."

"If you mean Joe Ryan, he's no man." Jake's denouncement of her ex-husband rang out bitterly. The truth didn't seem to matter, at least not when it came to healing the rift between him and Hayley. She only looked scornful, and her comparison of him to that bastard felt worse to Jake than a slap. All he wanted at the moment was to get shut of her. He wished now that he'd let Eden do the honors and make this trip with Hayley.

# CHAPTER TEN

UPDATING HAYLEY'S CLAIM report went without a hitch. The clerk at the recorder's office was more interested in popping her gum and talking on the phone than in paying attention to what Hayley put down as her most recent findings. Not wanting to take any chances, Hayley used the term Eden had suggested rather than mentioning opals by name. If Joe did hunt for her mine, she wanted to make it hard for him to figure out what she'd found at the Blue Cameo. Hayley couldn't shake the fear that he'd do everything in his power to claim what he'd already declared was his rightful share.

Even though talk between Jake and Hayley was still strained, he insisted they eat lunch in Nogales before returning to her camp. "We missed dinner last night and breakfast today, thanks to your ex. My stomach is near caved into my backbone. I'm not driving another mile without eating."

"That suits me. I'm famished, too. Have been since we left Tombstone. But you looked so grim I didn't want to ask any favors."

"If I'm grim, it's because I don't appreciate being lumped in the same category as that SOB you married."

"When did I do any such thing? You're nothing like him. I screamed when you hit him, but he had the local law backing him up. I was afraid Tilford would shoot you."

"I'm talking about later. It sure sounded like that's what you meant when you said that jerk fed you lies and now you won't trust *me*."

"I'm sorry," she said, lowering her lashes as Jake got into the drive-through line at a fast-food restaurant. "I guess it makes no sense to say my comments weren't aimed at you, but more at the promises you keep tossing around."

"You're right. It makes no sense." Jake drummed his fingers on the steering wheel.

Hayley bristled. "Look, Joe made the right promises, too. He just didn't keep them."

"So we're back to that. I'll have you know my word is good."

"I don't want to argue with you, Jake. Are you going to order? We've reached the speakerphone."

"You always make me forget what I'm doing," he said irritably. "What would you like?" She made her selections. Jake got huffy again when she pulled out her money and tried to pay her portion of the bill.

"Would you buy Eden's lunch?" she said, throwing the money down on the seat between them.

"Not as a rule. If Dillon's there, he pays for them. Times I'm in town by myself and I meet my mom and Eden for lunch, we go dutch. Generally those two carry more cash than I do." A dimple appeared in one of his cheeks.

"See." Hayley opened her milk carton and drank from it. "You admit to allowing them equal power. You don't assume they need to be cared for. Well, neither do I. I'm just as capable of providing for myself and my baby. I don't need anyone."

"Dammit, Hayley, if you don't beat all at twisting words to suit your purpose. Oh, never mind." Jake bit into his burger and muttered something dark and unrecognizable around the mouthful of beef and cheese. The milk painting Hayley's upper lip begged to be licked off. It was all he could do to look away.

She barely nibbled at the chicken she'd ordered, even after proclaiming to be famished. "Jeez, just eat," Jake said with a sigh. "Consider the subject closed."

Proving he was a man of his word, he steered their conversation to impersonal things. On the drive he pointed out a series of sun-blistered fields belonging to ranches bordering the Triple C. Jake lamented the ever-increasing need for measurable rainfall.

"I've noticed the spring isn't refilling as fast now as it did when you showed me how to open the valves. Has it ever gone completely dry?" Hayley asked worriedly.

"Five years ago it came close. The monsoons weren't just late, they blew past Arizona altogether. That year the J & B doubled their herd—a move that prompted Dad to speak to Ben about eventually acquiring his site. Ben agreed, but said he felt in his bones that the Blue Cameo would produce. He was the one who suggested the valve system. At the time it seemed the best and cheapest compromise."

"Isn't it still?" At Jake's arched brow, Hayley elaborated. "The men from the Cattlemen's Association who paid me a visit were antsy even before it became apparent there'd be a shortage of rain. Weren't they crying wolf? I mean, you said the system's been in place and working for five years."

"Yes, but all the valley ranchers have added to their herds. They had to or go under, the way beef prices have fallen these last few years."

Hayley sighed. "Everything always boils down to dollars and cents."

"My theory is there's enough to go around if no one ranch gets greedy." Jake's thoughts centered on John Westin and the rumor that he'd expanded his operation yet again. This time through leasing land in his daughter's name.

Hayley murmured agreement, her mind pulsing with Joe's threat to sue for half of her mine. Joe Ryan was lazy and greedy. A dangerous combination. "I suppose I should be happier with the news that Cindy Trent fleeced Joe. Turnabout is fair play, and he deserved it. Except that doesn't help me gain restitution. If Shad Tilford tracks Cindy down, he and Joe will split any money that's left." She paused. "You know what hurts worse than losing the proceeds from Gramps's mine? Joe telling people in Tombstone this isn't his baby."

She looked so downcast that Jake rallied, "Boy, we sure know how to pick depressing subjects. All this started because I mentioned a lack of rain. And I've seen some wet Novembers in the past."

"If that's the case, I'd better speed up the digging. The vein of opal is situated in a ravine I suspect feeds the waterfall during heavy rains. The more rough opal I stockpile, the more secure I'll feel."

Looking at her sitting there so small yet so determined to go it alone and beat the odds tripped a chord in Jake. A chord relighting the flame of desire he'd thought snuffed out during their earlier argument. Only this time he wasn't going to announce his feelings or restate his promise to help her dig. It could take a few days to clear things with his dad and Dillon, and he didn't want Hayley thinking he'd made a promise he wouldn't keep. No, what he'd do was show up and pitch in after he had his arrangements in place.

He knew exactly how he felt about her now. And he

knew he'd have another chat with his dad about clearing the property where he planned to build a house—for Hayley and for him. Of course he'd have to chip away at her barriers a little at a time. Perhaps, though, she'd believe he was serious if she actually saw progress on the building, and knew he really wanted to provide a home for her and the baby.

"Goodness, the clearing looks naked!" Hayley exclaimed as Jake topped the rise above her campsite.

He jammed on the brake, ripped headlong out of his plans for the future. "Were you robbed, you mean?"

Hayley gripped the dash with both hands. "No, silly. Eden and your mom must have transported all my samples. Oh, look. They left Charcoal to guard the place. How sweet. Would you consider letting him stay with me, Jake? I feel safer when he's here." With a guilty expression, she stammered, "I'll understand if you refuse. After all, I said I didn't need anything from anybody. I know you're still angry with me."

Jake let the vehicle roll down the slope. Killing the engine, he unsnapped his belt and moved toward Hayley. While she was confined by her belt, he leaned close and feathered kisses over both of her eyes and the tip of her nose. Then he gently nipped her bottom lip. "Something you need to know about the Coopers. We have a low flashpoint, but we're not ones to hold grudges."

She sighed, opening her eyes and lifting a hand to touch his cheek. "I'd feel horrid if I ruined our friendship, Jake. I'll need friends if I'm to consider staying in the area and apprenticing to Eden as she suggested."

Jake's breath caught. His heart clenched. He wanted more than mere friendship, dammit. But as he gazed into her still-wary eyes, he realized that this was a significant step. Asking to keep his dog was a start, however miserly. And he'd have to go slow if he ever hoped to win her love.

"Friends it is. Shall we cut our wrists and bind them together?" He grinned lazily.

His teasing apparently hit the right tone.

"The sight of blood makes me sick, Jacob. I doubt that comes as any great surprise, considering how fast I blacked out when you slugged Joe and blood spurted from his nose." She unbuckled her seat belt, picked up the satchel that held her dirty clothes and slid out of the Cherokee. "I cheered you on, even if I don't hold with violence."

Jake blocked her from closing the door. "This from the lady who took a potshot at me?"

"Are you blaming me for protecting myself? Men think they have a right to use muscles or kisses to overpower a woman. Well, they don't. *You* don't."

"I backed off, Hayley. There are men, of course, who wouldn't. Those same men might turn your gun on you. Sometimes it's smarter to hide or just plain climb in your truck and flee. Promise me you'll do that if need be."

"You mean if Joe shows up to jump my claim, don't you? I'm supposed to tuck my tail between my legs and let him take it? No, Jake, I won't."

"Dammit, Hayley. No amount of opals is worth putting your life or your baby's life in danger. You've recorded your find. There are legal avenues to beat Joe."

"Tell that to someone who believes in fairy tales. He forged my name on the sale papers for the Silver Cloud. He walked off with seven-eighths of the money. The law said it was his right as my husband. So much for your legal avenues."

"Shad Tilford does not speak for the real law in this

state. You have my word, Hayley. Joe won't get away with stealing from you again.''

Hayley wanted to believe him. The thought of Joe playing her for a fool twice frightened her. A rare sliver of luck had allowed her to land on her feet. But luck and Hayley Ryan weren't best buddies. ''Here we are, Jake, arguing over something that may never come to pass. I have work to do before the sun sets. As do you. So long, and stop worrying. I'll be fine. You said yourself it won't be easy for Joe to find the Blue Cameo even if he stumbles onto the recorder's files.''

''I said that, yes.'' Jake only wished he was as sure of that fact as he'd let on.

''Well, then.'' Hayley smiled softly as she circled a palm over her swollen belly. ''Junior and I will be right as rain. Speaking of rain, aren't there a lot of black clouds moving in?'' She squinted up at the darkening sky.

Hunching down to peer out the windshield, Jake saw she'd spoken the truth. ''Damn, I wish I didn't have to leave you alone. Heed your own advice and stop digging if those clouds do open up and dump on us.''

''I will. Jake, if you're headed to the Triple C to collect Mojave, would you mind taking a minute to call Eden and let her know I'm back?''

''Will do. I'm telling her to buy us tickets to the harvest dance, too. I don't care if you can't dance—I'm taking you.'' Jake shut the door, buckled himself in and threw the Cherokee into reverse.

He didn't want to admit that Hayley had scared him, talking about Joe's criminal traits. Jake intended to do more than notify Eden of their return and ask her to buy dance tickets. He planned to speak with his father about releasing him from his duties at the roundup. In view of Joe's threat, Hayley needed a full-time bodyguard.

The dark clouds had begun to roll with thunder and dance with heat lightning by the time Jake drove the Cherokee through the gates of the Triple C.

Wade Cooper glanced up from tying a tan slicker over a bedroll that spanned the broad rump of his favorite mare. He waited impatiently for Jake to alight. "About time you quit fiddledee-fartin' around the countryside with that fool woman and remembered it's getting our steers to market that pays your bills, as well as ours."

Jake froze, his hackles instantly raised. "Actually I came by to tell you I'm going back to help Hayley dig as many opals as possible before bad weather sets in. Dock my share of the profits from this sale, if it'll make you feel better. I already rounded up more than half the damned strays."

"Now they're *all* strays," his father roared. "I just got off the mobile with Dillon. A big clap of thunder spooked the herd. They scattered nine ways from Sunday. We need every hand we have to track them down. That includes you." He jabbed a finger in Jake's chest.

"A stampede?" Jake's jaw went slack.

"Has playing Romeo made you deaf? Throw a leg over Mojave and let's make tracks."

"You go on ahead. I promised Hayley I'd phone Eden."

"The hell with that. I already called your mom. Jacob, quit letting that little bloodsucker lead you by the nose. Before you know it, she'll have you convinced to move her lock, stock and barrel into our house."

Eyes narrowed dangerously, Jake cut his gelding out of the corral. As he slung a saddle on Mojave's back and cinched it tight, he said in a deadly quiet voice, "I'll thank you to keep a civil tongue any time you mention the woman I plan to marry.'' His sudden glimpse into the future shocked even Jake. An idea took shape in his head. He clearly knew his next step. ''I won't be bringing Hayley to the Triple C. After I round up the herd, I'm coming home and calling Carl Brown, that architect who designed Dillon's house. I want my own finished by December. I want to marry Hayley before she has the baby.''

''December? Holy hell!'' Wade almost spooked his own mount with his shout. His face turned beet-red as he hopped around with one foot in his stirrup. By the time he finally managed to drag himself into the saddle, his scowl was more formidable than the low-riding clouds. ''I told Nell not to visit that Ryan woman, I knew it'd only encourage your foolish interest in her. Marry her? You hardly know the woman. Do you hear what you're saying? It wasn't six months ago everyone in the valley laid bets on how soon you and John Westin's daughter would be booking a church.''

''I dated Ginalyn twice. Maybe three times,'' Jake said, getting as red in the face as his father. ''She's spoiled as sin. Hayley Ryan is a hundred—no, a thousand times more woman.'' Vaulting into his saddle, Jake clattered off without waiting for Wade to chew on his ear any longer.

Jake had the faster stronger horse. He managed to stay ahead of Wade until they got into rough terrain. Then the surefooted mare came into her own and drew abreast of Mojave. Together, father and son flushed eight or so bewildered-looking steers bearing the Triple C brand from a thicket of greasewood. Jake unlooped a lariat and swung it back and forth to try to head the cattle in the right direction.

Hearing steers bawling in the distance, Wade rode over the next rise. He had ten more head on the move when Jake rejoined him.

"Where's that cow dog of yours?" Wade asked. "He'd keep these strays on track and leave you and me free to hunt down the remaining delinquents."

"I left Charcoal with Hayley. By the way," he added, changing the subject. "Did you know Eden's offered to buy everything Hayley's mine can produce?"

"The lot of you encouraged her. If you'd let things be and hadn't taken her milk and garden greens, likely the little gal would've pulled up stakes by now. But no, my own family facilitated her operation, even though every last one of you knew I've been dickering for years to acquire that property."

"Don't forget the chickens I gave her."

Wade seared his son with a scowl.

"I was being facetious," Jake informed his dad. "But what's the big deal? Hayley's agreed to the same water arrangement you negotiated with Ben."

"Hell, Jake. I didn't want to spout off out of turn. All I have is an unsubstantiated rumor. When I collected our last stock check, Charlie Goodall, a rancher I know from Phoenix, asked what we thought down here of John Westin hobnobbing with developers."

"Developers?" To a rancher, *developer* was a scary word, too often synonymous with resorts and golf courses. It generally meant the demise of the government land ranchers leased to graze large herds. "Are you sure this Goodall didn't mistake John's chat with the governor on behalf of the co-op's water interests as a move to develop?"

Wade rubbed a thumb over a stubbled jaw. "Charlie sat near John's party at lunch. He knows who attended that meeting and what he heard. He'd have no reason to lie. Marshall Rogers from the Rocking R was hip-deep in it, too. I know for a fact that for the last two years he's made noises about selling out.''

''Are you going to confront John at the next cattlemen's meeting?''

''Not knowing the extent of his backing, I'm almost afraid to. What I need is control over the spring. Without a water source, the developers will back out.''

''Right now Hayley controls the water. So I can't understand why you aren't treating her more nicely.''

''She controls the mineral rights. Not water. Westin could make a case to the governor that the valley ranchers need the water rights split off from the mineral rights. It could happen as fast as that.'' He snapped his fingers.

Jake finished his father's thought. ''And if John's convinced a majority of our neighbors to go along with his scheme, he's nabbed a pot of gold. The Triple C either capitulates and sells to the developer, or we're eventually squeezed out.''

''That's about the size of it.''

''I can't believe John would be so sneaky. If he's of a mind to sell the J & B, why set Ginalyn up with a spread of her own?''

Wade scrammed three steers out of a thicket of mesquite. ''I figure it's a smokescreen for those of us not in on his racket. Think about it. A few of us have been on John's case for bringing in too much new stock and overgrazing the leased rangeland. I always suspected the guy was a wheeler-dealer out to make big bucks.''

''So you're saying Westin's depleted the rangeland and now plans to sell and make an even bigger killing on the property?''

''Much as I hate it, that's my theory.''

Jake charged off after a stubborn yearling bull who objected to being brought into the small herd they'd mustered. "Then it seems to me," he said, out of breath when he returned, "that'd be in the best interests of the Triple C for me to stick close to Hayley's operation. Won't John think twice about pulling any shenanigans if I'm on-site?"

They rounded up several more strays before Wade responded. "My druthers, plain and simple, is for you to talk that gal into revoking her claim so we can purchase the acreage fair and square. That would stonewall John."

"The mine is Hayley's insurance policy. Her ex swindled her out of Ben's property in Tombstone. I don't want her thinking we're shysters, as well."

Wade looked at Jake long and hard. "Don't talk to me again, boy, until you make up your mind where your loyalty lies. With your family or with that woman." Reining his mare sharply to the left, he kicked her into a gallop. Horse and rider soon disappeared over a rise, leaving Jake to swear at the steers they'd already rounded up.

His herd grew in size during the long grueling afternoon. Night had fallen by the time Jake merged his group of stampeded runaways with the main body of steers captured by Dillon and the vaqueros. Again the storm had rolled over the Santa Cruz Valley without dropping any rain. The milling bawling cattle were winded from their run and they were dry. The added humidity left herd and wranglers cranky.

Dillon rode out to meet Jake, who pivoted in the saddle, expecting his dad to be bearing down on him, too. Jake had been ganged up on by family more than once.

This time, apparently, Dillon was alone. Which was a relief.

Until Dillon skidded his mount to a stop, dropped his reins, dismounted and grabbed Jake right out of his saddle. Their noses inches apart, Dillon shook his younger brother hard enough to rattle Jake's teeth.

"It's not enough that you have Mom and Dad arguing over that little tramp you've befriended. Now she's got you turning your back on the blood, sweat and tears we've all put into the Triple C."

Jake broke Dillon's grip on his shirt. Seeing red from the moment his brother called Hayley a tramp, Jake lowered his head and rammed it hard into Dillon's midriff. With a huge *oof,* the two began punching wildly. Locked together, they rolled down a rocky incline. Furious though he was, Jake was the first to hear the cattle lowing in alarm. He stiffened an arm against Dillon's throat. "Listen, you dumb shit, maybe you like blistering your butt in the saddle all day digging these cows out twice. Once is enough for me." Though his chest heaved from the exertion, Jake stood and jerked his brother to his feet.

Dillon dusted off his hat and jammed it on. "I don't need your help, you—"

"Shoot your mouth off about Hayley again, and I'll say the hell with us causing a second stampede. Hayley's no more tramp than Eden is. Anyway, I don't believe Hayley caused an argument between Mom and Dad. They never fight."

"They are now. Dad fired Ernesto Torres for coming back drunk between the north- and south-area round-ups."

"What does that have to do with Hayley?"

"Mrs. Torres is a midwife. Mom told Dad right in front of the crew to give Ernesto back his job because she'd already talked to Mrs. Torres about moving out to Hayley's camp in case her baby comes early. I guess you'd know she's pregnant.''

"Mom did that?" Jake relaxed his shoulders. "She's brilliant."

"Well, Dad didn't think so. The vaqueros wouldn't respect him again if he reversed his decision. You know we can't condone drinking on the job."

"Ernesto has worked roundup on the Triple C for ten years. That ought to be reason enough to consider letting him dry out and stay on the crew."

"Exactly what Mom said. But she didn't let up. Dad finally blew his cork. They put on quite a show for the hands." Dillon sounded disgusted.

"So how did it end?"

"Dad won. Mom is pissed off. They're barely speaking. As if losing Ernesto isn't bad enough, according to Dad you're leaving us even shorter-handed while you go help that woman dig her damned opals."

"He never mentioned losing Ernesto. If you're in a bind, I'll ride back and forth, helping Hayley whenever I can—unless you badmouth her again. Then the deal's off."

Dillon stuck his fingers into his back pockets and leaned close to Jake. "You're serious. I can't believe it. Some days it'll be a two-hour ride each way. You'd give up sleep and stretch yourself thin for this woman?"

"I would," Jake said, his face stony.

Dillon bit back an oath and wrapped his reins around one hand. He mounted fluidly, the stiff set of his shoulders conveying his disapproval. "I certainly hope you're not expecting me to like a woman who'd pit husband against wife, son against father and brother against brother." He wheeled his star-faced gelding off into the darkness before Jake could formulate a comeback. Probably just as well, though. He was too angry now. And someday in the not-too-distant future, after he'd finished building his house and installed Hayley in it, Dillon would be forced to eat his words. Once she was no longer Hayley Ryan but Hayley Cooper, they'd return to being one big happy family.

Jake's good fortune continued. His path never crossed either Dillon's or their dad's over the next two days. Every last hand extended himself to help bring the herd's count to what it'd been before the stampede. The heat and dust, which had seemed to double after the passing of the rainless storm, sapped any will the cowboys might have had for bickering.

Jake didn't bother to check out with anyone at noon on the third day after he'd driven the last six strays he'd found into the main herd. Mopping sweat from his brow, he refilled his canteen from the water barrel and lit out for the Blue Cameo.

An hour later his heart did a fast jig as he rode into Hayley's camp. The fire was out, her camp empty of the ever-present piles of ore. Jake panicked.

But her pickup was there, so she hadn't taken a load of ore to Tubac. Then where was she? He called himself all kinds of fool for leaving her alone, unprotected.

*Wait!* He hadn't left her totally unprotected. Charcoal. Where was that dog?

Swinging down from his horse, Jake unsaddled the big bay and tied him to a tree near a patch of grass that wasn't completely brown. Though Jake hadn't the vaguest idea where Hayley's mine was located, he set off on foot to search the foothills. She'd said she was digging in a ravine that, if it rained, would feed the waterfall.

Considering how much ore she'd already gathered, Jake didn't think she could be hauling it far.

The longer he walked and the more barren his uphill ascent became, the greater his worry. His stomach bottomed out when he heard the muffled blast of dynamite.

He ran blindly and pulled up panting under the shade of a gnarled piñon. Placing a shaking thumb and forefinger against his teeth, Jake whistled for Charcoal. He was rewarded by a far-off but recognizable bark. At first delighted, then concerned that Hayley might be lying ahead somewhere hurt or disabled, Jake charged up the rocky cliff in the direction of the still-vibrating cloud of dust.

His boots slipped on the slick granite. He cursed the steep grade, but didn't slow down. Not until a shot rang out, coming so close it knocked the hat from his head. His heart slammed against his chest as he dived for cover behind clumps of desert bloom that wouldn't hide a flea. As his throat tightened convulsively, Jake's immediate thought was that someone had jumped Hayley's claim. The shot had come from a higher-powered rifle than she owned.

Sweat poured down his neck in rivulets. He buried his face in broken bits of shale and wondered how he'd let himself get pinned down so neatly.

No other shots followed, but it wasn't long before Jake felt eyes boring into his back. He had little choice but to raise his arms slowly. Maybe it would buy him time with the claim-jumpers.

He didn't even get one hand up before he felt a cold nose sniff his ear.

"Jake? Is that you?" Hayley shrieked. By then, Charcoal had all but deafened him, barking in his ear.

"What are you doing sneaking up on me when I'm

blasting?'' Hayley demanded, ejecting an unused shell from the chamber of a deer rifle Jake recognized as his own.

"Hey." He muzzled the Border collie with both hands and warned him to cease barking. "That's my old rifle. I can't believe you almost killed me with my own gun. How did *you* get hold of it?"

Hayley, who'd turned pale in spite of her tan, set the worn gunstock on the narrow trail and leaned on it as she massaged her protruding belly. "Your mother left it when she stopped by this morning to pick up another batch of ore. She heard from an attendant where she buys gas that two men, strangers, were asking questions about any new gold or silver mines in the area. Oh, Jake, I'm so afraid it's Joe and Shad. They don't know it's opals I've found, but…" She dropped the rifle, skidded down the sidehill and threw herself into Jake's arms.

It felt wonderful to hold her. To feel the ridges of her backbone. To breathe in the flowery scent of her shampoo.

Jake had no compunction about pushing the dog aside to fill his arms with the woman he loved.

"You scared the hell out of me, lady. I thought someone jumped your claim." Jake nuzzled her ear. Groaning, he tightened his hold and trailed damp kisses along her throat, down to a jutting collarbone that peeked out from under her sleeveless denim jumper.

"No wonder you were scared," Hayley murmured. "I shouldn't have shot without knowing who you were. But you shouldn't have sneaked up on me, either. Not while I was still half-deaf from the blast. I can't use a jackhammer because of the baby, and the ore's running deeper. The only way I can widen the vein is with dynamite.''

"That blast scared me even more than riding in and finding your camp empty. I thought something had happened to you." His hands roamed her back.

Hayley drew back. "Oh, right," she drawled. "I haven't seen you for days. You must've been really worried."

"Didn't Mom tell you the storm stampeded our herd?"

"No. In fact, she never said the rifle was yours, either."

"Wow, I hope she's not mad at me, as well as my dad."

Hayley managed to regain her feet, although it wasn't easy given the incline and her pregnancy. "Look, I need to go back and dig. Nell said she or Eden will drive out here every morning to pick up whatever ore I've managed to haul out. That way, if Joe does show up, he'll have less to steal."

Jake's control snapped. "I suppose it never dawned on any of you that he'd be mad as a hornet if he comes up empty-handed? Why didn't Mom call on the mobile and let me know Joe was closing in? Dillon has a phone at our base camp."

"It's not your fight, Jake. It's mine. I thought I made that clear."

"Oh? Then why did you throw yourself into my arms?"

Hayley stomped up the hill. "My mistake," she said, stooping to grab a pickax. "A reaction to having shot at you. Relief I didn't kill you. Go on back to your roundup. If Joe shows up, I'll take care of him."

Jake's anger crumbled in the face of her courage. "I've come to help, and you need me whether you admit it or not. I learned there's more people than Joe who'd like to see you gone. John Westin of the J & B promised developers access to the spring if they buy him out. They'd turn this area into a resort.''

She gasped, then swore they'd get it over her dead body.

Jake hesitated mentioning his dad and Dillon's wishes. Because when it came right down to it, he was one-third of the Triple C. Jake didn't see how he could allude to his family's interest in obtaining rights to the spring without implicating himself. He decided not to involve his dad and brother at this point.

''Until John pays you another visit, there's no sense trying to second-guess him. In the meantime I'm here to help you dig. Why don't we get to it?''

''Maybe it'd be better if you didn't know the exact location of my mine.''

Jake stared into her eyes, his own refusing to let her get away with questioning his integrity.

Eventually Hayley expelled an uneven breath. ''I take that back, Jake. I know you're a hundred percent in my corner. It's because of you that I have an outlet for my opals. I owe you a lot already.''

''No. I can't take the credit. That all goes to Eden. She overheard me asking my mother to visit you. Hayley,'' he said earnestly, ''I want you to trust me because I care about you. A lot.''

''We did agree to be friends. Come on. I'll show you the mine. And we'll see how fast you beg to go back to chasing cows.'' Her laughter trilled.

Jake followed her swaying skirt up the rocky trail. It was evident she still didn't trust him as fully as he wanted to be trusted. He tried not to let that matter. He'd known he'd have to win her over slowly. And once she saw that he was sticking around for the long haul, it might not be so hard for her to agree that the next logical step was marriage.

Coming to a halt behind her, Jake stared into a yawning pit of dynamited rock and wondered how on earth a man made himself indispensable to a woman capable of blowing up a hill and packing it out a piece at a time— all while she was seven months pregnant.

## CHAPTER ELEVEN

JAKE HAD DUG plenty of fence-post holes in this unrelenting ground. He knew how much muscle it took. He soon discovered that layers of blue stone Hayley sought were embedded in a tougher thicker clay she called bentonite. His hammer and chisel bounced ineffectively off the stuff five times for every bite he made into pay dirt. If he hadn't had respect for Hayley before, he sure did now. In plain speaking, mining was damned hard work for a strong man, let alone a small pregnant woman.

The two of them were wedged in a cut in the ground barely big enough to move around in. As the sun fell in its westward journey, it beat down on them without mercy.

Hayley seemed oblivious to the hardship. She chipped away steadily, pausing now and again to drink from a canteen she'd hung over a sturdy tree limb. Each time, she refilled the dog's cracked bowl, too. He whined, lapped up every drop of water and flopped down again in a narrow strip of shade that kept moving.

Jake took a long pull from his own canteen. He'd fetched it from his saddle when he'd gone after the jackhammer she hadn't been able to use, plus an extra set of mining tools she'd stored in her trailer. He'd never been inside her sleeping quarters before, so he'd spent a few minutes measuring what he was up against in trying to pry her away from here.

Her bedroom was little more than a cubbyhole. Her bed was a hard narrow mattress on a piece of solid plywood. A small clock sat on the floor beside a battery-operated radio. The cupboards above and below the bed must be where she stored her clothes, although Jake refrained from opening any doors.

The bathroom, which didn't look as if it had ever been used, was approximately the size of his mother's broom closet. Jake liked space; he found Hayley's present home claustrophobic. The tiny area that served as her living room and kitchen was uncluttered except for geological and mineral books piled behind a small rocker. The stack also included a few outdated western novels. A handknit baby blanket that Jake recognized as his mother's work and two terry-cloth infant sleepers occupied a prominent place on one of the built-ins. Other than that, no personal mementos sat among furnishings more masculine than feminine. This was probably the way Ben had left it.

Jake felt strongly that Hayley deserved to have a real home where she could hang pictures and decorate a nursery to suit her tastes.

And she deserved a soft wide comfortable bed. One where a man lay next to her every night and made her feel safe, made her feel loved. And not just any man. *Him.*

That last intimate thought had ended Jake's examination of Hayley's private space. On the way out, however, he'd tripped over a freestanding gem cutter and a barrel tumbler of the type Eden used at home and in her shop. It reminded Jake that he'd come for a hammer, chisel and spade, and made him feel less as if he'd snooped.

Now, while wedged tightly in a pit mindlessly hacking rock, he found himself thinking about Hayley's easy acceptance of hardship. He'd long since removed his shirt and was still sweating like a hog. Hayley wore a long denim jumper and seemed oblivious to the heat.

She'd sewn bags from canvas—to facilitate transporting of the rocks, she'd explained—and wore one now draped over her left shoulder. Nearly full, it hung past her knees. Jake didn't doubt that it bruised her calves.

"You ought to have something with wheels to haul this ore back to camp." he said, pausing to blot sweat from his face. "Like a wagon. The kind with wooden sides. We have one stored in the garage. I'll stop there tomorrow and bring it when I come."

"A wagon?" Hayley blinked as if drawn back from far away.

"Yes, a kid's toy. Mom saved a lot of Dillon's and my old stuff. For her grandchildren." Jake threw that out deliberately. It was time Hayley began to picture the Coopers not just in their work environments but as a family.

The rhythm of Hayley's hammer never faltered. "Thanks, but I don't want to leave any tracks to and from the mine that anyone could follow. That's why I quit using the sled you built. Well, it also put a lot of strain on my back."

"The ground at this level is too hard for a rubber-wheeled wagon to leave tracks. And below, through the trees, it's a bed of pine needles."

"The bags are fine."

"When they're full, they weigh a ton. Doesn't being pregnant already hurt your back?"

"I'm okay, Jake." Even as she said it, Hayley adjusted the canvas sack and without realizing it, stopped a moment to massage her lower back.

Jake didn't have to say a word. She followed the line

of his intent gaze, quickly yanking her hand away as she gave a short laugh. "Bring the wagon." She sighed. "I could probably carry two or three times the ore that fits in one bag. When I first sewed these, I lifted two at a time. Lately I've had to cut down to one."

"Lord, Hayley! Don't apologize as if you're shirking," he said gruffly. "Don't most pregnant women slow down before they're as far along as you are?"

"Dr. Gerrard said the majority of his patients continue normal lives throughout their pregnancy. I'll bet your mom never coddled herself."

Jake laughed. "Not having been around at the time, I'm afraid I can't say. On second thought, you're probably right. My mom's a doer."

"So am I. If you're going to stay and help me, Jake, you have to quit trying to pamper me."

"To an extent, I'll agree. While I'm on board, I want you to take regular breaks, though. I'll carry all loads of ore down the hill or wheel them once I bring the wagon."

Hayley might have argued, but the low nagging pain in her back had taken its toll. She'd awakened with it this morning, and it hadn't abated even a little. "Okay. How often are you going to be here?" she asked breathlessly. "Are you done with roundup?"

"No. For a few weeks I'm only available half days."

"It's too much, Jake. I'll pay you," she burst out. Almost at once her eyes filled with concern. She knew what miners earned an hour. Until Eden set and sold some of the polished gems, Hayley's income wouldn't cover what she needed for a hospital delivery, let alone the funds to tide her and the baby over until she could dig again next summer. How in the world could she pay Jake?

"I'm going to pretend you didn't make that ridiculous offer. Friends—" he emphasized the word "—don't pay one another for favors."

"Thank you, then." Those were perhaps the hardest three words she'd ever spoken.

"You're welcome. Now, about your breaks. It's time for the first one."

Hayley had been feeling shaky. It seemed hotter today, or was that her imagination? Without offering a single argument, she crawled out of the ditch and uncapped the canteen. She filled Charcoal's bowl and sank down beside him in the narrow band of shade, resting against the tree trunk.

Jake continued to chip away, breaking out chunks of colored stone. "I suspect you've been at this far too long today," he said. "Why don't you knock off and go back to camp where it's cooler under the pines? I'll fill both our bags and bring them down when I finish."

"I shouldn't." The way she lingered over the word said she was tempted.

"I saw a rock tumbler in the trailer. Start it, why don't you?"

"Can't. When I jumped at the chance to apprentice with Eden, I didn't think about needing electricity. I can't even watch the videos on cutting and polishing she sent with your mom."

"See? You ought to move your operation to the Triple C." He'd no more than said it when he could have bitten his tongue. Especially after recalling his dad's snide comment about moving Hayley lock, stock and barrel into their home.

"That's not necessary," she said stiffly. "Nell's going to talk to Eden. She thinks there are polishers that run off battery packs. If not, my training can wait until after I have the baby.''

"Did the doctor do an ultrasound?" Jake's question came out of the blue because he'd found himself wondering if Hayley was going to have a boy or a girl. Not that it mattered either way; he was just curious.

"No. Dr. Gerrard is a real country doctor. He doesn't do them routinely for women my age. And they don't always tell you if it's a boy or a girl, anyway. But that's okay. The prospect of learning my baby's sex after nine months of wondering may make the labor easier to handle.''

"Do you have a preference? Boy over girl or vice versa?''

"That's an odd question.''

"Why? Don't some women lean toward one or the other? Have you already picked names?''

Hayley grinned. "How about Opal if it's a girl?''

Jake shook his head. "Uh-uh. Too old-fashioned. She'd hate you when she landed in first grade with all the Ashleys, Nicoles and Caitlins.''

"Dr. Gerrard's receptionist said I can get a book of names from the library. I'll add that to my list of things to do after I leave here and go to Tombstone for the birth.''

"When's the baby due? Apparently Dillon arrived late and I showed up early. This isn't an exact science, you know.''

"The doctor said around Christmas.''

"So it could be Thanksgiving or New Year's?''

"I hope not. By New Year's Day, I'd be the size of an elephant. And I'm counting on being able to do Christmasy stuff after Thanksgiving, like trim a tree.''

Jake detected homesickness in her wistful words. He

felt badly about being the cause of her nostalgia, but she'd given him a better idea of when he'd need to have his house ready for occupation. The stab-in-the-dark date he'd thrown out to his dad for completion of the house was pretty much on target. Jake pictured cutting a tree and helping Hayley trim it. "I like real trees," he said. "How about you? You don't strike me as a person who goes for fakes."

"We never had a tree. I enjoyed the ones in the stores and Francesca's, although hers was plastic. I realize now that she probably bought the artificial tree out of concern for my grandfather's asthma."

"Who's Francesca?"

Hayley blushed and rose to her feet, concentrating on dusting off the seat of her jumper. "I never know what to call her. She and Gramps were, uh, lovers."

Jake thought about bowlegged old Ben O'Dell. Though generally clean, he rarely got a haircut and his clothes tended to be well washed and frequently patched. He'd shown virtually no interest in his appearance. Somehow, Jake would never have linked the old guy with a woman named Francesca.

"Does that shock you?" Hayley asked, looking back at him before she started down the hill.

"Shock? No. I just find it odd that Ben had two important women in his life, and all the times we sat and talked, he never mentioned either of you."

Hayley's fingers curled into her sides. "That's because prospecting was the most important thing in his life. Francesca accepted it. I was the one who always wanted more than he could give."

Jake's temper fired. "A relationship doesn't have to be that way, where one always gives and the other takes."

"Really? How should it be?" Her tone was...not sarcastic, but cynical. Unbelieving.

Damn, he'd stuck his foot in it now. Hayley nailed him with a look that said, *Go ahead, lie. Tell me life is beautiful.*

She waited, so he had to say something. Jake cleared his throat. "I can only explain my own views. All relationships have ups and downs. Ideally, more ups than downs."

Hayley snapped her fingers for Charcoal to follow her down the narrow path. "Funny," she called back. "I thought only girls believed in fairy tales."

It wasn't until Jake hit his thumb with the hammer, swore viciously, then dropped the heavy chisel on his knee, that he discovered how profoundly her defeatist attitude had affected him. Jaded as Hayley was, talking her around to accepting marriage presented a bigger hurdle than he'd first imagined.

*Patience, Jacob.* The admonition came out of nowhere. As a kid he'd never been known to have any. It was a phrase he'd heard from his grandfather and his parents as far back as he could remember. Grandpa Cooper used to say, "Hot will cool if greedy will let it." Not true, Jake thought now. At least not when it came to his desire for Hayley.

He'd prove to her that he could stick like a firefly to a screen door. Others had let her down. He planned to keep showing up until she learned to count on him. That was the answer, plain and simple. He'd outwait her.

Jake whistled a popular ballad as he filled his knapsack and then loaded Hayley's. The sun's face had disappeared behind the horizon by the time both bags were filled. The day was still far from cool. The humidity, which had risen the day of the stampede, had yet to subside. It might be a while before it did, Jake figured as he trudged toward Hayley's now-crackling campfire.

Charcoal whined a welcome and bounded out to meet Jake. After licking his hand, the dog ran back and flopped at Hayley's feet.

Reaching the lawn chair, Jake saw that Hayley had fallen asleep. A book titled *The Opal Challenge* lay open across her rounded stomach. Something that smelled like stick-to-your-ribs food bubbled in a pot hanging over the fire. Jake realized he hadn't eaten since five that morning. He'd grabbed a pancake rolled around a sausage before riding off to flush out strays, and he hadn't even gone back for coffee later because he was hoarding the time to spend with Hayley.

Jake wasn't sure he ought to wake her. She probably needed the sleep. He should saddle up and take off so he could catch a few winks himself before he had to do his part in the roundup again.

He set the bags of ore near her chair as soundlessly as possible. Looking at her, so tuckered out, Jake suffered a barrage of conflicting emotions. He was torn between leaving her to go uphold his obligations to the Triple C and skipping out on them to give her a few full days of relief.

While he debated, her eyes flew open. She sat up fast, tumbling the book into the red dust. Charcoal leapt to his feet and began a frenzied barking.

"Whoa, there." Jake caught Hayley's arm with one hand and Charcoal's collar with the other. "I didn't mean to scare you. It's late. It got too dark to see what I was digging. I left the tools in the ditch and covered them with a tarp." He jerked a thumb toward the mountain. "I'm glad you're awake," he said, dusting off her book. "I was about to saddle up."

"But...but..." Hayley stuttered. Gripping the chair arms, she heaved herself up. She made her way to the fire and stirred what was in the pot. "How long did I sleep? The stew is sticking. Give me a minute to make biscuits. I won't hear of you leaving without my feeding you first."

"Believe me, I'd rather stay." Jake meant it. "But I have the midnight shift riding circle on the herd. If I leave now, maybe I'll be able to snag an hour's sack time before I trade places with Dillon."

It dawned on Hayley, the sacrifices he was making for her. It was *why* he put himself out that worried her. Frowning, she moved the pot off the center of the heat. "Then by all means, don't let me keep you. You've done far too much already. It's silly for you to ride back and forth every day. There's simply no need, Jake."

"There *is* need," he said, removing his hat to rake his fingers through sweat-matted hair. "You have no idea how my gut churns and burns at the thought of you out here alone while I'm doing nothing but rousting the same stupid steers again. The thunder stampeded them. Regrouping set us back two weeks or more."

"All the more reason you should stay there and tend to your own affairs."

"You may not want to be my affair, Hayley," Jake said, walking up behind her and gently pulling her back against his chest, "but you are." When she stiffened, so did he. "A poor choice of words," he acknowledged, brushing light kisses over her temple. "Nothing you say will make me stay away. You may as well save your breath."

"Why, Jake?" She pushed ineffectually at his grasp. "Look at me. I'm big as a barn with another man's child. I'm virtually homeless. This mining claim is all I have that someone like you could possibly want. Well, I won't abandon it, Jacob. I won't, and that's final.''

Jake tried hard not to let her accusation wipe the hope from his heart. The hope that she'd take a second look at herself and revise her opinion. She might be technically correct in what she'd said—except the part about the mine being all she had of value. God, no. To him, her mine was irrelevant. It was *her*. And her baby.

Turning her to face him, he stood quietly until she was forced to lift her eyes. Jake did his best to pour everything he was feeling into the loving look he bestowed. He eased her toward him by inches. The minute their bellies bumped, he leaned forward and put everything left inside him into a goodbye kiss. She tasted warm and inviting and honeyed. How could she not want this forever and ever?

Maybe she did. He thought they were connecting, at least on the physical level, when her mouth softened and her tongue explored the contours of his. And when she grabbed his belt, then his waist, and hung on for dear life as her knees wobbled and banged against his legs.

Her weight, or rather the imbalance caused by the baby's weight, dragged him forward until he opened his eyes and saw they were nearly horizontal to the ground. Afraid he'd drop Hayley accidentally and hurt her, he broke the kiss and righted them swiftly. ''I promise we could have a good life together, Hayley.''

Hayley blinked at him. Her heart beat madly like an orchestra of kettledrums. It annoyed her that the shame she wanted to feel wasn't there, even though by now it couldn't be a secret that Jacob's kisses made her totally forget her scruples. There were people in Tombstone who would claim she'd done the same with Joe. It wasn't true, of course. Joe's kisses didn't compare to Jake's.

Joe had sabotaged her with promises she'd naively believed.

But she was no longer naive. At least she shouldn't be, Hayley reminded herself as Jake released her. Crossing her arms, she rubbed away the goose bumps peppering her bare skin. She willed her voice to be cool, her words methodical. "According to my booklet, during pregnancy women sometimes start to dislike kissing, touching and the like." She moved out of his reach. "I think it's obvious. A woman in this shape isn't exactly desirable. I'm sorry, Jake. I don't feel anything when you kiss me. Now, please leave and take Charcoal with you. Our goodbye tonight is final. I tried to tell you earlier. There's nothing here for you, Jake."

He scooped up his hat, which had fallen off without his knowing, and settled it far enough down his forehead to hide the firestorm of desire his eyes must surely reveal. It cost him dearly to keep his tone as flat as hers. "The pooch stays. And I'll be back tomorrow." He hoisted the heavy saddle and cinched it solidly around his horse. Hayley's back remained toward him as he cantered off. She'd delivered a nice little speech. One that might have discouraged a less-determined man. A man who could ride out of sight and put her out of his mind. That wasn't him. He saw Hayley's face every minute of every hour, whether or not she was around.

For some time after the clip-clop of Mojave's hoof-beats faded, Hayley did her best to feel bad that she'd failed to convince Jake to stay away. But some rebellious portion of her heart refused to fall in line and insisted on looking forward to seeing him tomorrow. "Where is my backbone?" she asked Charcoal as she fed him. He tilted his head, wagged his tail and whined. His empathy, if that was what his actions meant, was short-lived. He almost knocked her down diving for his bowl.

She watched him wolf his kibble and lick the bowl clean after she'd dished up her own stew and sat toying listlessly with her spoon.

She was nothing more than kibble to the whole Cooper clan. Or rather, opals to Eden. An avenue to the springwater for Jake and his dad. Nell was still a puzzle.

Hayley performed her nightly chores and went to bed, unable to get a fix on what Jake's mother wanted from her. Eventually, she guessed it would become clear. Meanwhile the analogy she'd drawn put Jake's persistence into perspective. Hayley drifted off to sleep feeling stronger and more able to rebuff his many charms.

THREE MEN RODE into her clearing the next morning while Hayley tidied her breakfast dishes. This time she didn't question Charcoal's loyalty when he edged between her and the riders, and bared his teeth. Grateful for his presence, she kept a hand on his furry head.

John Westin climbed off a long-legged palomino.

Hayley tensed when she recognized him. His last visit had been to represent the cattlemen's concerns. She supposed he'd come here now to give her dates and instructions on opening the valves for his roundup.

Westin tipped his hat before introducing his companions. "Little lady, the tall drink of water is Marshall Rogers, owner of the Rocking R ranch that sits due east of my spread. The shy dude is Tully Mack. He owns the Eagle's Nest, directly south as the crow flies." Westin laughed at his own joke.

Hayley noticed the other men seemed nervous. They

barely cracked smiles. "I'm Hayley Ryan," she said. "I don't own anything but the claim you're standing on."

Westin's laughter cooled. His ice-blue eyes honed in on Hayley's protruding stomach. "Now, me and the boys want to discuss your claim. It appears to me that your mining days are about over."

"I'll be pulling out after Thanksgiving. Expect to be back next July."

The man confronting her exchanged an unreadable look with his pals. Slapping his reins against a gloved palm, Westin took a couple of steps closer to Hayley. Charcoal checked his forward motion by nipping at his ankles.

"Ouch! Damned dog bit me! Say, is that pup kin to Jacob Cooper's cow dog? The two look enough alike to be from the same litter."

While Westin was distracted, Hayley walked over to a log and picked up Jake's deer rifle, which she'd left there earlier. She threw a shell in the chamber. "He's a guard dog, Mr. Westin. Prospectors have to be careful. Why don't you gentlemen state your business?"

"Put that down before you shoot somebody, little lady." Westin scowled, but he moved out of range.

Marshall Rogers nudged him with a foot. "Tell her our deal, John. I don't mind saying a woman with a gun makes me skittish."

Westin snatched off his hat, a high-crowned, broad-brimmed monstrosity like Hayley had seen Hoss Cartwright wear in TV reruns of "Bonanza." She wanted to laugh, which wasn't a good idea when faced with three men who had no legal right to try to pitch her any kind of a deal.

"I'll get right to the point," Westin said. "You need

money or you wouldn't be out here, alone, pregnant and scratching for nothing in this godforsaken land.''

In Hayley's opinion, he paused a little too long on the words *alone* and *pregnant*. Obviously news of her opal discovery hadn't yet reached the ears of this trio. She could make a couple of deductions from that. One, the Coopers kept their own counsel, and two, Joe and Shad weren't behind Westin's deal, whatever it was.

''Last offer I made you was fifteen grand. We're prepared to fork over eighteen right this minute. All you have to do is stop by the county recorder's office on your way out of town and rescind your current claim. We'll even help you hitch up the trailer. A woman in your condition shouldn't be lifting that heavy trailer tongue.''

''Eighteen thousand dollars?'' Hayley smiled at that.

Westin pulled out a wallet he had chained to one of his belt loops. ''Twenty-one, then. Come on, Mrs. Ryan,'' he snapped, when the increase didn't appear to move Hayley. ''Twenty-one thousand dollars is a lot of money for nothing. If you're frugal, it should get you through confinement and maybe give you time to find a sitter and a job.''

''I have a job,'' Hayley said mildly. ''Mining. And you're trespassing.'' She didn't exactly threaten them with the gun, but her hold on the rifle tightened, and she might have shifted and brought the barrel in line with John Westin's heart. If he had a heart.

Hayley would never know if her show of bravado could have dissuaded the men from turning surly because that was when Nell Cooper appeared. She bounced and jounced into the clearing in her dusty Range Rover. Westin's wallet disappeared into his pocket, and he'd mounted up by the time Nell set her brake and climbed out of her vehicle.

"Morning John, Marsh and Tully," she said cheerfully. "Guess you three are about to wind up your tallies and are heading into roundup. I suppose you stopped by to coordinate the valve-release schedule with Hayley."

Hayley wondered if she was the only one there, except for maybe Charcoal, to notice that Nell's easy banter belied her tension.

John leaned an elbow on his saddle horn. "Is that why you're here? Did Wade and the boys send you to release water? Tell 'em I said shame on them. That old valve wheel is rusty. Too tough for a lady to unscrew. Lucky for you I happened to be around to help." John started again to swing out of the saddle.

"Actually Jacob's been handling our water needs." The look she shot Hayley asked her to play along. "Wade suffered a setback. Thunder from that last storm caused a stampede. I came to tell Hayley they're running a few days behind the schedule they'd originally planned."

"They wouldn't cut into *my* water schedule, would they?" Westin danced his big palomino across the clearing until he loomed over Nell. "Tell Wade I said this parceling out the water is damn crazy." He shook a ham-size fist at Hayley. "And while you're here, Nell, convince this little lady it's dangerous to think she can turn back ranchers with that peashooter." Dragging on the reins, he wheeled the palomino around. Then he gestured to his companions and the lot of them disappeared up and over the ridge.

It was several minutes before either of the women moved or relaxed her guard. Nell did first. Walking toward Hayley, she wore a smile on her face, even though she never took her eyes off the grip Hayley maintained on the rifle. "Whew. What was that all about?"

"One-upmanship. Your husband's friends offered me cash again to clear out."

Nell gave a subtle shrug. "Unfortunately they're friends no longer. John, Marshall and, I suppose, Tully, since he was here, are undercutting the Cattlemen's Association. They want this spring so they can sell out to developers. You need to be careful of them, Hayley. Wade doesn't know what they might do to gain their objective."

"Ah, but your menfolk were prepared to have the state revoke my mining permit."

Nell's lips parted. "That was before you found opals."

"Which Eden wants. So now I'm supposed to believe the Triple C no longer cares to purchase this property? Did your cattle stop drinking water?"

"Of course not. But you agreed to give us access to the spring, the same as your grandfather did." Nell smiled easily again. "By the way, Jake rang through on the mobile unit. He asked me to deliver a wagon. It's in the back of the Range Rover. Let me open the tailgate, and I'll trade the wagon for your latest batch of ore."

"You and Jake are making all these trips to my site out of the goodness of your hearts? Neither of you expects a payback?" Hayley felt nasty saying it, but once the words were out, there was nothing she could do.

Nell wrestled the cumbersome wagon over the tailgate and set it on the ground, the friendly light extinguished from her eyes. "My son with the big heart has it in his head that you're a nice young woman who needs rescuing. Period."

"I'm not. I don't. I *am* nice," Hayley sputtered, "but

I don't need rescuing. Why would he choose me? A man like Jake must have an oceanful of women to choose from.''

Nell looked startled, then tipped back her head and laughed. ''I must remember that to tell Eden. I suppose if you're likening women to fish in the sea, I'd have to say that while many swam by, both my sons are picky fishermen.''

Hayley realized she still had a tight grip on the rifle. She pumped the shell out of the chamber and returned the gun to its place on the log. Mulling over Nell's comments, she carried the first box of ore to the pickup.

''Let me do that,'' Nell demanded. ''Honestly, Hayley, I can see why Jacob worries. If I didn't think you'd accuse me of having an ulterior motive, I'd invite you again to come stay at the ranch. Pregnancies aren't always smooth. Unpredictable things happen. When they do, you need to be within reach of a phone.''

''I'm sorry if I sounded bitchy, Nell.'' Hayley hugged the older woman. ''I don't want you to worry. After my experience with Joe Ryan, it's hard to trust anyone. I can't even trust my own judgment. I'll work on the attitude, okay?''

Nell brushed Hayley's dark hair back from her face. ''I confess that before I dragged Eden over here to meet you, my biggest concern was that you'd break Jake's heart. Now...I'm just as concerned about you and the baby.''

Tears seeped from Hayley's eyes. ''I've been as honest as I know how to be with Jake. I'm feeling well—really I am. I promise that in approximately two months I'll be out of here, and Jacob will forget all about me.''

''Hmm.'' Nell handed her handkerchief to Hayley before she loaded the remaining ore. She made no further comment, and the women waved gaily to each other as Nell drove off.

Hayley kept a bright smile on her face until she could no longer hear the crunch of Nell's tires. Nell Cooper had a good heart. Kindness and generosity were part of her makeup. But deep inside her ran an implacable need to protect her family—her son—from the Hayley Ryans of the world. Hayley felt it, and Lord only knew she accepted the strikes against her. For very soon she'd be a mother who'd go to any lengths to protect her own child. Unconsciously Hayley rubbed her stomach.

If—no—*when* Jake showed up this afternoon, she'd have to work that much harder at convincing him to stay away.

## CHAPTER TWELVE

HAYLEY'S VOW to treat Jake in such a cavalier manner that he'd stop slipping around every afternoon lasted ten minutes, tops. She wouldn't have found it so blasted hard to give him the cold shoulder if he hadn't blown in each day wearing one of his impossible-to-resist grins.

Jake had called out from the bottom of the steep grade to announce his arrival today, but Hayley already knew he was there. Charcoal, roused from doggie sleep, had lunged awake to sniff the air. His whine of recognition was pitched differently from his earlier growl.

"Good dog," Hayley praised him. She doubted if her compliment made any impression. His joyful barks drowned her out as he leapt a foot in the air to lick Jake's face. Charcoal wriggled all over and poked his nose into Jake's shirt pocket.

"Ha! Smart dog. You know I swiped some bacon from the chuck wagon." Jake dug out the treat he'd wrapped in a bandanna. Instead of wolfing it down, Charcoal closed his eyes and almost daintily savored each morsel.

That was when Hayley's indifference flew out the window. She laughed in spite of herself. "I've seen him lick his lips before, but never smack them. He must not like bacon the way I fix it."

"You probably don't burn it. Manny burns almost everything. That's how Charcoal got his name. I took him to roundup right after I got him. Manny was new then, too. The crew tore off the charred edges of their meat and tried to discreetly toss them in the fire, but the pup kept catching them in midair. At that point I hadn't named him. The wranglers called him the charcoal mooch, and the charcoal part stuck.''

''You still have the same cook? I would've thought you'd fire him.''

''Don't kid yourself. Cooks are in big demand with so many ranchers shipping beef to market at the same time. We're lucky to get anyone who wants the job.''

''I thought you staggered roundups. At least, I think that's what the men who came by this morning said.'' Hayley dislodged a blue-layered rock and reached out of the open ditch to set it in the wagon.

Jake's gaze had narrowed to a frown at her announcement. ''Mom delivered the wagon. Who came with her?''

''They weren't together.'' Hayley coughed. She hadn't intended to tell Jake. Now that she'd let it slip, she grudgingly gave him details.

''I don't like Westin's bully tactics. Why would Mom tell him we're on to his development scheme?''

''She didn't. It's okay, Jacob. The men left. Everything's fine.''

Not mollified in spite of her assurance, Jake yanked on a pair of leather gloves and climbed into the hole he'd made with the jackhammer the day before. ''I think you ought to shut down this site until next summer. Like right now. After we finish today.''

''I'll do nothing of the sort.''

''It'll be two weeks, maybe more, before I can give you full days. When Ryan and Deputy Dawg were your only threat, it was bad enough. I figured they'd have to hunt long and hard to locate you. But Westin and his cronies know where you are and they know you're alone most of the time. That makes two threats too many.''

''Oh, not three?'' Hayley grit her teeth and drove her chisel deep. Now she was back on track. It wasn't hard to spurn Jake's advances when he provided an opening like this. ''Haven't you conveniently forgotten that the Coopers tried to weasel me out of this twenty acres? Funny how everyone else is the bad guy for wanting me gone, but *your* intentions are so pure.''

Jake wanted to fly out of the shaft and refute her every word. But his family *was* guilty. And so was he. Not just guilt by association, either. All night, as he circled the restless herd, he'd hatched a plan of his own to halt her digging. Even though his motives were based on love, that wouldn't matter to Hayley. She still didn't trust him. Until he overcame that obstacle, one plan to displace her would probably sound pretty much like another.

Hayley more than half expected Jake to make excuses, or at least object to the way she'd lumped his family in with a bunch of thugs. The longer the silence drew out between them, the more she battled a cold sweat. Each time he whacked hammer to chisel, a knot in her stomach clenched tighter. Pretty soon she wanted to scream at him to deny her accusation. He had before. Why not now? She felt hot and cold. Nauseated. Sick. She crawled from the trench, wanting to blame her symptoms on her pregnancy. Hayley hated the need to give Jake the benefit of doubt.

''Break time?'' he asked, poking his head above the fissure. Though he was glad she hadn't continued her indictment, the fact that she was taking a break without his pressuring to told Jake he ought to step up the time-table for closing down her operation.

She didn't answer his question, and Jake noticed that her face was pale under a sheen of sweat. Her grip was so unstable she almost dropped her canteen.

Flinging down his tools, Jake vaulted out of the hole. "Are you ill?" He scrambled to her side. His boots slipped on loose rock, knocking two large pieces into the shaft where she'd been working.

"It's nothing." *As if she'd admit the real problem*, she thought.

"Not a breath of air gets into these troughs. How long have you been working today? Since first light, I'll bet." He planted a flat palm to her forehead, then pressed it softly against her stomach. "I'm glad Mom brought the wagon, but dammit, Hayley, you were supposed to fill it and leave it for me to truck back to camp. How many loads have you hauled down the mountain today?"

His devotion and solicitude seemed to contradict his earlier silence. Maybe he hadn't heard her question before…. Spurred by hope, Hayley smoothed a finger over the worry lines bracketing his lips.

A shudder coursed through his body. Turning his head slightly, Jake buried his mouth in her palm and planted a kiss. "Hayley, dammit, honey, you scare me to death. It's plain foolishness for you to keep at this. To stay out here alone."

She felt the reverberations all the way to her toes. From his admission and the brief touch of his tongue to her palm. It produced a string of tiny contractions—low, where the baby was forever doing somersaults. *Or it could be the baby.* Hayley quickly snatched her hand from Jake's.

His grave gray eyes assessed her. "I realize I'm

crowding you. Last night, riding back to the roundup, I promised myself I'd quit rushing you. I just did it again. I want to start over. Take things slower. Next time I swear I'll let *you* say when you're ready to be kissed." He made an exaggerated cross over his heart.

*She was ready.* Hayley hitched in a long ragged breath, which Jake misread.

He stepped back to give her some space. "No dice, huh?" he said gloomily.

Hayley grabbed her canteen. "Does starting over mean that we'll start off equal?" she ventured in a shaken voice. "You won't give me orders?"

"Promise." Jake leaned forward and urged her free hand up for a limp high-five. He felt a whole lot better, glad to be given another chance. "I'm asking, not ordering, okay? But would you like to play hooky this afternoon?" He capped her canteen and traced a finger over her dusty nose. "We could use your truck and go into town. You've never seen Eden's store or her design room where, with any luck, she's going to make you a rich woman." A dimple flashed in Jake's cheek.

Hayley shook her head, yet smiled tentatively. She thought he was kidding, but wasn't altogether positive. "I can't just quit work in the middle of the day."

"Sure you can. You're the boss, aren't you?"

She ran nervous fingers down the front of her dirty jumper. "It's impossible. I'd need to take a bath and change clothes."

Jake could tell the idea appealed. "A quick shower under the waterfall and throw on a clean dress. Meanwhile, I'll finish loading the wagon. We can be on the road in, oh, twenty minutes." He made a show of checking his watch.

"It's tempting." The frown that had settled on her

forehead began to fade. "I want to see Eden's shop. I should bank the check she gave me. I hate to leave it lying around the trailer." She paused suddenly. "We'll get back here late. Aren't you riding herd tonight?"

"Nope. Not till tomorrow night. We'll have time to take my mom and Eden to dinner. Tubac has this great Mexican restaurant. Wait...will that upset Junior?"

"I don't know. I haven't thrown up in a while." A new sparkle lit her eyes. "I shouldn't listen to you. But...oh, I want to go."

"All right. Go shower. Take Charcoal in case anyone rides in unexpectedly."

"What about him?" Her face fell. "We can't leave him here."

"He can stay to guard the place if you prefer. But he loves trips to town."

"Let's take him. I'm afraid he might tangle with the wolves if he's here by himself. I've heard some close by the last few nights."

"Probably the Mexican grays the state reintroduced along the border last year. They were released south and west of here. The drought is driving wild animals from their natural habitats to look for water. I hope you're not bathing at the spring after dark. It's not safe, Hayley. One of our vaqueros sighted jaguar tracks again."

"Still safer than during the day when two-legged animals are on the prowl."

Jake started to say something, thought better of it and offered a hand to help her up. She climbed to her feet, obviously embarrassed by her awkwardness. "Easy, easy," he cautioned. "Your center of gravity is off. You need to lean backward a little to compensate."

"I refuse to waddle like a duck, Jacob Cooper. It's bad enough that I have to get patterns from Omar the

Tentmaker for these jumpers.'' Calling to Charcoal, she marched off down the hill with her shoulders squared and her chin high.

After she'd disappeared, Jake let a small whistle escape his lips. He hadn't had a lot of experience with pregnant women. He'd heard from married friends that pregnancy was a touchy time. Hayley looked fine to him. Damned fine. But she'd probably bite his head off if he told her so.

Once he, too, had washed up and they were ensconced in her battered pickup, he decided to compliment her, anyway. The plum-colored maternity top she wore with denim pants brought out the lavender in her eyes. ''You're very pretty in that outfit, Hayley,'' Jake said lightly as he turned the key and stepped on the gas pedal.

''It makes me look as round as I am high,'' she grumbled.

''It does not. What's wrong with this damn truck? Does it always growl like it's on its last legs?''

''What do you expect? It's older than dirt.''

Jake gave up and closed his eyes. ''Great. For God's sake, Hayley. You need reliable transportation. What if you went into labor early and needed to get to the hospital fast? Not only doesn't this beast have air conditioning, it's cantankerous starting.''

Charcoal, who sat between them, barked as if in agreement.

''The baby isn't due for ten weeks. I'm going to leave here the first week of December. I'm sure the truck will last that long. Gramps drove it for years without incident. Pop it into gear and pump the foot feed. That's generally all it takes.''

Jake muttered things best not repeated. He did as she suggested, and the engine caught. Except for an occasional miss, it ran smoothly after that. They made it into town without further malfunction.

Edging forward, Hayley craned her neck around the dog to see out both side windows. "So this is Tubac? I've never been past the general store out on the highway."

"In that case I wish we had more time to explore. Anthropologists call Tubac the City of Nine Lives. It's been a lot of things. Indian village, Presidio, boomtown, ghost town, mining town and now an art community that lives its motto, Where Art and History Meet."

"It's charming. Did anyone ever tell you you'd make a good spokesman for the Chamber of Commerce?"

His laughter filled the cab. "As kids, Dillon and I pretended we were Juan Bautista de Anza, Presidio commander, and Fray Francisco Garces, the Spanish explorer who established the fort. I could impress you with my knowledge of Tubac's history, but I won't. I'll leave the hard sell to my mother and Eden."

"I'm already sold," Hayley said around a nervous laugh. "It's more a matter of being able to afford to live here. And Francesca's in Tombstone to help me with the baby."

If Jake hadn't promised to back off and give her space, this would be the time to tell her about his house, the one he wanted her to share. With Hayley, though, he was beginning to see the importance of laying solid groundwork first. So he merely pointed out Eden and Nell's combined shop, then found a place to park.

"Jacob. Hayley." Nell poked her head out from a back room as the bell over the front door tinkled. "What are you doing in town? Nothing's wrong with the baby, I hope?" She hurried to meet them.

"I'm fine," Hayley assured her. "Jake came to help

me dig, but talked me into goofing off, instead. Don't ask me how.'' Glancing at him, she smiled.

Eden appeared in the doorway Nell had just vacated. She wore goggles and held a small bright torch. "My brother-in-law is a smooth-tongued devil." She grinned wolfishly. "This time he did good. Come see the pendant I'm making. The first of your opals, Hayley. I hate to brag, but it's beautiful. Only fine opals are cut into cabochons.''

Hayley and Jake followed Eden. "I'll have a look," Hayley murmured. "However, you may as well be speaking Greek.''

"Stick with me and you'll learn gem terminology. Opal is so fragile it sometimes has to be underlaid. Depending on the number of layers, those are known as doublets or triplets. Substantially less valuable than cabochons, like the one I cut from your ore. It looks like the sky with a trace of clouds," she finished rhapsodically.

Jake slid his hand over Hayley's shoulder and squeezed. "I think Eden's trying to say your opals are top quality.''

"Thank you, Jacob, for interpreting," Eden drawled. "Why are you off playing when you should be helping my husband with roundup so he can get home faster?''

"I've been pulling my weight out there and then some. I had business in town. Carl Brown has my blueprints ready. Could you or Mom give Charcoal a bowl of water and show Hayley around while I dash over to Carl's office? And if you lose that nasty tongue, I'll take all you ladies out to dinner.''

"Nasty, is it?" Eden hissed the acetylene in the torch in his direction before she shoved up her goggles and shut off the flame. "But far be it from me to turn down a free meal. Can you get away, Nell?"

Nell's hands and arms were covered in clay. "Sounds good. The pot I'm working on is a lost cause, anyway." She folded the clay together and shut down the wheel. "Eden, give Hayley the grand tour. I need a word with Jacob. I'll walk him to the door," she said, shucking her apron.

He clutched his heart with both hands. "What did I do now? If you've lost more of your prize chickens, my fingerprints aren't on them this time."

"You really did steal those laying hens you sold me!" Hayley yelped.

Jake gave a helpless shrug as Nell marched him toward the front door. "I fessed up to Mom—and I didn't take your money," he declared firmly.

Eden and Hayley could be heard giggling. Jake noticed that his mother looked serious, however. She trailed him outside the shop before she spoke, and when she did, her voice was furtive. "Andrea Sheldon, who sells my pottery at her gift shop in Arivaca, came by today to pick up a new supply. She said two men were in town, one flashing a badge. They mentioned you by name and had a picture of a woman resembling Hayley."

Jake lost his teasing manner. "Did anyone direct them here? Damn, obviously Ryan and Tilford meant what they said. I thought they were all talk."

"Andrea said they knew she handled my pottery. She told them all roads leading out of Arivaca dead-ended on private land. Which is true. She also said she sold my work, but didn't know me personally. I thanked her for fibbing."

"Hayley won't listen to reason. I don't know what to

do, Mom. It'll be mid-November before I can hang around her mine full days. This roundup isn't going well.''

"Big as that baby's getting, Hayley shouldn't be out there digging anymore.''

"You tell her. It won't do any good. Eden told her you worked right up until the day both Dillon and I were born.''

"At home. Sitting on a stool, moving my foot up and down to turn the pot carousel, doesn't compare to crawling in and out of holes, shoveling tons of dirt.''

"Don't get huffy with me. She's not ready to accept what I'm offering. Every time I think I'm making headway, she pulls back.'' He sighed. "She's been badly burned, and she's afraid to trust another man.''

Nell reached for his arm, saw the clay caked on her hand and let her hand drop. "Jake, maybe you ought to give up. Stop knocking yourself out.''

He looked her square in the eye and put his feelings into words. "I can't, Mom. I love her.''

"I know you think you do. But are you sure that when the chips all fall, she won't go back to Ryan? It's his baby she's carrying. That's a powerful tie.''

"She's smarter than that. I'm sure of it. Hayley's like an injured rabbit. One who doesn't know who to trust or which way to run. Eventually she'll see that I'm not going to let her down.''

"Oh, Jacob. I hope you're right, son.'' Nell's troubled gaze remained on Jake's broad shoulders as he zigzagged across the street to Brown & Brown architectural offices.

He returned with a spring in his step, whistling a chipper tune. "Mom, you and Eden head on over to the restaurant and snag a table on the patio. Hayley wants to stop at the bank. We'll walk through the plaza—that way she can see some of the other shops in town.''

"Okay, but where are your house plans?" Eden asked. "Carl said you're interested in the hacienda he first designed for Dillon and me."

"You guys turned it down. It's exactly what I want. I initialed the blueprints and sent them to the builder. Art Wahl's going to break ground on Monday."

"So soon?" Both Eden and Nell gave a start. Hayley had wandered over to inspect one of Eden's display cases. If she was curious about Jake's house plans, she didn't show it. His pensive gaze tracked her every move.

Eden, who'd been unsure of the real situation up to now, let her mouth form a soundless "oh." Even then she turned to Nell for confirmation. "I'll fill you in on the way to the restaurant," her mother-in-law whispered. "Let's go, everyone!" Nell said aloud.

The four went out, leaving Charcoal behind. Nell locked up while Jake took Hayley's hand and crossed the street. He didn't let go as they sauntered past one of the art galleries and paused to look at the paintings in the window. He released her at the bank while she opened an account, but recaptured her hand as they left.

She'd relaxed by then and was laughing at something he said when he shoved open the door to the restaurant where they were meeting the others. Jake slipped an arm around her waist as they stepped aside to let a boisterous trio of young women make their way out of the building.

"Well, I declare. Jacob Cooper." A well-made-up blonde stopped and gushed his name. Her attention faltered on the woman he had tucked under his left arm. The blonde's expression changed. "Oh, look, Tina. I do believe this is the shabby little gold digger. Daddy said she plans to turn our valley into a wasteland. With Wade Cooper's help,'' she added, pouting at Jake.

Hayley tried to duck out from under Jake's arm, but he tightened his grip. "Ginalyn, apologize to Mrs. Ryan." Jake momentarily blocked the women's exit.

"Mrs.?" Ginalyn Westin cooed, her eyes firmly locked on Hayley's stomach. "Gosh, Jacob, maybe the girls and I ought to add up the months you've been out of circulation." All three women snickered.

A muscle jumped along Jake's jaw. "Spread whatever dirty rumors you'd like about me. But apologize to Hayley."

Ginalyn, who'd probably mastered the coy look at age two, ran her gaze over Hayley's home-sewn outfit. Ginalyn and her friends were wearing designer jeans and silk blouses tucked into narrow waistbands. "I'm positive I didn't misunderstand Daddy. Isn't she digging for gold out by the springs where we used to go skinny-dipping?" This time Ginalyn made no attempt to soften the derogatory twist of her lips.

Hayley finally broke free of Jake's suddenly lax grasp. Midflight she ran into Eden, who'd evidently come to see what was keeping them. Eden had only caught the tail end of the conversation, but she, who had a stature in town equal to Ginalyn's, caught Hayley's arm. "Actually," Eden exclaimed loudly enough for everyone to hear, "Gordy White told me Jake's the only guy in the old crowd Ginalyn hasn't been able to coerce into skinny-dipping with her."

Smiling sweetly, Eden faced Jake. "Nell's ordered a pitcher of iced tea. I hate to break up this reunion, but I'd like to finalize my contract with Hayley for her next shipment of ore."

Jake knew he ought to thank Eden for bailing him

out, but he felt like strangling her, instead. Ginalyn would rush right home and report to her dad; John would think Hayley had found gold on her claim. The minute they sat down at their table, Jake unloaded his fears on Eden.

"I'm sorry, Jake. Blame the devil in me. Ginalyn Westin is a bitch. Someone should have given her a taste of her own medicine long before this."

Nell shushed them. "Could you keep it down? The Triple C still has to do business with the J & B. I thought you two had more finesse." She waggled her brows toward the surrounding tables filled with interested onlookers.

"It's my fault." Clearly stricken, Hayley started to rise.

Jake stopped her. "It's not your fault. You didn't say a word. Let's order. We have a long drive ahead of us in a pickup that's iffy at best."

Hayley watched him bury his nose in a menu. Of course, he had to regret the unfortunate encounter with those women, who obviously knew him well. While it was true she'd forgotten who she was for a minute and had begun to dream of fitting in here, the exchange at the door had opened her eyes. Jake's attention came with conditions attached. His family and all the ranchers in the valley wanted the spring. Hayley supposed that eventually he'd get around to asking her in his own words; it was foolish of her to pretend otherwise. She should have put a stop to his visits from the beginning. But Lord help her, for all her big stubborn talk, she—who ought to know better—had fallen head over heels in love with Jacob Cooper.

Dinner was strained. Nell remained miffed at Jake and Eden, who'd let themselves be drawn into a catfight in the foyer of a restaurant where half the people in town could hear. Eden was irked at Jake for scolding her when she'd only come to his rescue. And Jake hated watching Hayley pull back into her shell. He cursed himself for bringing her to town and exposing her to spiteful women like Ginalyn Westin and her friends.

He'd planned to talk to Hayley about his house on the drive back to her camp. But from the minute they'd collected Charcoal, she huddled into a corner of the cab with the dog and feigned sleep. Jake didn't know how to scale this latest barrier she'd thrown up.

Her old truck sputtered for most of the trip. It up and died at the top of the incline overlooking her clearing. All Jake's efforts to restart the engine failed.

Hayley roused, rubbed her eyes and yawned. "Are we there?"

"Did Ben keep a tool kit behind the seat? The engine coughed for the last twenty miles. Now it's stopped. The carburetor may need an adjustment." He opened the door. Charcoal bounded out into the trees.

"There was a box of tools—but the truck doors don't lock. After you said transients might steal me blind, I put the toolbox inside my trailer."

"That's great! I suppose the flashlight's in the toolbox, too."

"No. In the glove compartment."

Jake reached past her to open the catch, but she admitted meekly, "The batteries are dead. I've been meaning to replace them. They're larger than the ones I bought for my radio."

Jake's temper erupted, then quickly fizzled. One look at her, sleepy, disheveled and contrite, and his heart spiraled into a free fall. He'd promised both of them he wouldn't touch her again until she issued an invitation.

But she seemed so forlorn he couldn't help himself. Cupping her chin, he lightly drew a thumb over her softly protruding lower lip and bent to steal the kiss he'd been wanting all day.

The kiss felt right to Hayley. Right enough that he didn't have to beg her to come into his arms. Nor did he steam the windows alone. She was a willing participant.

Jake went wild. He wanted to do more than kiss her. Kisses weren't enough. Had never been enough. From the noises she made in her throat and from the way she moved against him, it was evident she wanted more, too. "Hayley, honey, I've never made love to a pregnant woman," Jake murmured as he kissed her ear. "Did Gerrard cover that subject? Is it safe?" He ran his hands underneath her maternity top and choked on a groan as he realized she wasn't wearing a bra. For a minute Jake thought the shear joy of feeling her beaded nipples against his palms would make him explode prematurely. He kissed her again hard, hoping to regain control.

Hayley stirred. The little contractions she'd experienced in the midst of their last kiss had brought dampness between her legs. "The book has a chapter," she moaned, pulling away from his warmth. "I skipped it. Why would I need to know what it said?"

Jake dropped his head to her forehead and sighed. "Why indeed?" He'd hiked up her top. Unconsciously his thumbs circled and scraped her swollen nipples.

"Oh. Ohh. Jake, stop."

He did, pulling his hands away. "Sorry, you must be tender. I didn't mean to hurt you."

The cool air striking her bare breasts hurt more than the curl of heat winding tight inside her. Here she was—falling apart in Jake's arms again—dreaming of the ecstacy they might share, not in a truck, but in a real bed. She'd been ready to lead him to hers in the trailer. Would still do it, if only she could be sure he didn't have an underlying agenda.

Hayley struggled to sit up straight and breathe normally. Her top fell back into place. "Jake." She reached for his hands, needing the connection because he'd turned off the lights and the cab was pitch-black. "I deserve to know what plans you have for the spring. Not knowing is making me crazy. It's driving a wedge between us."

Jake's heart sped up. He did have a plan. One he'd fashioned last night as he idly blew his harmonica to calm the herd. How could she know? He'd told no one. Maybe Hayley was beginning to trust him.

Hayley held her breath. If there was a God and he heard her prayers, Jake would keep quiet or categorically deny giving her any reason not to trust him with her heart.

Jake combed his fingers through her hair. "I've chewed on this idea since your ex and his partner threatened to find your mine." He didn't mention what his mother had said about Joe and Shad showing up in Arivaca. Jake hated to complicate matters or add to Hayley's worries. If she agreed to his plan, her troubles with Joe would be over.

"All we have to do to get Joe off your back is go to the county recorder and switch your claim to my name. It's brilliant, really. You get the ore, but Joe loses his leverage." Jake started to add that as soon as her divorce was final, he and she could get married and there wouldn't be any further need for these machinations, but Hayley reared back and planted a fist in his left eye before he got that far.

"Ow! What was *that* for?" Jake strove to see her through the dark.

"I don't like getting the shaft."

"Shaft? What? I said the ore is all yours. This would be a transfer in name only—for your own protection."

Hayley fought with the stubborn door until it finally creaked open. Fuming, she got out and slammed it on Jake's sputters. With the Blue Cameo in his name, he'd have everything his father needed to purchase the property. Maybe he'd give her the opals and maybe he wouldn't. Did he really think that because she went weak in the knees when he kissed her it also made her weak in the head? She might have fallen for him like a nitwit, but she'd get over it. She'd once thought she loved Joe Ryan, too.

*Damn him. Damn Jake. Damn them all.*

"Oh, Charcoal," she moaned as the dog loped up and pressed against her legs. "Lead me home, boy. Then go with your master."

Jake heard Hayley talking to Charcoal. He stumbled after her through the darkness, making so much noise he couldn't hear what she'd said. Why was she so mad? She'd asked for his help, hadn't she?

He figured out pretty fast, after he reached the clearing and heard her go into the trailer and slam and lock the door, that he'd said something wrong. Dead wrong.

"Hayley. Come out here. We need to discuss this rationally."

"I'm not rational. Go away and don't come back."

"I damn well will be back. I don't want your stupid opals. Is that what you think? That I'd gyp you?"

Charcoal sat on the top wooden step leading into Hayley's trailer. He raised one paw and scratched the metal door, whining.

"Just because you're mad at me, don't take it out on the dog." Jake heard her moving around inside the trailer, but she didn't answer.

"Well, hell! Stay, boy," he said sternly, patting the wood. "I'm riding out to the herd. You guard the lady. Hanged if I know why I don't give up," Jake grumbled, now petting the dog's head. "But I swear," he said through gritted teeth, "she's going to be my wife one day and your mistress."

Though Jake hated leaving Hayley virtually stranded, he left the old truck at the top of the hill. Lacking proper light and tools, he had no other choice.

THE NEXT AFTERNOON he brought tools and tinkered with the engine until he got it running.

"It might only be temporary," he explained after he'd climbed the sidehill to continue helping Hayley dig. "That engine can't be trusted. I wish you'd wind down here."

She gave him the silent treatment.

Not only that day, but every day thereafter for the next week. She spoke only when spoken to. She was a damn stubborn woman.

But Jacob Cooper was stubborn, too.

He knew that his parents suspected Hayley was at the bottom of his surliness, and that the whole family talked behind his back. The day they'd corralled the last steer, Wade approached his son. "Dillon deserves time with his wife now. Jake, you're taking our beeves to market."

"No. I'd have to be gone too long. I can't—*won't*—leave Hayley alone. She's too far along in her pregnancy to be doing what she's doing."

"A break will do you both good," Nell advised

gently. "Go on up to Phoenix. Buy Hayley a present while you're there. Or get her something for the baby."

His face lit up for the first time in a week. "A cradle. Early on she talked about wanting a cradle. I'd hoped to build her one. I haven't had time. I'll buy one. And a really nice maternity dress. One suitable for the harvest dance."

Wade grunted and stomped off. Nell hid her concern. "I'll go see her a few times while you're gone, Jacob. I'll take her some acorn squash."

"And milk," Jake reminded her, heading to his room to pack. "She's looking so peaked. Dammit, Mom, she's got it in her head that all I want is access to the spring. I've told her I love her a hundred times. She doesn't call me a liar, but she might as well. Her eyes say it loud and clear."

"I wish I could advise you, son. Hayley's distanced herself from Eden and me, too. She's never had a family, Jake. Maybe we overwhelm her."

"I don't think it's that. But I'm telling you right now, so clue Dad in. When I get back, I'm pitching a tent at her site until she's ready to stop and go have the baby. I'll pay Dillon to do my chores and keep an eye on Art Wahl. I want that house finished in time to bring Hayley and the baby home from the hospital."

"Oh, Jacob. Seeing you like this breaks my heart. I'll talk to her. Plead with her. There'll be frost soon. Maybe by the time you get back, she'll be ready to give up. At least move her trailer to the Triple C."

"Or not," Nell whispered to the four walls after Jake left.

## CHAPTER THIRTEEN

BEEF BIDS WENT SMOOTHLY. Jake managed to shave three days off his trip; instead of a week, he'd been gone four days. Though he was eager to get home and shed the trappings required for wheeling and dealing in the stockyard, he took the time to swing by his mother's shop. She and Eden were both busy with customers. Although he was anxious to hear about Hayley and also to see her, he nevertheless cooled his heels until one of the women was free to talk.

He'd gone into the back room and helped himself to coffee, and now stood over Eden's workbench, studying her latest designs, when his mother joined him.

"Isn't that ring gorgeous? Too bad it's presold, or I'd buy it for myself. Eden's having the time of her life with Hayley's opals. I heard her tell a dealer yesterday that the fire and the passion of these stones inspires her creativity."

"I'm glad for Eden and for Hayley. How is she, Mom?"

"Still at the site and not at the Triple C, if that tells you anything. I tried, Jacob. So did Eden. Art Wahl phoned Dillon. He said it's impossible to finish your house before late January. Over the weekend Eden helped me paint Dillon's old room. We papered one wall in a nursery print. The antique store down the street had a crib and chest they'd taken on consignment. Solid ma-

ple. Fabulous condition. I hauled them home. Wade
helped me wrestle the pieces into the house. He only
grumbled a little.'' Nell smiled, then sobered. ''Hayley
cried when I told her what I'd done. But she kept saying
I shouldn't have and refused to even come back with
me to look at the room.''

Jake's expanded lungs deflated like a pierced balloon.
He pressed the heels of his palms to his forehead, shut
his eyes and massaged the deep furrows away. ''Why is
she being so stubborn if Eden's sales are taking off? I
know she was fretting about not having enough money
to take proper care of the baby until she can open the
mine again—but that shouldn't be a problem now.'' He
shook his head. ''She can't seem to trust anyone but
herself to provide for them.''

''You told her you love her. I said we'd welcome her
at the ranch. Dillon's old room is ready and waiting. I
hate to say it, honey, but the rest is up to Hayley.''

''I know.'' Jake turned bleak eyes her way. ''I'm going home to change out of this suit and give Dad the
check from the sale. Then I'm going to see her.''

''Did you find a cradle?''

''Yes. That's one less item she needs to save up for.
I bought other stuff for the baby, too. Two of everything
a kid needs in the first week of life, or so the clerk at
the store said.''

''Oh, Jake. That was sweet of you.'' Nell smiled at
her son through misty eyes. ''I wish your love was re-
ciprocated. Over the years I've watched so many local
girls toss their hearts at your feet. I never thought I'd be
sorry you hadn't caught and held on to one. Now I am.
If you'd chosen one of them, you wouldn't be going
through this heartache.''

Jake hugged her awkwardly. ''I distinctly remember

you telling me hearts go their own way—regardless of what the mind says.''

Nell slipped out of his arms and blotted her eyes with the sleeve of her blouse. ''That was when Eden chose Dillon and I knew you were dreadfully hurt.''

''I got over Eden. She and Dillon are right for each other. Hayley...'' He tried to articulate how this was different, but words failed him.

Nell's every feature conveyed sympathy.

Eden bounced into the room and stopped inside the door, darting a puzzled glance between the two. ''Oops. Sorry if I'm interrupting.''

''You're not. I'm headed home,'' Jake said briskly. ''Then on to see Hayley.''

''Tell her the customer who just left ordered an opal pendant for each of her five sisters.'' Flinging her arms aloft, she danced around the room. ''Our winter visitors are really going for the opal jewelry. Wait until I exhibit at the gem show this spring. Will you ask Hayley if she's still interested in becoming my apprentice? If not, I'll place an ad in next month's *Rock and Gem* magazine. At the rate I'm selling, I'll need to start training someone soon.''

Jake stroked his chin. ''Before Hayley has the baby? I know she wants the job, but she's facing so many big decisions all at once, I don't think she knows which way to turn. She's sort of hung up on the cost of living here, too. If it wouldn't put you in a bind, could you cut her some slack?''

''Sure.'' A puzzled look settled between her brows as Eden looked at Nell. ''What's with the cost of living? Are you going to charge her rent?''

''Hayley turned down my offer of a room. I was disappointed, to say the least. I didn't let you know because I'm still hoping Jake can change her mind.''

"Don't count on it." He heaved a sigh. "She's one stubborn lady. But if Dillon and Dad can spare me around the ranch between now and the harvest dance next weekend, maybe I can help Hayley dig enough ore to satisfy her. That's a couple of weeks earlier than she intended to shut down. As far as I'm concerned, any days she lops off would make me worry less about her health and welfare."

"You've got to admire her guts," Eden said. "She's out to here." Eden linked her fingers approximately eighteen inches away from her flat belly. "Most women would have called it quits already."

Totally in agreement, Jake turned to go. "Oh, hey," he said, poised at the door. "I take it there's been no further evidence of Hayley's ex?"

"He's still out there bumbling around." Nell combed a hand through her short curls. "Link Thompson bought a bull in Nogales on Saturday. He told Dillon there were two men in the café attempting to throw some official weight around. They mentioned Ben O'Dell and you in the same breath. Link's ears perked up. He said he didn't like the way they acted, so he kept his mouth shut."

"Nogales, huh? How long before they stop at the recorder's? Don't those dudes have jobs? How can they afford to keep searching?"

"People with vengeance on their minds make the time, Jake. I don't like them including you in this. It's not your fight," his mother reminded him. "There's plenty to keep you busy at the ranch. But I suppose any hope of getting you to stay at the Triple C is just wishful thinking."

Jake didn't even bother to reiterate his decision to

devote his days to Hayley; he knew his mother had read his intentions in his wry smile. She'd know where to find him during the hours he wasn't asleep. If he thought Hayley wouldn't pitch a royal fit, he'd roll out a sleeping bag in front of her door and spend his nights at the Blue Cameo, too. But he was positive she'd never go for that.

Jake missed the days he'd been out of the saddle. He'd have preferred to ride Mojave to Hayley's, were it not for the gifts he'd bought. This once, he'd drive his pickup over the longer bone-jarring route. After today, he'd ride his horse.

The sun was on the wane by the time he actually pulled in and parked next to Hayley's truck. Jake was surprised to see her in camp rather than up the mountain digging. She appeared to be sitting in her lawn chair, staring into the fire, one hand aimlessly stroking Charcoal.

In spite of her added bulk, she'd moved fast enough to grab the shotgun before Jake even got out of his vehicle. He recognized her gun as the weapon with which she'd first greeted him. This time, though, even his dog stayed close to Hayley and snarled.

Jake approached with his hands up and laughter in his voice. "Except for the fact that I'm not riding Mojave, this is déjà vu."

"Jake! I didn't realize it was you."

Was that relief he heard in her voice? Maybe absence *had* made her heart grow fonder.

"Your truck's hidden by mine. I didn't know who or what to expect. I suppose this is like the first day you rode in and surprised me. I was looking smack into the sun then, too. Could hardly see you."

Jake could see her well enough, though. She looked beautiful, but more tired than when he'd last seen her.

"Knocked off early, huh? Is that a case of while the cat's away the mouse, play?" he joked.

Charcoal, having identified Jake, raced around in circles, wagging his tail.

Hayley set aside the gun and raked twitchy fingers through her hair. "About an hour ago Charcoal alerted me to another visitor. One of your co-op cops. I wasn't sure if he was gone or not. I left my tools at the mine and decided to light a fire and sit a spell. I thought you might be him sneaking back."

"Co-op cops? You mean Westin?" At first Jake's gut tightened. Then he relaxed and dropped to his haunches beside the fire. "John and Marsh Rogers would be into their roundups. I imagine they needed to open the valves to release water."

"That, and to dispense advice."

"Such as?" Jake brushed dog hair off his hands.

She settled gingerly down on the chair, taking care not to meet Jake's eyes. "Nothing. His message was personal."

The light dawned on Jake. "So Ginalyn got around to complaining to her daddy about that night at the restaurant. I'm sure she bent his ear good. I hope you told him to buzz off. Dammit, Hayley, you don't have to take guff from them."

She laced her fingers across her stomach. "I'm the gate-crasher. Your Ginalyn belongs here. I understand why Mr. Westin would take up for his daughter."

"Piss on him," Jake said savagely. "John's the outsider, if you want to get technical. You were at least born in Arizona. Westin blew in a few years ago from Virginia. And we know how much he cares about this land. He's after a fast buck."

"Jake!" Hayley sounded shocked.

He sliced a hand through the air as if to say the conversation was finished as far as he was concerned. Rising smoothly, he leaned over and dropped a kiss on the tip of her nose. "I brought you some stuff from Phoenix."

She tried to keep a childish anticipation in check. Few people in her life had ever brought her gifts. She couldn't contain her curiosity and finally capitulated. "What? What did you bring? It wouldn't be milk. Not from Phoenix." She clapped her palms soundlessly, at last pressing her fingertips, prayerlike, against a quivering bottom lip. "I know, a new drill bit. You said mine is hopelessly dull."

When Jake straightened and grinned, she started to rise. "Wait," he told her. "Sit and relax. I'll bring everything to you."

"Everything? You bought more than one thing?" Sudden wariness extinguished the excitement from her eyes. "You shouldn't spend money on me, Jake."

He ho-ho'd merrily. "If I hadn't shaved, you'd call me Santa."

Hayley giggled in spite of herself. Before she could again deny his right to buy her presents, he jogged off. During their chatter, darkness had cloaked the area in and around the clearing. Both Jake and Charcoal blended with the evening shadows.

Hayley strained to see what Jake carried a few minutes later as he walked toward her again. Slowly. He'd brought something large, judging by the way he staggered under the weight. What on earth...?

"Close your eyes," he ordered, still several feet from the fire.

"Honestly, Jake. Oh, all right," she agreed when it became obvious that he intended to stay out of sight until she complied with his request. "Hurry. The suspense is killing me."

One-handed, he untied the old quilt he'd wrapped around the cradle to keep it safe from dust. The layette had needed three department-store sacks, and they'd all been stuffed into the cradle. Still in his truck, inside a box from a Phoenix maternity store, was the dress he'd bought her to wear to the harvest dance. But that could wait.

"Can I look yet?" Hayley eyed him through splayed fingers.

"Okay, now." Jake had removed the baby clothes from their bags and arranged them on the cradle mattress. He wished he'd taken time to tie on the bumper pads and put the brightly patterned sheet over the mattress. He gazed at the hodgepodge, wondering how it would look to Hayley. As if in answer, she suddenly burst into tears.

"Hayley, oh, God! You hate it. The cradle's nothing like what you wanted."

"Noooo." She kept shaking her head and wiping her cheeks. "I *love* it, Jake. In my whole entire life no one's ever given me such a wonderful surprise."

"Then why are you crying?" Jake was genuinely perplexed.

She ran a finger tentatively over the maple spindles. The cradle didn't sway.

"There's a metal pin at the foot." Jake pointed to a ring. "Slide it out and you can rock the baby. Shove it in and it remains stationary. A good feature, I thought."

She nodded, not trusting herself to speak. Hayley swallowed around the huge lump in her throat and picked up a tiny pastel undershirt. Refolding it carefully, she brushed at the front of her jumper. "I need to wash before I touch anything more. Jake, you bought too much. I'm only having one baby, you know.''

He knelt at her feet and solemnly tucked a stray curl behind her ear. "The clerk said this is barely enough to get started. Otherwise, you'll be doing laundry every day. And that's just for the baby, she said.''

She clamped her teeth over her bottom lip. "I know so little about caring for a baby. You must think I'll be a horrid mother.''

"You're going to be a great mother. Parents can't do more than put their child's welfare before their own. That's what I see you doing, Hayley.''

Without warning, Hayley flung her arms around Jake's neck. She kissed him soundly on his lips. As tears trickled down her cheeks, she peppered his face with soft damp kisses.

"Hey.'' He wobbled backward, dangerously unsteady. "We'll be in a real mess if you tumble out of that chair and flatten me.'' He laughed.

Smiling at last, she turned him loose. "Is that a nice way of saying you'd rather not have a hippopotamus land on you?''

"No way.'' Jake scowled. "Will you quit putting yourself down? The only weight you've gained is baby. I don't know where you get these notions. To me, you're perfect exactly the way you are.''

Hayley blushed. "I've never met a man as intense over little things as you are, Jacob Cooper. You don't really know me.''

"I know all I need to know.'' Rising fluidly, Jake started for his truck again. "I have another package. If you want to wash up, do it while I'm gone.''

"More gifts?'' She blinked. "Oh, Jake, no more, please. I'll be indebted to you until I'm a hundred.''

"Gifts don't come with strings, Hayley."

He'd stopped in the deeper shadows to deliver the rebuke. Hayley couldn't see his eyes, but she imagined they burned like liquid silver. She'd noticed they did that whenever he was serious, angry or trying to make a point. "All right. No strings," she agreed. "You've made me so happy I couldn't possibly pay you back properly if I tried."

Jake shifted restlessly from one foot to the other. It was on the tip of his tongue to tell again that he loved her. But it would sound too much as if he was trying to extract payback, after all. He wanted her to love him not because of the comforts he could provide, but because life itself would be bleak without him. Fearing he wanted what could never be, he retrieved the last package.

He had to wait for Hayley to return from the spring. And then she made him wait while she held up and exclaimed over each item in the layette. Disposable diapers. Shirts, sleep sacks, receiving blankets, bibs and booties. At the bottom of the stack, Hayley discovered a rattle and a plush yellow squeaky duck.

She cried again, harder. She'd been weepier than usual. But Dr. Gerrard's pamphlet warned that might be a side effect of pregnancy. Jake tugged her upright into his arms, and he held her patiently until her tears dried. "Come on," he wheedled, fanning his hands across her back. "Open the last box. This one will make you smile. Especially when I tell you how ill equipped I was to buy it. The saleslady asked me fifty questions I couldn't answer. In the end I picked it because I could picture you wearing it. So if it doesn't fit or you really hate it, you've got to promise to tell me. Eden's going to Phoenix tomorrow. She can return it and replace it with something you'd rather wear to the harvest dance."

"Jake, I told you I don't dance!" Hayley gasped. "Look at me. Do I look like someone able to dip and swing?" She stepped away, drawing his attention to her misshapen form.

"So? You can sit around and look pretty with the best of them, Hayley."

"Sure," she croaked. "Tell that to Ginalyn Westin and her fashion-plate pals. I suppose she's going to the dance," Hayley muttered.

Jake ran his hands from Hayley's elbows to her shoulders and back again without commenting.

"I thought as much." Hayley withdrew again and took a deep breath before picking up the gaily wrapped present. "The bad thing about this is that I know automatically I'm going to love whatever you bought. You can't imagine how tired I am of wearing these sacky jumpers. I sewed them up fast before I left Tombstone. I had the material and the pattern was easy. I'd make something more fashionable, but my machine needs electricity."

"Mom would let you set up your machine in one of our guest bedrooms," Jake said as she dropped into the chair again and untied the big pink bow.

Her fingers stilled. "I know, Jake. But I'm not going to impose. And I'm reasonably sure your dad would hate to have me hanging around. How would it look to the members of the Cattlemen's Association, anyway?"

"What do they have to do with who we invite to the Triple C?"

Hayley pried the lid off the box and rested one hand on the thick folds of tissue paper. "Are you kidding? I saw how upset you were when you found out that Mr. Westin tried to deal with me behind your dad's back. Don't you think that's precisely the view other association members would have if I took up residence at your house?''

''The difference is that Dad wants the spring so *all* the ranchers can share the water equally. Westin plans to stab us in the back by selling his spread—*and* the spring property—to developers. Without water rights, all the valley ranchers will go under. So you're absolutely right. I wasn't pleased about Westin dickering with you.''

''How do I know your dad's on the up-and-up? Maybe he asked you and Nell and Eden to treat me nice just to throw me off guard.''

The hiss Jake made in his throat brought Charcoal to his feet. ''What kind of person can't tell who's lying and who's telling the truth?'' Jake's stance was belligerent. Charcoal edged closer to Hayley and bared his teeth at Jake.

''Obviously not me!'' she snapped, becoming as agitated as Jake appeared. ''Otherwise I wouldn't have been so gullible as to believe Joe's big fat lies. I even believed Shad Tilford when he told me he'd bring Joe in for questioning. I know I'm a sucker. And I attract con men. So why wouldn't *you* have an ulterior motive to hang around me, too?''

Jake did more than hiss. He couldn't get the words out and practically choked as he tried. Giving up, he threw his hands in the air and stalked toward his truck. ''This is getting us nowhere. I intended to come back tomorrow and help you dig. Although I'm sorely tempted to let you sit here for a few days to realize how idiotic your off-kilter analogy sounds to a rational human being.''

It took three tries for Hayley to heave her pregnant body out of the low-slung chair. ''Ha! As if the way *you're* acting is rational.'' She crushed the partially open gift to her fast-beating heart. Seeing him continue to stride away, she said with less fervor, ''Please don't go, Jake. I *want* to trust you. If you only knew how much…'' He didn't turn, but climbed into his truck.

He drove off, and Hayley didn't understand why the fear of abandonment overtook her unpredictably and at random. It twisted her tongue and her thoughts. Only a person who'd been through such an experience could possibly sympathize. Which wasn't Jake. Just the opposite, in fact. He knew nothing of betrayal or real loss.

It was just as well she'd driven him off. He belonged with someone pretty and rich and confident. Hayley got sick every time she thought about Jake matched with someone like Ginalyn Westin, but she had to admit they were better suited than the two of them.

She could imagine the whispers Jake and Eden and Nell would have to endure if he took a pregnant guppy like her to the harvest dance. Nell herself described the event as the biggest one of the year for all the local ranchers. No, it was better to make Jake mad than have him end up the talk of the town.

Hayley's hand strayed to the dress box. She had no right to even look. But she couldn't resist. Peeling back the tissue carefully, she exposed a beautiful red dress. Made of silk crepe, it rustled when she held it up and let it drift over her lumpy body in a perfect A. The collar and cuffs of the long sleeves were pristine white satin, and there was a white satin rose at the neck. It was by far the finest dress Hayley had ever owned.

She quickly folded it back into the box, not wanting a new flow of tears to stain the material.

How could she have tears left? As she made neat piles of the baby things, placed them on the mattress and dragged the cradle and its contents into her trailer, Hayley knew she'd cry buckets of tears over losing Jake. She had missed him terribly during the four days he'd been in Phoenix. She'd never missed Joe as much. Never.

Sitting on her bed, calling herself all kinds of names for not leveling with Jake about the truth of John Westin's visit, Hayley dried her tears. Westin had said he was aware that her *husband* was trying to find her. Westin said if she didn't take his offer and turn over the mine, he'd direct Joe to the Blue Cameo.

The threat was still very much on Hayley's mind when Jake showed up lavishing her with gifts. But Joe Ryan was her albatross, not Jake's. Hayley knew that if Jake had any idea Westin had threatened her, he'd take it upon himself to shoulder her burdens—and that chilled her to the bone. Jake was too kind. Too sweet and decent a guy to ruin his life fighting with scum like Shad and Joe. If she could hold out another three weeks, Joe would legally be her ex. Then he'd no longer have any claim on property that belonged to her. Anyway, Westin might have been bluffing. Joe was probably off hitting on some other woman. He had the attention span of a gnat.

JAKE ARRIVED at the breakfast table looking like a thundercloud. When Nell and Wade greeted him, he grunted something unrecognizable.

Nell rose and removed a check from her purse. "Eden wonders if you'll give this to Hayley today when you go to help her dig. If Hayley asks why it's more than the previous amount, Eden said it's because sales have increased considerably."

"You take it to her," Jake said, staring at the check as if it might bite him. "I'm riding fence today. I talked to Dillon last night. He said we had a report of several miles down. Apparently he promised to plow Eden's garden to get it ready to replant, so that leaves me.''

"Yes,'' Nell said. "When he's finished with hers, he's going to plow mine. I can't visit Hayley today. Business at the store is booming.''

"She won't die without these funds,'' Jake said nastily. "I doubt she'll take time out from stockpiling ore to go and bank them.''

Nell dabbed her lips with a napkin. "Did Hayley refuse the cradle and layette?''

"She didn't have a choice. I left them. We didn't argue over that.''

"But you did argue?'' Surprisingly it was Wade who asked.

Jake snorted. "She thinks you're a bogeyman. Has herself convinced the Coopers will use treachery to get clear title to the spring.''

Wade looked shocked. "I've only met the woman once. I had my say and I listened to her. Yes, I want the water rights, but when you and Nell and Eden took up for Mrs. Ryan, I backed off.''

"I know. Hayley sees enemies at every turn. Do you mind if we change the subject? It'll give me an ulcer if I keep thinking about it.''

Nell curled her hand over Jake's. "I'm sorry, Jacob. I like Hayley. I prayed it would work out for you two. But some things will never be. I guess I'd better take the crib and chest I bought back to the store. I'd hate them to be a sad reminder each time you pass Dillon's old room.''

"Keep them, Mom.'' Jake rose and plucked his hat off a rack by the door. "One of these days Dillon and Eden will give you grandkids. Undoubtedly they'll ask you to baby-sit. Anyway, in a couple of months I'll be in my own house.''

''Yes.'' Her eyes remained troubled. ''A home you built for her. I know it's probably too soon for me to say this. But, Jake, the right woman is out there somewhere. Give it time. You'll find her.''

''Hayley's the right woman. The only woman, Mother. Aren't you the one who's always said that when a Cooper falls in love, it's forever?'' Stalking through the kitchen door, he tried not to slam it shut. He wasn't giving up, dammit. Oh, he'd stay away a few days. Maybe all week. Call him a glutton for punishment, but he *would* go back. He worried too much about Hayley being out there alone, working like a stevedore, with her due date so close.

By Wednesday Jake had blisters on his hands from setting posts and stringing wire. The project required another day, but he needed a break. He decided to ride over to check on Hayley from the top of the ridge, if nothing else. Before he could head in that direction, his general contractor called, asking him to take a look at the location of the kitchen and living-room fireplaces. They were back-to-back, and Wahl thought the nook on the living room side would be perfect for built-in bookshelves. If Jake approved, his men wanted to rough in the change today.

The decision didn't take five minutes after Jake had driven the ten miles out to his property. On his return to the house, he saddled Mojave, deciding he'd just go finish the fence project, after all. While Jake had been gone, his brother had unloaded a tractor to plow Nell's garden.

The two men exchanged waves. As Jake started to ride past, Dillon killed the tractor's engine. ''Are you going out to Hayley's?''

Jake tugged on his hat brim. "North pasture. Why?"

"Didn't Mom reach you? She phoned me looking for you. She didn't leave a message, but I gathered it had something to do with Hayley."

Jake's heart took a dive. Icy sweat slid down his backbone. "Do you have your cell phone on you? I'll ring Mom. Save me going back and unlocking the house."

"Sure." Dillon dug the phone out of his shirt pocket and handed it over. Jake connected with Nell on the first try.

"What's up? Dillon said you'd phoned. Regarding Hayley?"

"It may be nothing," Nell said, unable to keep the worry from her voice. "I find it hard to believe, but according to Eden, Ginalyn told friends her dad had met with Joe Ryan this morning. She indicated the men made some deal involving the spring. Like I said, it may be rumor, nothing more."

"Hellfire! Westin just might be that underhanded. I'll ride out and take a look-see. If you hear anything else— or if Ryan shows up in town—leave a message on the recorder. At this point I won't say anything to Hayley. In fact, I may look things over and not let her know I'm there. Whatever I decide, I won't stay. I'll be home in time for dinner. We'll touch base then."

"Trouble?" Dillon asked as he accepted his phone.

"Maybe. Maybe not. It concerns Hayley's ex. He's a jackass. A jackass with an ax to grind. They're the most dangerous kind."

Dillon stared silently as Jake wheeled his horse around. "Take care, little brother. If you're not back by suppertime, shall we send the dog with the brandy?"

Jake laughed at that. "Hayley already has Charcoal," he said. "So you can go ahead and drink the brandy."

He wasn't one to ride a horse into a lather. But something had a grip on Jake's spine and it wouldn't let go. He rode hard and fast. Where he'd planned to nose around quietly, the sight of a dirt-spattered Jeep parked up against Hayley's pickup changed everything. Jabbing his heels into Mojave's flanks, Jake galloped down the incline like a madman.

It was a good thing, too. Joe Ryan and Shad Tilford were shoving Hayley back and forth between them. Her face was ghost-white, except for a trickle of bright red blood running from one edge of her upper lip.

Charcoal barked and ran in frenzied circles. Shad kept trying to kick him.

The two men evidently heard Mojave's hoofbeats. Both turned. Jake could see Tilford's shiny badge. Too damn bad. That badge bought him nothing in this territory. Not one damned thing.

Jake rode past the trio, sprang from his saddle and scooped up Hayley's gun, which leaned against the log where she kept it. "Touch her again and I'll fill both of you full of lead." At the time Jake fully intended to follow through. His face must have reflected his intentions.

"Jake, no!" Hayley's voice caught in a sob as Joe backhanded her hard and sent her flying across the rough ground. She landed against a jagged boulder. Though her face twisted into a mask of pain, she threw a protective arm over her swollen stomach, and the other she flung out to block Jake. "Don't shoot them, Jake. They aren't worth spending your life in jail." He voice caught in an agony of shuddering breaths.

Jake didn't agree. However, the truth was, he could never kill anyone. He wasn't the one on the ranch who dealt with putting down horses who'd broken their legs or cows mired in sandy bogs. He knew that. These bastards didn't.

Pumping shells into the double chambers, he laid a row of shot so close to Ryan's boots the man danced back and back until he smacked into Shad.

"I'll have your ass in jail for attempted assault so fast you won't know what hit you," the deputy screamed.

"The authorities will have to find your bodies first," Jake snarled back. "You're forgetting this is my territory. And it's awfully remote. I can dump your remains in Mexico." He slammed the butt of his rifle into Ryan's soft gut. "Who'd be the wiser?"

Something like fear entered the men's eyes. Turning, they ran as fast as they could toward the Jeep. Jake sailed another smattering of lead past their ears. Bounding after them, Charcoal tore at their pant legs, growling ferociously.

From the safety of the Jeep, Ryan and Tilford shouted obscenities at Jake and his dog. They made a series of dire threats that he countered with a single one of his own. "You're dead if I ever see you near Hayley again."

Tilford, the driver, laid rubber out of the clearing and left a rooster tail of red dust behind. Not before Joe threatened to sue Jake for attempted murder and Hayley for the mine. One hundred percent of it.

Trusting they'd gone and wouldn't risk returning without backup, Jake rushed to Hayley's side and dropped to his knees. His heart slammed erratically.

She was curled into a ball and made terrible sounds. It scared the hell out of him. Especially as the lower part of her jumper and one of her boots was wet.

"Jacob, my water broke," she sobbed, tears mixing with the dust on her face. "It's too early. More'n a month too early. Oh, God, my baby. I'm going to lose my baby.'' Her fingers clawed at Jake's shirt.

"Hold on, honey. Let me start your truck. Then I'll come and carry you up the hill. We'll get you to a hospital.'' His hands shook so hard Jake had difficulty grabbing the key off the hook inside her trailer. Charcoal barked sharply and punctuated it with howls, as if to hurry him along.

The ignition clicked once, then twice. Not a shred of a spark reached the engine. Swearing, Jake tried it six times and almost lost his lunch when each attempt failed. Her battery was dead as a doornail.

Racing back to Hayley, he lifted her gently into his arms and tried to put on a confident face. "Dead battery,'' he informed her. "I'm taking you to the trailer.''

"Jake, no! I need a doctor. This baby is coming.''

"Listen, woman,'' he growled softly. "I've delivered hundreds of cows and a few horses. Hell, I delivered Charcoal. There's nothing going to happen to you or your baby. Not while I'm around.''

His speech seemed to calm her. It did nothing to settle the tennis tournament going on inside his own stomach. Nor did it help that the inside of the trailer was hot as an oven. And Jake had zero room to manipulate in the cubbyhole she called a bedroom. He ended up placing her in a chair while he dragged her mattress out into the living space, where it was only marginally cooler. It was eighty outside, but it felt like a hundred in the closed-up trailer.

Hayley was too shaky to remove the wet jumper by herself. Jake helped her, then gave her privacy to don a soft cotton nightgown. He really hoped that when she lay down, the contractions would stop.

They didn't.

He timed them and noted they were ten minutes apart. Then eight. As they continued, it became obvious that he was indeed going to have to deliver the baby. At her request, he placed a makeshift waterproof pad underneath her, then began gathering supplies. A basin for water. A pair of scissors. Towels.

All the while he prayed, and prayed hard, for the skill he'd need.

# CHAPTER FOURTEEN

AFTER SEEING to Hayley's comfort, Jake took a quick turn around camp. Mostly to satisfy himself that Joe and Shad hadn't parked somewhere and sneaked back. Jake carefully dusted away any wagon prints leading to Hayley's mine. Then he collected his rifle and Hayley's shotgun, stationed Charcoal by the trailer door, and inside the cramped trailer again, he closed and locked the door.

Hayley watched his deliberate actions. "You think they'll come back?" she asked.

"I never should have left you alone," he said tightly. "I knew they hadn't given up. Last I heard, they were hanging around Nogales. God, Hayley." Jake slid to his knees and clasped her hands. "What if I'd gone off to mend fence and hadn't come here?"

"You're not to blame, Jacob."

"I sure as hell am." He stared down at her in anguish, not looking for absolution. "If I'd been more vigilant, you wouldn't be lying here in early labor."

Hayley moved restlessly on the mattress. "No, Jake. The day Westin and his friend stopped by, he said if I refused to leave the property, he'd tell Joe where I was."

"Why in hell didn't you tell me that? I'd have stayed with you. I wouldn't have gone off in a huff."

"If I can't take care of myself, how can I care for a child?" Even as she finished saying the words, a contraction left her breathless and moaning in pain.

Jake turned her and massaged her lower back until her muscles stopped their siege of spasms.

"Better?" He took note of the time between this spell and the last. He felt self-conscious about asking to check Hayley's progress, yet the contractions had been six minutes apart for an hour. Jake worried that something might be wrong. If she lost this baby because he was too squeamish to do the job, he'd never forgive himself.

He avoided looking squarely into her pain-clouded eyes as he smoothed back strands of sweaty hair and brought one of her clenched fists to his lips. "I need to check to see how far dilated you are, sweetheart. Can you let me do that?"

"Check? You mean, like a doctor would?"

Jake saw that her cheeks had gone from white to pink to a blaze of red. "I, ah, don't know any other way to measure your progress," he stammered.

"Jake, I wasn't thinking straight when you offered to deliver my baby. I can't let you…well, I mean, I won't embarrass you like that. Leave me. Ride to the ranch and get a vehicle to drive me to the hospital. I'm sure I can last that long."

"Hayley, I love you. What kind of man would I be if I left you to deal with this alone?" Jake collected both her hands, and this time he met her panicked expression with a warm assured smile.

Another contraction struck. Hayley was swept away by the pain, and as a result was saved from having to respond to Jake's declaration. One he'd made before, but she'd steadfastly refused to give it credence.

Nor did she really believe him now. Quite frankly, she hurt too much to think about anything beyond the pain. The booklet Dr. Gerrard's receptionist had given her said that when the time came to deliver, she should pant like a puppy and ride through the wave of contractions. She tried. Amazingly it did help. When the latest paroxysm loosened its grip, Hayley was too tired to argue with Jake. "If you insist on staying," she muttered weakly, "I won't argue. I'm scared to death of having my baby early."

Jake wiped her face with a cool washcloth he'd prepared. "You're what? Just over four weeks early?"

She nodded, catching his hand and squeezing it in fear.

"Is there any possibility the doctor could've been off in figuring the date?"

"I didn't know I was pregnant. I thought I had the flu. Dr. Gerrard set the date after his exam. I think he's right. Joe...well, he'd found someone else. The doctor's prediction works out to the last time Joe joined me in bed. Not that he did *that* very often."

Jake brushed her cheek with the back of one hand. "Don't you act guilty. Joe was the fool."

Hayley smiled. "You do know how to make a lady feel better. Do whatever needs doing, Jake. I'll try not to be prudish."

He checked her as discreetly as possible and saw she probably still had a few hours to go at the present rate. "All systems are go," he said lightly, pulling her gown down over her knees. "I remember hearing a friend who had a new baby say her doctor sped up the process by having her walk the hospital halls."

Hayley rolled her head from side to side. She could easily see from one end of the trailer to the other. "I might manage walking in circles." Pursing her lips, she levered herself up on an elbow.

Jake helped her to her feet and steadied her when she

bent double and clutched her abdomen. "Another contraction?" he asked, glancing at his watch.

"No." She blushed. "Standing feels funny. It's ridiculous, I know, but I'm sort of afraid the baby will fall out on its head." Deliberately standing erect, Hayley moved away from Jake's support. Her grimace confirmed what the effort cost her.

"Birth is an awesome process," he murmured. "In all honesty, though, I'm glad God gave the chore to women. Cross my heart, I won't make fun of a single thing you say or do. If you want to scream or cuss at me, go right ahead."

"I hope I can be more reserved. Now that I'm up and about, shall we get the cradle ready? If you hand me the mattress and a sheet, I'll fix it while you tie on the bumper pads. Please? It'll take my mind off what's happening."

Jake jumped at the chance to do something worthwhile to help pass the time. "Pick out what you'd like the baby to wear. I'll find a place to store the rest of this stuff."

"Good luck. There's not an empty drawer in the place. I had to leave everything in the cradle." She shuffled across the room toward him.

"I'll put everything back in the sacks, at least."

"When I first looked at these, they seemed so tiny. If my baby is premature, he or she may swim in these." She held aloft a nightgown with bears on it and started to cry. "Darn." She hiccuped, swiping at the tears. "I hate crying and that's all I've done lately. It doesn't do any good. Why can't I just accept that I've botched my life again?"

"You didn't botch anything. It's just the changing hormones." Jake gave up trying to keep his hands to himself. He slipped his arms around her and swayed to and fro until the rough hitches in her breathing began to subside.

"Oh, Jake," she said quietly, twisting the wet sections of his shirtfront in her hands. "This is above and beyond the limits of friendship."

"Yes, it is," he agreed dryly, taking care to cradle her face against the hollow of his shoulder. "But it's easily within the bonds of love." He let the simple statement stand. He was through tiptoeing around her silly objections. If ever he hoped to convince Hayley how much he cared for her, he had a ready-made situation at hand. If he hadn't gotten through to her by the time the birth was said and done, he probably never would.

Hayley fell silent and hobbled through several more contractions, letting Jake assemble the cradle alone. When her pains became harder and closer together, he helped her lie down. Pulling a harmonica out of his pocket, he began to blow softly.

"I never knew you played harmonica," she said, pillowing her head in the crook of her arm.

Taking it from his lips, Jake grinned at her. "Some of our hands play guitar when we're circling a big herd. I couldn't seem to get my fingers on the right strings. Any idiot can blow a harmonica."

Smiling, Hayley tugged on the hem of his jeans. "You're too modest, Jake. Play me a lullaby and calm this baby down." She rubbed her taut stomach.

He leaned forward on the straight-backed chair. "Calming isn't the object, Hayley. Now that the little rascal's started, we want a swift appearance."

"Speak for yourself. I'm not ready." Tears welled in her eyes again. "I thought I was so smart setting a timetable for everything. I shouldn't have argued with Joe this afternoon when he demanded I sign over half the mine. In retrospect it would've been the smart thing to have done. I honestly never dreamed he'd hit me.''

"He'd better never lay a hand on you again." Jake scowled fiercely.

"I'm sorry for involving you, Jake. I heard Shad say you'd be sorry for interfering, that the local sheriff would back Joe's claim."

"Our local sheriff should have retired years ago. He's up for reelection next month, but he's going to lose. It's the case of another jerk like Tilford throwing his weight around. He can't hurt you."

"I wish I was as certain. Whoever thought Joe could forge my name to my grandfather's papers and get away with it? He did it slick as you please. Oh, oh, oh!'' she cried, curling into a tight fetal position.

Jake tossed his harmonica aside and went down on his knees beside Hayley. He gripped her hand tightly as she gasped and panted like a puppy.

"A rough one?'' he whispered consolingly, again sponging her feverish cheeks with the cool cloth.

She barely had time to straighten out before the next hard pain hit. By the third one, Hayley uttered some words she'd never used in her life. Gritting her teeth, she swore like a miner and ordered Jake to leave. "No, don't you dare go,'' she proclaimed in the next breath, grabbing for his hand.

"Easy, easy, honey." Jake smoothed the fingers she'd clamped around his wrist. "Wild horses couldn't drag me away. Here, hug this pillow. Don't let go, no matter what. I think Junior is about ready to put in his appearance.''

"Oh, help!'' she cried in increasingly jerkier sounds.

"Names. I haven't thought of names. Jake, I need to push. Oh, Lord, what shall I do?"

Jake had hurriedly washed his hands in the basin and moved to the foot of the mattress to rearrange her nightgown and allow him room to work. He smiled at her. "Our kidlet has crowned, so push away. Whatever you're having, Hayley, boy or girl, this kid has a mop of black hair."

The next rolling cramp brought out the full head and shoulders. A heartbeat later, the baby was born.

"We have a girl!" Jake proclaimed excitedly, holding a wizened red-faced infant, who waved skinny arms and wailed feebly. There were tears in Jake's eyes as he cut the cord, tied it off in an economy of motion. Lifting the baby from Hayley's stomach, he wrapped her in a thin blanket and placed her in her mom's shaking arms.

Outside, Charcoal howled a long mournful howl, as if announcing the new arrival to the outside world.

"Uh-oh, is she all right? Jacob, she's so tiny. And homely." Hayley burst into tears even as she rained kisses over her baby's furrowed brow.

Jake, busy with matters that came after the birth, stopped and moved in closer. He cradled mother and child tenderly. "She's beautiful," he said, his voice husky with emotion. "When she gets a little food in her tummy, she'll start to fill out and she'll be as beautiful as her mother." Jake touched Hayley's face reverently.

Through a curtain of tears, she gazed first at Jake, then at her new daughter. "I've waited so long," she sobbed. "I was afraid Joe had hurt her. Oh, she's gorgeous. Simply gorgeous." Hayley smoothed fingertips over the red wrinkled cheeks and wiped away the tears that had fallen on a matted shock of dark hair.

Jake curved a palm tenderly around the baby's perfect

skull. "Prettier by far than the calves I've delivered. And Charcoal…well, he was runt of the litter. This little miss will clean up just fine. Speaking of which, I'll do that as soon as I make sure Mom is A-OK. Why don't you count her fingers and toes?" he suggested, wanting to make Hayley less self-conscious about the final phase of the birthing process.

His method of distraction worked.

"Look how long her fingers are," Hayley said when Jake came to take the bundle away for a wash in the warm bath he'd prepared. "Maybe she'll play the piano. I always wanted to learn," she added softly.

Jake responded to her wistful tone. "Why didn't you? Don't they have piano teachers in Tombstone?"

"Yes. But music wasn't high on Gramps's list. To him, even radios and TVs were frivolous."

"Well, then, you and the little miss here will have to take lessons together." He opened a clean towel and stood where Hayley could watch him dry the baby.

She shifted awkwardly and curled one arm under her head. "You handle her so easily, Jake. Aren't you afraid of dropping her?"

He grinned. "I've had a lot of practice throwing and branding calves."

"Branding. That's like naming, in a way." Hayley yawned and struggled to partially sit. "What do you think of naming her Cameo, after the mine? With a middle name of Joy because…well, having her is a joyous occasion, and I feel so wonderfully incredibly happy."

"Listen to your mom," he said, crooning to the baby as he patted her dry and put a diaper on her before tucking her into a cheery yellow night sack. "Your mother certainly wasn't saying such nice things half an hour ago, as I recall," he teased.

Hayley made a face. "So much for not poking fun at me. You promised."

"That's right, I did. Okay, no more jokes. As for the name, Cammy's a lot more appealing than Opal." He handed Hayley the baby and then arranged several pillows behind her back. Already it seemed the redness was fading from the infant's tiny cheeks.

Sitting cross-legged beside Hayley, Jake curled the baby's thick damp hair over his forefinger in one long sausage curl.

Hayley touched it and smiled. "You did that like a pro. Are you sure you don't have a wife and six kids stashed away at the Triple C?"

Jake gazed at her so seriously Hayley wished she hadn't given in to the urge to tease him. Especially after he said, "You've had plenty of offers to see the ranch and everything there, Hayley. You can take the grand tour anytime."

To cover her uneasiness at this turn of the conversation, Hayley focused on the baby, who'd begun to root around the front of her nightgown. "Cammy acts hungry. Could she be this soon?"

"It's hard work being born. Uses up a lot of calories. You need to try her at the breast. Get her into the habit of sucking. She's not likely to get much at first. I boiled water and it's cooling in a bottle in case she's too fussy."

Hayley pulled uncomfortably at her gown. "Obviously I wasn't thinking about breastfeeding when I bought this." A hot blush colored her cheeks.

Jake knew she was back to feeling ill at ease around him. Which he thought was silly. What could be more intimate than assisting someone you loved through childbirth? But he didn't want her to feel awkward. "I have a clean shirt or two out in my saddlebags," he offered. "I carry them in case I unexpectedly have to spend the night at one of our line shacks. My shirt will hang to your knees, but it buttons down the front."

"Thank you. That's thoughtful, Jake."

He didn't like her stiff tone of voice. Or maybe he just felt like an outsider, watching her gaze at Cammy with her heart in her eyes. He remembered that his married pals sometimes complained of feeling shut out from the mother-infant bond. And they were attached to their offspring in ways he wasn't attached to Cameo. Rather than risk sounding jealous, Jake went out to get the shirt.

Charcoal greeted him with a miffed expression and an uncomprehending whine. "Ah, you're a lot like me, old boy. Except you were truly exiled. Still…Hayley lets you sleep in her house. Hell, in her bed. I've only had that privilege in my dreams."

Returning with the shirt, Jake left the dog outside again. "While you change," he told Hayley, "I'll feed Charcoal. After that, I'll rustle us up some food. It's getting late. Past suppertime."

He took the mewling baby from Hayley's arms and placed her in the cradle. "Do you need help?" he asked her. Frowning, Jake watched Hayley gingerly pull herself upright with the aid of a chair.

"You've done more than enough already. Pioneer women didn't have men waiting on them hand and foot. Thank you for—for everything. You probably want to get on home. Don't worry about me. I'll mail your shirt back from Tombstone. I'll loaf around here a couple of days and then hitch up the trailer and leave. I want Dr. Gerrard to check Cammy as soon as possible."

Jake's frown grew darker. "Apparently you didn't hear me say your truck has a dead battery. That's why you didn't deliver Cameo in the nearest hospital. And I don't give a good goddamn what pioneer men did—I'm not letting you fend for yourself. Got that?''

Her shoulders slumped as the baby started to wail. Darn it all, she was trying to show responsibility for her life and that of her baby. But her legs were shaking and she was more tired than she'd ever been. She really didn't want Jake to go off and leave her alone. After struggling to get up off the mattress, she sank to her knees and bawled in a very unladylike manner.

Jake didn't know whether to try to comfort her or not. Eventually his need to hold her won out over having her possibly bite his head off. He gathered her fully onto his lap and rocked her in a chair that wasn't a rocker.

''I'm tired,'' she mumbled into his neck. ''I didn't even dig today, yet every muscle in my body aches. And…and the slightest decision seems overwhelming.''

Jake resisted reminding her that a short time ago she'd said she felt incredibly happy. ''Shh,'' he whispered, instead. ''Why do you think they refer to giving birth as labor? It's hard work. I know you want to be in command of your life, honey. You will be again in a few days. Please, let me help you through this rough patch.''

''All right.'' She snuggled closer before drying her eyes. It felt good to be held. Her grandfather had never been much for dispensing hugs. Nor had Joe. But touching came easily to Jake.

''I'm okay now.'' Hayley eased off his lap. ''Feed Charcoal while I change. When he's finished eating, why don't you bring him inside? I've liked having a pet. If I can swing getting an apartment where they allow pets, I'd like to have a dog.'' Hayley made a stab at smiling.

Jake didn't have to be asked twice to go. It bothered him the way she talked about living on her own. Was he a fool to keep beating his head against a stone wall? If he hadn't witnessed moments where Hayley lowered her guard and showed him a vulnerable side, he'd give up. But he'd seen her melt into his arms almost as often as she'd shoved him away. Somehow she had to figure out that he was nothing like the men she'd known, that he wouldn't turn on her or let her down. To convince her, he had to find a way to keep her from going back to Tombstone.

Cammy was wailing by the time he returned to the trailer carrying a steaming pot of beef barley soup. "Hey, hey, what's the trouble?" He set the pot on the tiny stove and hurried to Hayley's side.

"The baby acts hungry, but she just cries, instead of trying to nurse. Maybe I don't have what it takes to do this. Where did you put the bottle of water?"

"Nursing is better for her," Jake declared. "Maybe you're too tense."

"I am not," Hayley declared. She'd barely said it than both she and Jake recognized the fallacy of her words. Their shared laughter vented the pressure that had built between them. And Cammy finally latched on to Hayley's nipple.

"Ohh." Hayley dragged out the sound. She gazed down in wonder at the tugging rosebud mouth. Lightly she ran a finger over the baby's soft cheek.

Jake was blinded by the love that sprang instantly into Hayley's eyes. This was the woman who'd said in so many ways that she was incapable of love. Now he had proof it wasn't true. The moment bolstered his spirits and renewed his patience. His goal was to be a husband and a daddy-by-choice. Someday—and he hoped it was soon—Hayley Ryan would become Hayley Cooper. She'd gaze lovingly not only at Cammy but at him.

Cammy fell asleep suckling. Jake hated to disturb them, but Hayley needed nourishment. Her eyes had begun to droop. ''I'll put the baby in the cradle and bring you a bowl of soup,'' he said. ''Then you ought to nap for a while. From what the new parents of my acquaintance say, the adults need to grab some sleep when the baby naps.''

''How will I ever get anything done?''

Jake smiled. ''It won't be that way forever. I doubt you'll feel like dashing out to dig opals in the next few weeks.''

She stared into the bowl of soup Jake had placed in her hands as if it were a crystal ball that held all the answers. ''You're right. How will I accomplish the things on my list, Jacob? I can't drag Cammy around while I hunt for housing. Even if I find a furnished apartment I can afford, I'll need to stock it with groceries. Go ahead, say I didn't plan very well. I should have closed down earlier like you said.''

Jake curved the fingers of her right hand around a spoon. He checked on the baby and let Charcoal in before he sat down to his own soup. ''Eat, Hayley. There's nothing you can do tonight. Unless I miss my guess, by tomorrow part of your problem will be solved. Mom will come roaring in here to see why I didn't come home. She'll go all crazy over Cammy, like all women do with babies. Unless I don't know her as well as I think, you and the baby will be installed at the Triple C before you can say Winnie the Pooh. That's how she and Eden decorated the nursery, you know?''

Hayley stopped with the spoon halfway to her mouth. ''Jacob, I can't impose on your parents like that. It's out of the question. I already explained to Nell.''

''Okay, so you explained. I know Eden has another

check for you. That should make you feel better. Now, eat,'' he said again, feeling sorry about her distress. He and his dad and brother had been bulldozed by his mother's decisions more times than he could count. Even Eden had succumbed. That was how she and Nell had ended up sharing a work space. However, his mom's intentions had been good—they normally were—and she'd been hurt when Hayley refused to so much as look at the room. Jake didn't want to take sides. But he would if his family tried in any way to strong-arm Hayley.

After they ate and he washed the dishes, he moved the mattress back into the cubbyhole. Charcoal, who couldn't seem to understand the changes, sniffed the cradle once, then flopped down under it. After Jake helped Hayley into bed, Charcoal hopped onto the foot, and dog and woman slept.

Jake was reluctant to awaken either of them when an hour later he heard the crunch of approaching tires. The night was so dark he couldn't see a vehicle out of the small trailer windows.

''Hayley.'' Jake tiptoed up to her and shook her gently. ''We've got company. In case Joe and Shad have come back with the sheriff, I need you awake enough to stand watch over Cammy. If it's me they're after, I'll go peacefully. But only if they swear to leave you alone and let me notify my folks to look after you and the baby.''

Too sleepy to comprehend all he'd said, Hayley crawled out of bed. ''Someone's coming? Why isn't Charcoal barking? He's always warned me before.'' She stared in confusion at the collie, who'd blinked awake in a massive yawn.

''Beats me. Maybe it's because I'm here. At any rate,

I'm leaving him inside as protection for you and the baby.''

Hayley bit her bottom lip. "Stay, Jacob. I'm scared. Make them come to the door.'' Though Hayley moved slowly, she managed to insert herself between Jake and the door.

He was torn between doing as she asked or keeping danger as far from her and Cammy as was humanly possible.

He'd let the time for decision pass. The vehicle had apparently been closer to the clearing than he'd judged. The next thing Jake knew, there was a series of loud raps on the door.

Startled, Cammy awoke with a scream that became a long high-pitched wail. "See to her and stay out of sight,'' hissed Jake, motioning Hayley away from the door. He picked up the shotgun and quickly checked to see that it was loaded.

Charcoal padded to the door, sniffed along the threshold and whimpered. Jake had no ready answer for his pet's unusual behavior. Not until he threw open the door and thrust the muzzle of the gun into his father's ashen face. Wade jumped backward off the makeshift step and landed on his wife's foot.

Nell cried, "Watch what you're doing, Wade. Jacob? Why in heaven's name are you pointing a gun at your father?'' In the next breath she covered her mouth with both hands. "Oh, dear. Tell me that's not a baby crying.'' Tears glistened in her eyes.

He ejected unspent shells from the shotgun. "Yes, it's a baby. Now suppose you tell me why in hell you two are creeping around Hayley's place in the dead of night.''

"Ask your mother,'' Wade growled. "She came unglued when you missed supper. As if you weren't full-grown and never missed a meal before. She was hell-bent on driving out here. Would've come alone if I hadn't pulled my boots back on and driven her.''

Nell shoved past Wade while he was still explaining. She zeroed in on the crying baby. "How precious! Hayley, she's an absolute doll. But she's early. Oh, I knew something was wrong. See, Wade? I had a premonition, didn't I?"

Jake's father stepped inside, filling the doorway with his stocky frame. He was a big imposing man, but looked less so when he snatched off his hat and gazed at his wife, pure adoration darkening his eyes. "I learned to listen to your mother's hunches, son. Nine times out of ten she's right on the money."

"Ten out of ten," Nell chided, rubbing her hands to warm them before she scooped the tiny squalling bundle from Hayley's arms.

Jake had never heard his mother talk baby talk. He found it humorous. Yet something indefinable clogged his throat and impeded his breathing when his dad got into the act. Wade Cooper tickled the baby's tummy with a big work-roughened forefinger and did his own version of cootshy-coos.

Jake could tell that Hayley didn't know what to make of them. She'd never had a family.

Afraid she'd tear Cammy away from his parents, Jake shut the door, then casually slipped his arms around Hayley.

"Cammy's only a few hours old," he informed his folks. In low tones he followed that news with a condensed account of the scene when he'd ridden in. He mentioned the failure of Hayley's pickup to start and ended by saying the baby had decided to put in an early appearance.

"That horrid man hit you?" Nell glanced up at Hayley with fire in her eyes. She touched the purplish bruise marring Hayley's cheek and chin. "He ought to be jailed for assault. Wade, you and Dillon take care of that right after we get Hayley and this little sugar pie settled at home. Jacob, you and Dillon can come back tomorrow with whatever parts you need to fix Hayley's pickup. We'll store it and her trailer in one of the vacant barns until she needs it again."

Jake watched the play of emotions across Hayley's face. "Mom," he said earnestly, "Dad and I are used to you arranging our lives. Hayley calls the shots when it comes to Cameo Joy."

"Cameo?" Nell beamed at Hayley. "You named her after the mine. It's perfect. And she's beautiful. But she *is* premature, and the nights are beginning to get colder. Wouldn't you rather have her in a heated room? Oh, and there's a retired pediatrician who bought a small farm east of the Triple C. We'll ask him and his wife by for coffee tomorrow. I'm sure he'll be happy to give this sweet child a quick exam."

Jake sensed the minute Hayley lost the battle to his mother. "It's all right," he whispered close to her ear. "Her heart is as big as the whole outdoors. Cammy couldn't be in better hands."

"I know. And I'm too tired to make a fuss. Not only that, she's right—it is getting colder at night." As if to punctuate her words, she shivered. Hesitantly she said, "Thank you. I guess it won't hurt to spend a day or two at the ranch."

Hayley had no sooner agreed than Nell began to bark orders. She rebundled the baby to travel. Jake did the same with Hayley and carried her to the Range Rover. Wade collected the cradle and the layette Jake had purchased. Spotting the blanket she'd knitted, Nell covered Cammy with it before dashing to the vehicle.

In less time than it had taken Jake to fix their evening soup, he'd saddled Mojave and was trailing behind the precious cargo being transported at a crawl over the bumpy unpaved path. Smiling, Jake wondered how many times his mother cautioned his dad to drive more slowly. Wade Cooper wasn't one to go easy on the gas—except that he'd do anything his wife asked.

Once they'd reached the house, Jake hovered while Nell settled Hayley and the baby in their rooms. Instead of placing Cammy in the nursery, Nell directed Jake to set the cradle next to the bed, where Hayley now lay wearing one of Nell's frilly silk nightgowns.

"The warm shower felt like heaven," Hayley murmured, her eyes drifting closed. "Funny, but I hardly missed the convenience before."

Smiling, Nell fussed with the covers. "If you need any help with the baby during the night, just yell. Promise me you will, child. I won't hear of this notion that you're imposing. You must think of us as family." Stepping back, Nell nudged Jake forward.

*Family.* The word had a nice ring. Hayley glanced up and saw Jake.

"I sleep light," he said. "Mom, too. When Cammy cries, it'll be a stampede to the cradle. Don't you worry. You need to rest."

Wade stuck his shaggy head around the door. "Make that three light sleepers. I'll probably lead the stampede. It's been too long since I rocked a baby at night."

Hayley gazed from one smiling face to the other. The fear that had clutched at her heart since Joe blew into her camp began to unravel. She smiled at Jake as he ambled over to take a last peek at Cammy. And she didn't act embarrassed or push him away when he turned and kissed her good-night. She slid fully beneath the warm covers in a room that felt totally secure. Her heart accepted Jake and his family—even if her brain was slower to come around.

## CHAPTER FIFTEEN

AT MIDNIGHT, again at two and sometime after four, Hayley awakened to Cammy's crying, only to have Jake or Nell or Wade place a freshly diapered baby in her arms for nursing. Now it was almost nine-thirty. Jake stood over her bed, smiling and holding a breakfast tray.

Hayley cast a sleep-fogged glance at an empty cradle. Panicking, she bolted upright and threw aside her covers.

"Whoa! Mom has Cammy in the kitchen. The pediatrician has come and gone—Cammy got a clean bill of health. The doctor left you a note. Mom sent the tray. The doctor ordered a healthy breakfast to, uh, help produce milk," Jake stammered. "Cammy was slugging down a two-ounce bottle of water when I left them," he said, his voice growing stronger. "Can you manage the tray by yourself?"

Hayley fluffed two pillows and eased back against them, taking care to restore the quilt, although she couldn't say why she'd suddenly be self-conscious around a man who'd seen her all. She focused on the stack of toast, bowl of cereal and tall glass of milk, but those blasted tears plagued her again.

"Don't you like toast and cereal? Why are you crying?" With his hands full, Jake felt at a loss to console her.

Unable to speak through a constricted throat, Hayley

staved him off with a hand. "I...I... No one's ever served me breakfast in bed before."

"Then you'd better eat, before it gets cold," Jake urged gently. "In the Cooper family, it's a treat reserved for special occasions, like anniversaries or Mother's Day."

Hayley let him settle the tray across her lap. "I feel like such an impostor. You're all doing so much for me, and I'm not a Cooper."

"Not yet." Jake left her to digest that, along with her breakfast.

As Hayley ate, she studied the sunny room with its hand-rubbed oak furniture and oval braided rug. There were watercolor paintings on the walls and knickknacks on the dresser. Grandpa Ben had never owned a home; he'd always rented. Only now did Hayley realize how long they'd lived with secondhand junk.

She wished Francesca could see this room and the nursery Nell had let Hayley peek at last night. Francesca insisted no one lived in homes like the ones that were pictured in the magazines Hayley collected. They were just for show, she'd said. But the Coopers' house was beautiful yet obviously well lived in. Hayley understood in a way she never had before that expensive furnishings and lush carpets and shining oak floors didn't make a home; the people who lived there did. The Coopers had created a place of beauty and shelter and love. A home.

Wade himself came in to take her tray. He seemed incongruous in the elegant feminine room, Hayley still felt ill at ease in his presence. She sat very quietly, expecting him to try to harass her into revoking her mining claim.

"Nell's busy playing grandma," he told Hayley with a huge grin. "I'm relegated to being your waiter. Jake and Dillon have gone to put a new battery in your pickup. They'll have your truck and trailer here by noon.''

"Good. Tomorrow or the next day I can be on my way to Tombstone.''

"What's the rush? And why Tombstone? I thought Eden said you were going to learn the jewelry business by starting out as her apprentice. Isn't Tombstone a far piece to travel?''

"Oh." Hayley inspected her ragged fingernails. "Yes, we discussed an apprenticeship. I realize now, with the baby and all, I wasn't being very realistic.''

"I expect Eden will change your mind when she gets here. She and Nell are already conspiring on where to fit a crib and a playpen in their office." A fond look softened his craggy face. "Nell and I always took the boys to work with us. That's the best thing about being your own boss—setting the rules.''

Hayley weighed what he'd said as he left and Nell breezed through the door, bringing Cammy for a feeding. "I'll leave you two to your privacy. Eden just drove in, and right behind her is the county sheriff. Jake told his dad that no-good ex of yours threatened to file a lawsuit to gain half your mine. Don't you worry. If that's why the sheriff's here, Wade will set him straight in a hurry.''

"I can't ask you to fight my battles, Nell." Hayley shifted Cammy so she could wriggle out of bed. But the baby set up a howl.

"You didn't ask us. It's become a family matter. Get your body back in bed and feed that poor starving child." Nell grinned and winked as she leaned down and kissed Cammy's nose.

The baby quieted enough to blink unfocused blue

eyes. Hayley sank back into the pillows. She really ought to object more vigorously to all this pampering. ''On the other hand, cupcake,'' she whispered to the baby after Nell had gone, ''let's wallow in it while we can. They're all so darn nice, how can we *not* love them?''

Hayley was asleep when Jake tiptoed into the room two hours later. Cammy had begun to stir in her cradle. He lifted her and carried her into the nursery next door for a diaper change. Returning, he sat in the rocking chair in Hayley's room.

It was there that Hayley saw him when some small noise happened to wake her. He was concentrating so hard on singing to the baby he obviously didn't realize Hayley had opened her eyes. Which suited her. She liked looking at the way Jake's big strong hands tenderly swayed the small bundle, as if he held something precious.

Hayley couldn't recall the size or shape of her father's hands. Or if he'd ever held her like that. But he must have. Ben said she'd been her parents' pride and joy.

Hayley had always intended that her children would have the love of two parents. Sadly that wasn't to be. A hole seemed to open in her heart and left her feeling drained and empty.

''Well, hello, sleepyhead.'' Jake stopped rocking and bestowed a loving smile on the rumpled woman in the bed. ''Your daughter was just telling me her tummy's growling and I should interrupt your nap.''

Hayley scrambled into a sitting position, hoping Jake hadn't been able to read her dark thoughts. As he leaned over her and placed Cammy in her arms, another wave of emotion swamped her. Jake smelled like sunshine and soil and car grease. Earthy scents Hayley associated with good memories. It shook her to realize she still did have good memories of men. Her dad. Gramps. And now Jake Cooper.

"Before you get started feeding the wee one," Jake said, straightening to slide a hand into his snug jeans pocket, "I have something for you."

"Jake, you can't keep buying me things." Even as she said it, Hayley was curious to know what kind of gift would fit in his pocket.

He pressed a pendant into her hand. A white-gold modern bas-relief sculpture of the Madonna and child. Where their faces should have been were two ovals of pale blue. *Her opals.*

"I asked Eden to specially make it for you," Jake murmured. "I know it'll never replace your mother's cameo, but I wanted you to have something to commemorate Cammy's birth and your opal discovery."

Hayley's tears began to flow. They fell like rain, wetting Cammy's blanket.

Jake, who was better prepared for Hayley's tears this time, kissed them away while he fastened the chain around her neck. "It has a safety catch on the back of the pendant if you'd rather pin it on a jacket."

His smile held more than warmth and friendship. Hayley recognized love in the depths of his eyes. Her trembling fingers blindly sought and found the smooth pendant. Clutching it, she stammered out a wholly inadequate thank-you. Twisting to stare at the delicate piece, she whispered, "I've never told a soul, but Joe…didn't buy me a wedding ring. At the JP's, I gave him a gold band. He refused to wear it. I saved out of my grocery money and bought myself a band. He got mad. Said it was a waste of money. Oh, I don't know why I'm telling you this. It's just…your mom said the sheriff came by. If Joe knows I have anything this nice,

Jacob—'' her voice turned to a sob ''—he'll find a way to take it away.''

''Shh.'' Jake tipped her tear-streaked face up and kissed her lips. ''I'm not going to let Joe near you. Dad's phoned our lawyer. He said for you not to worry. Joe's bogus lawsuit will be laughed out of court.''

Eden knocked on the open door. ''Excuse me. I hate to interrupt this touching scene, but I'm dying to know what Hayley thinks of the pendant.''

Hayley could do little more than telegraph Eden a wet radiant smile.

''I told Jake it was a bad idea, that you'd hate it.'' Eden entered the room, nudged Jake and winked. ''I guess you won't mind if I steal this precious lamb while you pull yourself together,'' she teased Hayley. ''Oh, I can see now she's a future Miss America,'' Eden breathed, gazing reverently at the baby.

Still with a death grip on the pendant, Hayley tried again to articulate her deep appreciation.

Eden brushed off Hayley's gratitude. ''It's a simple design. Jake sketched what he wanted. The hardest part was finding matched opals. The stone is a joy to cut and polish, as you'll soon learn. Well, not too soon,'' she added, smiling into the infant's sweet face. ''Some time this spring. How does March sound? By then, you guys will be settled in Jake's new house. Besides, if you bring Cammy to work too soon, I'll be tempted to badger Dillon into starting our family a year earlier than we've planned.''

Hayley clutched the Madonna so tightly her knuckles turned white and she almost snapped the slender chain. ''I...I'm not moving in with Jake.''

Eden shot her brother-in-law an apologetic glance. ''Oops. Nell and I thought we'd given you time enough to pop the question. Shall I call Dillon? Do you need a script?''

Jake closed his eyes. "Scram, Eden," he muttered gruffly.

"Sure. But get on the stick, Jacob. Nell and I are itching to decorate for a holiday wedding."

"Eden!" Jake roared. His harsh voice startled Cammy. She screwed up her small face and let out a cry. Rising, Jake relieved his sister-in-law of the baby. Holding Cammy on his shoulder with one hand, he used the other to hustle Eden out.

She muscled her way back into the room and grinned at Hayley. "I'm counting on being your matron of honor. I've got a new bronze-colored dress just begging for such an event. And Nell reminded me that the boutique across the street from the shop has a gorgeous, pale-peach empire-waist dress that would go great with your coloring. With Nell's pearls, it'd make a perfect wedding—"

Jake shut the door. He stood, facing away from Hayley a moment, catching his breath before he found the courage to turn and look at her. When he did, he felt awful. She'd turned white as the sheet clenched in one hand. "Well," he said lamely, "now that Eden's let the cat out of the bag, I guess I'll have to hold you prisoner until you agree to marry me." He kissed the baby, who'd quieted.

"Dammit, Hayley, I was going to soften you up with the pendant and then drag out the big guns." Fishing in his shirt pocket, Jake produced a flat velvet pouch. He sat on the edge of her bed and laid it in Hayley's lap while he pried her cold fingers open. It wasn't easy, but he eventually managed with one hand to dump out a pair of wide gold bands studded with diamonds and opals.

"If you'd rather have a set with an engagement ring, I'll have Eden trade yours. Unlike Joe Ryan, Hayley, I want the world to know I have a wife. I want everyone to know we're a matched set."

She picked up the smaller of the two bands. Her lower lip quivered, but this time she was determined not to cry. "I love you, Jake. But I've been so afraid to let that happen. I don't need fancy rings or houses. Only regular hugs from someone who'll love me and Cammy unconditionally."

"I know," he said, tears springing to his eyes as he moved closer and urged her to share his grip on the baby. "What I need is for you to trust me completely."

"I do. I think I have from the beginning."

"It's done, then. And there'll be no more doubts, Hayley. From here on, you and Cammy are part of the Cooper family." He kissed her and drew back. "Feed this hungry child while I go alleviate everyone's anxiety. Mom, Dad, Dillon and Eden are all in the kitchen waiting for your answer."

Hayley detained him a moment, stealing another kiss. Jake backed from the room, wearing a goofy grin. "Hold that thought," he said.

THE WEDDING WAS SMALL, but more lavish than the harvest dance, which not one of the Coopers had attended. They'd had too much going on. Their ranch house rang with the laughter of family and close friends.

Hayley wore the peach dress, but she refused Nell's pearls. The opal Madonna-and-child pendant and her new wedding band were the only jewelry she wanted.

The minister christened Cammy at the same time—Cameo Joy Cooper. Jake had tracked down Joe Ryan—in jail—and convinced him to relinquish his rights to

Hayley's daughter. It hadn't been difficult. Adding to his sleaziness, Joe couldn't wait to sign away any responsibility. Of course, he wasn't in any position to offer support. Mere days after the incident at Hayley's camp, Joe and Shad Tilford had been arrested for smuggling illegal substances across the border. Cammy would be ready for college before Joe finished serving his sentence. And Hayley's opals would more than pay her way through.

Following the wedding ceremony and before Jake spirited Hayley away for a one-night honeymoon at a bed-and-breakfast in Tubac, Nell and Eden took Hayley aside. "Come into the kitchen," Nell urged. Eden proudly displayed a new sign for their shop. "Wade carved it," Nell said, tracing the letters spelling out Triple C Southwest Art Gallery.

Eden gave Hayley a spontaneous hug. "Wade renamed the ranch the Triple C when Dillon and Jacob became his partners. We three Cooper women are partners, too. It's only fitting we trade on such a distinguished name, don't you think?"

"I promised myself I wouldn't cry tonight," Hayley said, sniffling. "Darn, I lied." She broke down completely as Nell thrust a tissue into her hands.

The Cooper men crowded into the doorway. Their eyes weren't exactly dry. Jake covered his tears fairly well by twice repeating instructions to his mother for taking care of Cammy while he and Hayley went away for the night.

Dillon broke the tension. He walked over and clapped Jake on the back. "When you get back, I have a housewarming gift. It's a sacrifice, but what are brothers for? I'm giving you guys Coronado."

"What?" Eden shrieked. "Give them my parrot? No

way! You should be ashamed. The poor bird just needs
more attention.''

"I was kidding. Only kidding.'' Dillon captured Eden
and kissed her silent, making everyone smile. "Believe
it or not, I've made peace with that fowl.''

"Wait.'' Hayley hung back as Jake dropped her new
wool coat around her shoulders and eagerly shepherded
toward the door. "I have a gift, too.''

The group eyed Jake, all assuming it was some sort
of bride's gift to her groom. What Hayley pulled from
her purse was a bill of sale for the twenty acres on which
her mine, and the spring, were located. "I asked your
lawyer to handle everything, Wade,'' she said shyly. "I
wanted to make sure the land belongs irrevocably to the
Triple C.''

No one knew quite what to say. "The opals from the
mine are all yours, Hayley,'' Jake said, cupping her face
softly as he turned up her collar. "I'll help you dig the
ore, but everything earned goes into your private bank
account.''

Dillon and Wade quickly seconded Jake's promise.

Rising on tiptoe, Hayley pressed a lingering kiss to
her husband's lips. "Last week when Eden drove me
into town to try on the dress, I had the bank move everything from my account into the joint one you established for us, Jake. Cammy and I are Coopers now. It's
share and share alike.''

Jake almost didn't get out of the house to go on their
honeymoon, although Dr. Gerrard had given Hayley the
okay to resume all normal activity a few days before the
ceremony. And Jake had been counting the minutes until
they could consummate their marriage. Her announcement came as a shock. Trusting him with the nest egg
that had for so long spelled her independence and

Cammy's future was like announcing to the world that she embraced his love fully and completely.

"Come on, Mrs. Cooper," Jake whispered, tracing her lips with his tongue. "Tonight we share a bed, setting a precedent for the rest of our lives."

Eden, Dillon, Wade and the remaining guests followed the couple outside into the cool night, pelting them with laughter and birdseed. Charcoal raced around trying to catch the seed in midair.

A smiling Nell Cooper stood framed in the living-room window, her first grandchild cradled in her arms.

"Look, Jake." Hayley stopped him before he backed the new reliable Land Cruiser he'd bought her out of the drive. "With the lamp shining behind Nell, she and Cammy could be models for my pendant."

"Mom wasn't my model, Hayley. Even before Cammy was born, it's how I pictured the two of you. My wife and my child." Straining against a seat belt that held him fast, Jake kissed her fully and deeply. A kiss that brimmed with love.

"I love you, Jacob Cooper. I'm about the luckiest woman alive," Hayley murmured in a husky whisper.

"Likewise," he returned. "I'll show you exactly how much after we check in tonight." Jake framed her lovely face with his hands momentarily before drawing away. "But I'm the lucky one. No man could ask for more than a wife like you to make his house a home. You and Cammy complete my life, Mrs. Cooper."

Hayley snuggled happily against his shoulder. "And you, Mr. Cooper, are the fulfillment of all my dreams."

# HARLEQUIN *Super*ROMANCE®

*They spent a snowy night in each others'*
*arms. Now there's a baby*
*on the way....*

## *SNOW BABY* by *Brenda Novak*

(Superromance #939)

Chantel Miller has fallen for Dillon Broderick, the man
who held and comforted her during the blizzard. Then
she learns that her estranged sister is in love with him.
The sister whose affection Chantel's trying to regain. The
painful coincidence becomes even more devastating
when Chantel discovers she's pregnant.

*On sale September 2000*

*Available wherever Harlequin books are sold.*

# HARLEQUIN®
*M*akes any time special ™

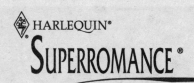

# SUPERROMANCE®

## *You are now entering*

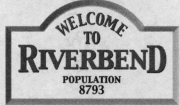

WELCOME TO **RIVERBEND**

POPULATION
8793

Riverbend…the kind of place where everyone knows
your name—and your business. Riverbend…home of
the River Rats—a group of small-town sons and
daughters who've been friends since high school.

The Rats are all grown up now. Living their lives and
learning that some days are good and some days
aren't—and that you can get through anything
as long as you have your friends.

Starting in July 2000, Harlequin Superromance brings
you Riverbend—six books about the River Rats and
the Midwest town they live in.

**BIRTHRIGHT** by **Judith Arnold** (July 2000)
**THAT SUMMER THING** by **Pamela Bauer** (August 2000)
**HOMECOMING** by **Laura Abbot** (September 2000)
**LAST-MINUTE MARRIAGE** by **Marisa Carroll** (October 2000)
**A CHRISTMAS LEGACY** by **Kathryn Shay** (November 2000)

*Available wherever Harlequin books are sold.*

## HARLEQUIN®
*Makes any time special* ™

# HARLEQUIN
## Duets™

*Pick up a Harlequin Duets™
from August–October 2000
and receive $1.00 off the
original cover price.* *

*Experience the "lighter side of love"
in a Harlequin Duets™.
This unbeatable value just became
irresistible with our special introductory
price of $4.99 U.S./$5.99 CAN. for
2 Brand-New, Full-Length
Romantic Comedies.*

Offer available for a limited time only.
Offer applicable only to Harlequin Duets™.
*Original cover price is $5.99 U.S./$6.99 CAN.

# Romance is just one click away!

## online book **serials**

➤ *Exclusive* to our web site, get caught up in both the daily and weekly online installments of new romance stories.

➤ Try the Writing Round Robin. Contribute a chapter to a story created by our members. Plus, winners will get prizes.

## romantic **travel**

➤ Want to know where the best place to kiss in New York City is, or which restaurant in Los Angeles is the most romantic? Check out our Romantic Hot Spots for the scoop.

➤ Share your travel tips and stories with us on the romantic travel message boards.

## romantic reading **library**

➤ Relax as you read our collection of Romantic Poetry.

➤ Take a peek at the Top 10 Most Romantic Lines!

## Visit us online at

# www.eHarlequin.com

## on Women.com Networks

Daddy's little girl... **THAT'S MY BABY!** by

# Vicki Lewis Thompson

Nat Grady is finally home—older and wiser. When the woman he'd loved had hinted at commitment, Nat had run far and fast. But now he knows he can't live without her. But Jessica's nowhere to be found.

Jessica Franklin is living a nightmare. She'd thought things were rough when the man she loved ran out on her, leaving her to give birth to their child alone. But when she realizes she has a stalker on her trail, she has to run—and the only man who can help her is Nat Grady.

## THAT'S MY BABY!

On sale September 2000 at your favorite retail outlet.

HARLEQUIN®
*Makes any time special*™

x

---

### #930 THAT SUMMER THING • Pamela Bauer
*Riverbend*

Charlie Callahan is the original good-time Charlie. At least, that's what everyone thinks, especially Beth Pennington. After all, she was once briefly—disastrously—married to him. And now she's sharing an inheritance with Charlie! Isn't it ironic?

*Riverbend, Indiana: Home of the River Rats—small-town sons and daughters who've been friends since high school. These are their stories.*

### #931 P.S. LOVE YOU MADLY • Bethany Campbell

Darcy's mother and Sloan's father are in love. But Darcy's sister is aghast and Sloan's aunt is appalled. And that leaves the two of them trying to make everyone see sense. No problem, right? But then their parents break up just when *they're* falling in love.... Compared to what these two go through, Romeo and Juliet had it easy.

Guaranteed to be one of the funniest romances you'll read this year!

### #932 CATHRYN • Shannon Waverly
*Circle of Friends*

Cathryn McGrath of Harmony, Massachusetts, is the ideal wife and mother—her children are happy, her house is beautiful, her marriage is perfect. Except it's not.... Her husband is having an affair with another woman! Then Cathryn's marriage irrevocably ends, and she resumes her friendship with Tucker Lang—former bad boy of Harmony, who shows her that there's life after betrayal, love after divorce.

### #933 HITCHED! • Ruth Jean Dale
*The Taggarts of Texas*

Rand Taggart may have been swindled out of a fortune by his old college roommate, but he can inherit a *second* fortune—provided he's happily married by his thirtieth birthday. In order to save her sister's name, Maxi Rafferty is going to help him out—and complicate her life and Rand's with this seemingly straightforward marriage of convenience!

### #934 HIS DADDY'S EYES • Debra Salonen
*A Little Secret*

There's one thing in Judge Lawrence Bishop's past that could come back to haunt him. Two years ago he spent a weekend in the arms of a sexy stranger. Then Lawrence learns the woman is dead—but her fifteen-month-old son is living with her sister, Sara Carsten. Lawrence does the math and pays Sara a visit. What he tells her—and what he sees with his own eyes—rocks both their worlds.

### #935 DEEP IN THE HEART OF TEXAS • Linda Warren

Heiress Miranda Maddox has been kidnapped and held prisoner. Jacob Culver, a fugitive and the man known as "the hermit," rescues her, and against his own inclinations, agrees to guide her back to her home. In the process, Miranda discovers that someone in her family ordered her kidnapping—and she learns to trust Jake. She also learns that sometimes trust leads to love....